supper
club

ALSO BY THE AUTHOR

The Girl Made of Clay

The House of Bradbury

the second chance supper club

NICOLE MEIER

LAKE UNION
PUBLISHING

Published by Lake Union Publishing, Seattle

www.apub.com

Amazon, the Amazon logo, and Lake Union Publishing are trademarks of Amazon.com, Inc., or its affiliates.

ISBN-13: 9781542041560
ISBN-10: 1542041562

Cover design by Faceout Studio, Tim Green

Printed in the United States of America

To sisters everywhere, especially mine.

PROLOGUE

As the plane descended low into the valley, the landscape came tightly into focus. Bright sunshine bled through the windows, casting an aureate glow on everything in its path. Farther out, the tip of the airplane wing dipped gracefully, like a brushstroke across a watercolor sky.

Glimpses of a craggy canyon emerged next. Mounds of earth rose up to form impressive foothills, extending toward the horizon and beyond.

Lower still, the view gave way to miniature pink stucco dwellings braided throughout the landscape. Towering cacti sprouted up in random patterns. More colors appeared: a spot of fuchsia, hints of ivory, and soft shades of brown. All amid a blanket of green.

How alive it all seemed. How unexpected.

Every so often, a thin stream or riverbed could be seen winding its way through the parched terrain. A surge of hope. A watery glimmer of life.

The airplane lowered again, now gliding toward its destination. Wings level, wheels down, a slowing of momentum. A voice echoed from an overhead speaker.

Welcome to the desert.

Welcome home, Julia thought to herself, and what a strange homecoming it was.

CHAPTER ONE
JULIA

One day earlier

The rain drenching Manhattan hadn't let up for three miserable days. On Thursday morning, an orchestra of percussive drops tapped at the window and woke Julia like an incessant faucet leak. At the same time, her phone vibrated just inches away. She blinked back confusion and raised her head from its spot on the living room sofa. To her dismay, a paper plate containing day-old bits of pizza crust clung to the side of her cheek.

She'd fallen asleep in her clothes again.

With one palm, she swiped the plate to the floor and rubbed her eyes. The beginnings of a muted dawn peeked through the neighboring buildings outside. Everything was blurred.

Her phone buzzed a second time.

"Okay! Okay!" she groused. The heel of her hand rose to press against an uncomfortable thrumming in her head. She smacked her dry lips and grimaced, detecting a layer of film coating her tongue.

Trying to focus, Julia studied the screen. It read 5:45 a.m.

Oh no. She tensed. Without hesitation she punched "Answer."

"Hello?" Clearing her throat took considerable effort. She really needed to stop working such late hours.

"Julia? Where the hell are you?" A woman's voice on the other end was sharp and insistent.

Catrine.

"At home," Julia blurted, a shot of adrenaline sending her to her feet. Surveying the room, she noticed work papers strewn everywhere. Her eyes widened at the full realization of her mistake. She'd drifted off without setting an alarm. Her much more punctual other half, her fiancé of nine months, James, was away on business, which meant there hadn't been anyone around to insist she set the alarm. Or not fall asleep on top of a plate of takeout. She should have left for the studio forty-five minutes ago.

Catrine's tone turned to worry. "Are you sick?"

"No, I'm not. I overslept." Julia groaned. With the phone pinned under one ear, she scurried about, urgently gathering up files. "I can still make it! You'll just have to work quickly. I have a feeling I look like a train wreck today."

"Well, you better hurry." Catrine's voice dropped to a stage whisper. "You-know-who is already getting his hair blown out."

"I'm on my way!" *No! No! No!*

The pinpricks of alarm were multiplying.

She was unbelievably late. Of all days. To make matters worse, Miller "Perfectly on Time" Warren was already in the studio, probably rolling his eyes at Julia's tardiness and savoring how he'd deliver the news to the executive producer. Their EP, Peter Henry, was not known to show mercy. If he detected an iota of weakness among his staff, he seized upon it. Julia both admired and feared this about him. Currently, fear was winning out.

This morning's slipup would be used against her for sure.

Without so much as stopping to brush her teeth (she kept spare toiletries at work), Julia snatched her tote bag and phone, buttoned up her wrinkled blouse, and cast about frantically for something to put on her feet. She opted for the closest thing, a pair of running shoes with neon swooshes. Pausing to glimpse in the oblong mirror above the entry table, she recoiled.

"Oh hell." She scowled at her reflection of electrified hair and purple half-moons drooping under bloodshot eyes. "This is bad."

There wasn't much choice in the matter. Swallowing back horror, she used her fingers as a makeshift comb. The clock was ticking. She had to go. She yanked the door open and uttered a little prayer as she raced downstairs to catch a ride.

As her driver snaked through Midtown and Julia urged him to speed up, she balanced on the edge of the back seat and agonized. She counted the milliseconds as blocks went by. *Please hurry. Please hurry. Please hurry.* She chewed on her lip and considered what kind of excuse she could possibly give for holding up the morning show so dangerously close to airtime.

If Peter found out, heads would roll.

If the other execs found out, it would be curtains for her.

Just yesterday, after Miller had hijacked nearly the entire news segment, Julia had been summoned to her boss's office. Her presence was hardly ever requested upstairs at the network, but that morning, she'd been seated at an imposing mahogany table and scrutinized.

Julia shuddered at the memory.

All those sets of eyes bearing down on her, the executives accusing her of not meeting expectations. It was awful.

"We count on everyone to pull their own weight around here," announced Mr. McBride, a member of Gamen Broadcast Network's executive team. He was an unforgiving older man, lean and sinewy, lacking any ounce of softness. Julia watched, terrified, as he tapped a pencil with a stern and unyielding gaze that made her squirm. It was a test of some sort, and she wasn't prepared. Even so, she smiled meekly in his direction.

"Yes, of course." She nodded and wished her wobbly response hadn't betrayed her. For some reason, none of her team were in the room with her. If anyone else had been called on the carpet, she wasn't aware. This meeting was all about how her performance, and hers alone, was disappointing the network. "I, uh, I thought the show had been going pretty smoothly," she responded.

There was a pulse of silence before someone from marketing, a Paul Something-or-other, sprang up from his chair with terrier-like reflexes and passed around a mind-bending spreadsheet to everyone in the room. From what Julia gathered, the focus was her recent dip in ratings.

"We're concerned about this," McBride said, stabbing the spreadsheet with the point of sharp lead. "Your viewers just aren't staying engaged. They're tuning out."

"You don't have a brand," the Paul guy piped up. His eyebrows arched just below a perfectly coiffed hairline. Julia instantly hated him.

"A brand? Isn't that something the show should have?" She was confused. She'd been hired to do a job and she was doing it. Wasn't she? Sure, the morning show was less than a year old, and perhaps she was still finding her footing. But initially she'd received all kinds of positive responses on social media. Viewers had likened her to a breath of fresh air. That counted for something. But that was early on, she glumly realized. The numbers apparently no longer reflected this.

Miller's larger-than-life personality had begun to drown her out. That was why her cohost's numbers had spiked higher than hers. What was Miller's brand? she wondered. Julia had no idea why the media company had paired the two of them together eleven months ago. She and Miller coanchored *Daybreak*, a weekday program that included headline news and light elements of pop culture. Her producer had claimed he detected a "chemistry" between the two of them upon their hiring.

She gazed desperately at the spreadsheet for answers. The data distorted in and out of focus. Pretending to study the math, she stalled.

What on earth was she supposed to say? It felt as if she'd been called into the principal's office for an offense of which she wasn't guilty.

"We want you to think about how to turn these numbers around." McBride interrupted her contemplation. "This is a prime spot, your morning show. And it's imperative the ratings swing our way. Understand?"

No, not really, she wanted to say. She'd shown up for work every day, reported the news in front of her, and put up with her slimy cohost. Julia needed to say something in her own defense, but before she had the chance, she was swiftly excused from the room. It seemed her time was up.

The door swung open as someone mumbled instructions, and she was ushered into the hallway. To her shock, a much-younger woman was seated just outside, wearing a tight-fitting dress and a smug smile. Julia glimpsed down at her own boxy pantsuit, which suddenly seemed wildly outdated, and then watched, dumbfounded, as the woman was welcomed into the room just as quickly as she'd been whisked out.

The heat of humiliation had engulfed her.

GBN was considering firing her. And that younger model would be her replacement.

A surge of newly formed rage washed over Julia now as she willed the car to drive faster. But emotions weren't going to do her any good. What she needed was a plan.

CHAPTER TWO
JULIA

Landing hard in her seat facing the teleprompter, Julia ignored the annoying trickle of perspiration running down her spine. A finger tugged on the collar of her blouse as Andy, the tech guy, came from behind her and attached a mic. Julia tried to shrug away the feeling of discomfort. She was overheating by the minute, both from the exasperating rush to get into position and the glaring studio lights. It was a miracle she'd pulled it off, actually. She'd whizzed through hair and makeup, ripped a clean blazer off its hanger, and parked herself in front of the camera just in time for the show. All before Peter had the chance to catch up with her.

By the gawking faces of the staff, though, it appeared no one was impressed.

The clock on the wall counted down ninety seconds until *Daybreak* went live. Julia hadn't had any cushion time to scroll through the newswires or even review the notes the writers had left on her desk. She was going to have to fly without a safety net for the next hour, with a coanchor who was most assuredly far more prepared than she and wanted her to land on her chin.

Her hands twisted together under the news desk as she waited. She silently prayed for a smooth show. Any more mistakes and she'd be out of a job.

"Well, well, well." Miller appeared just then, coming through the studio doors all lacquered and sneering. His fingers crawled along the buttons of his dark suit jacket, smoothing the already-taut fabric, as he slid into the seat next to hers. Unyielding cologne drifted in Julia's direction. Her eyes watered.

"Look who decided to grace us with her presence after all." He leaned back and gave her a slow once-over. "Rough night?"

"Hello, Miller." Julia straightened and reshuffled the stack of papers set before her. A pair of reading glasses was retrieved, and she pretended to be distracted by her notes. But her nerves were too jumpy. The words just floated around on the page like black ants. It was all she could do to keep her heart from hammering out of her chest. Agitated, she cleared her throat. "Just following a lead on a story, that's all. No need to worry."

"Oh, really? Which story is that?"

She faltered. There was no way she was going to let Miller know she was bluffing. Her hand swatted the air. "Something I'm developing for Peter. I'm not ready to share just yet."

"You could've fooled me," Miller quipped. Julia thought she heard one of the cameramen snigger. She scowled out into the bright lights.

Despite her best effort to not be ruffled by Miller, his remark delivered a fresh stab of humiliation. Catrine, usually a magician in the makeup room, had been heavy-handed with the application of under-eye concealer. Maybe she had just added insult to injury. Julia was suddenly desperate for a mirror, but the digital clock on the wall showed they were mere seconds from airtime. Instinctively, she fanned her face with her fingers, hoping the heat in her cheeks would diminish.

"Are you ready?" A production assistant hustled in, lowered his clipboard, and addressed Julia with a tone of uncertainty. His questioning glance ricocheted from her to Miller and then back again.

Julia squirmed against the dampness collecting at the small of her back.

"Julia?"

"What? Oh yes. I'm all good." She could feel his expectant eyes probing her. *Just get through this,* she told herself. Willing her roiling stomach to settle, she pulled the familiar facade of success over her shoulders like a well-worn shawl. "Really, I'm fine. Ready to go." Ignoring the stink of her own perspiration, she nodded.

The assistant gave a thumbs-up and swiftly exited back to his position in the control room. A cameraman held out his hand, counting down with each finger. "Five, four, three, two, and go!"

The studio lights shone brightly, the cue was given, and the theme music swelled to a climax. Miller turned robotically to the camera. "Good morning from GBN's *Daybreak*. Our top stories today . . ." And Julia snapped into focus.

~

Twenty minutes into the show, they paused for a commercial break. The news, so far, had been fairly vanilla. Nothing terribly substantial or exciting happening in the world that morning, apparently. Julia had found her rhythm, masking her trepidation, and read the teleprompter while Miller took his usual number of liberties with some ad-libbing.

At the break, Miller went for his water and Julia for her notes. Scanning the segment schedule, her eyes widened.

"Wait, we have Mayor Rossetti coming on next? For an interview?"

"How nice of you to finally tune in. Don't worry, I'm interviewing him." Miller lifted his chin with satisfaction. "It took me weeks to get this guy booked. He's all over the media, but for some reason he hasn't agreed to do our show until now."

Julia's mind raced. This topic hadn't been part of their weekly news editorial meeting. As far as she knew, Rossetti coming on the show wasn't ever formally discussed. Miller had obviously changed things without informing her. But that was typical. He liked to put Julia in the position of playing catch-up.

And now she was caught unawares as the mayor was about to do a live interview.

Julia pictured the city's most prominent figure, rotund and flush-faced, usually photographed pumping hands with the residents of New York, always smiling and showing off his pearly teeth. People liked him. Rumor had it he was on an upward route to the governor's office.

But Julia knew something else.

"What's Rossetti going to talk about?" Her voice inched up an octave.

Miller cast her a sideways glance. "What do you think he's going to talk about? Mayorly things, you know, like the status of the city. Pretty light stuff. But still, it's a prize that we got him. All thanks to yours truly and my brilliant powers of persuasion."

Julia perked up. She looked down at her papers, trying to concentrate. There was something she'd overheard at a black-tie affair she and her fiancé, James, recently attended. James was always being invited to those things, and she'd been his plus-one. And while he was usually the one to do all the schmoozing, there'd been a conversation to which only she was privy. Quickly, she recollected the details.

The night of the party, two men had stood outside the bathroom door, talking in hushed voices, without realizing she was inside listening. She recognized one of the voices as a staffer from the state attorney's office, someone whom she'd met several times before. He had a distinctly nasal tone that was difficult to forget. Who the other person was, Julia wasn't sure.

"Did you hear about Rossetti's office?" the staffer asked.

Ever on the lookout for news, Julia stopped washing her hands and strained her ear to the door.

"Oh, that business about tax fraud? Is that true?"

A chuckle could be overheard. "I can't confirm or deny. But don't be surprised if you see something in the papers soon."

Something else was said, but it was too muffled for Julia to make out. She leaned on the bathroom door and it jiggled. The men must've heard her, because footsteps quickly fell away and down the tiled corridor. Julia had emerged, stunned. Was Mayor Rossetti being investigated for tax fraud? Could she have an exclusive story?

Miller was now rattling on, but Julia was too distracted. Her mind raced. If only she'd had more time to follow up, to gather her sources, whatever she'd overheard had the potential to be a big scoop. The cocktail party hadn't been too long ago, and she'd intended to sniff out the truth of what she'd overheard.

Only she hadn't, and unfortunately, the only thing she had to base her claim on was idle party gossip.

"And we're back," a voice from the control room signaled.

Julia's head swiveled as the assistant's words came over her earpiece. Suddenly, there was Rossetti's large face, hovering on the screen before her.

"Good morning, Mayor Rossetti." Miller was already laying it on thick, swapping toothy smiles with his guest. "How nice to see you."

"Thanks for having me, Miller and Julia. I'm a big fan of the show." His plump cheeks pushed back into a greeting.

Julia nodded with a tight smile.

Miller beamed. "Why, thank you. It's an honor."

"The honor is all mine."

Oh, for god's sake, Julia steamed. The men were wasting valuable airtime fluffing one another up. *If Miller doesn't get into it soon, I'm jumping in.*

"You're nearing your one-year anniversary as New York City's mayor. Your State of the City address is going to be delivered next week. Can you give our viewers a hint at the status of things?"

"Why, yes. I'm looking forward to celebrating the accomplishments our city has achieved as well as previewing the year ahead and what's in store for revamping parts of downtown."

"The city has a lot to celebrate. From what I understand, we're seeing a record low for homelessness. Isn't that right?" Miller asked.

"Yes, that's right, Miller." Rossetti's chest puffed slightly. "In just one short year, I've brought together various leaders and businesses to address what is a very big problem in our community. The system isn't perfect, but I'm hopeful for more progress in the future."

Miller nodded and glanced briefly at his notes. "You've started a campaign to collect private dollars to build more housing for the city's homeless. How's that going?"

Julia's ears pricked up. *Money.*

"Yes, that's true. My office has been facilitating this campaign. But we're also working with several nonprofits to handle aspects of this new program. It's a team effort, after all."

"Mayor Rossetti," Julia jumped in. "Which agency is collecting and distributing the funds for the program?" She couldn't resist. Miller was practically leading her down the path. If she didn't take her opportunity now, then she might not get another one. These guys were going to do nothing more than slap one another on the back for the next five minutes, and then the interview would be over.

"Where are you going with this, Julia?" The producer's voice came over her earpiece with a distinct tone of caution.

"Who's handling the funds?" The mayor repeated her question, his expression quizzical. Julia swore his ruddy color turned a shade deeper. She watched as his lips parted, closed, then parted again.

"Yes, does your office handle the donations?" she pressed.

Again, her earpiece buzzed. *"Julia."*

She ignored her producer's second warning and fixed her focus on the screen.

"Oh no." Rossetti averted his gaze and shook his head. "Like I said, we're working with businesses in the nonprofit sector. My office is merely facilitating."

Miller kicked her hard with the toe of his loafer under the desk. Julia winced but ignored the painful warning.

"Is that because—"

"What my colleague is trying to say, Mayor Rossetti"—Miller's eyes flashed with abhorrence as he pitched forward to interrupt; Julia caught the muscles of his jaw tightening before he continued—"is that you've taken on a lot of responsibility only one year into your term. You've been able to get a lot of people working together in such a short amount of time."

"Thank you." A strained smile returned. "Yes, we work hard around here. I've got a great team. And we live in a great city. It's the best city!"

He's covering something up, Julia thought. She just had to jump back in and find out what. She parted her lips to speak.

"Julia!" her producer hissed into her ear. "Let Miller take it from here."

Julia scowled. She knew her boss was more than annoyed. But it was a risk she was willing to take. This could be breaking news.

Her producer didn't know what she knew. None of them did. It was the kind of information that would keep viewers in their seats, their eyes glued to the screen. If Julia could pull this off, she might secure that spot on the evening news after all. She had to try.

Julia's gaze flicked to the digital clock on the wall. Three short minutes to go until the segment ended. And then they'd lose Rossetti. Adrenaline coursed through her veins; her heart thumped against her rib cage. If she was going to do this, it had to be now. There wasn't any time to analyze. No time to ask for a break and bring her producer up to speed. They had a potentially juicy story right there in the palms of their hands, and Miller wasn't going to stifle her.

Your viewers just aren't staying engaged. They're tuning out. McBride's harsh words from yesterday's meeting echoed in Julia's mind. She'd practically been given an ultimatum: produce something big or step aside.

She had to make a decision. It was now or never.

"Mayor Rossetti," she broke in. Her breath was suddenly shallow. "Is it true that your office is being investigated for tax fraud? That you've been accused of mishandling state funds?"

The teleprompter wobbled.

Everyone froze. The room fell quiet. Both Rossetti and Miller looked on with gaping mouths. Julia's remarks were met with utter disbelief.

After a beat, she heard her coanchor suck in his breath. Miller was at a loss for words. It was in that instant that Julia realized she'd made a terrible mistake. She hadn't any proof or evidence to back up her accusation. And Rossetti wasn't about to admit his crimes to a lowly newscaster who was obviously bluffing.

Now what?

She swallowed and waited for Rossetti to form an answer. She suddenly had the nauseating feeling of time standing still and her entire future crumbling down around her. There on the screen in front of her was a purple-faced man of great power and influence, whom she'd just accused of a crime on national television with no evidence to support it.

There was no taking this back.

"Julia," Rossetti uttered through gritted teeth. "I'm not sure where you're getting your information, but that is false. For the record, I am not being investigated for any such thing, and you, I'm afraid, are the victim of salacious gossip. And because of that, I can't continue this interview or support the integrity of this network. I have to say goodbye."

A high-pitched ringing flooded Julia's ears.

Rossetti ripped his mic from his jacket lapel, shoved his chair backward, and stormed off camera. The air went dead and *Daybreak* immediately went to commercial. There was more commotion in her ear as Julia registered profanities and the sound of something being thrown in the control room. Out of self-preservation, she removed her earpiece and backed away from her desk. The floor under her feet felt as if it had dropped away, leaving her dangerously in limbo. It was clear things were on the edge of going from bad to worse.

"Holy shit, Julia! What have you done?" Miller gaped at her, all color draining from his face as he appeared genuinely afraid. His hands flew to his hair, suggesting he might rip it out.

Julia's mind blanked. A swirl of McBride's threats and Miller's outbursts filled her brain. The only thing she could focus on was the sheet of sweat blanketing her body. "I . . . I didn't want to let the opportunity slip away. I heard from a source that his office—"

"What source? What are you talking about?" He stopped her stammering, new rage coming to the surface. "You can't just break a story like that, something of that magnitude, on a show we do together, without telling anyone. You just accused the mayor of New York City of tax fraud. What the *hell*, Julia? Is it even true? Because we're all screwed if it's not!"

Julia blinked back the stinging in her eyes and dropped her head into her hands. With the full weight of what she'd done bearing down on her, she became acutely aware that her career had just officially come to an end.

~

Riding in the back seat of an Uber an hour later, Julia placed her forehead against the cool glass and watched the GBN building fade into the distance. It had all happened so fast. A piece of her had been left inside that building, and she wondered how she'd manage to get it back.

Her exit had been a nightmare. After being lectured and then accused of perpetuating "fake news" by her boss and summarily ordered to vacate the premises until further notice, Julia had packed her things and left. There'd been just enough time to snatch a few belongings from her desk, say goodbye to members of her team, and hustle out among a din of whispers and empathetic murmurs.

In a single act of foolish impulse, she'd allowed poor judgment to dismantle everything she'd worked so hard to achieve. She had no hope of gaining it back.

Julia sank farther into the seat and lamented. The clouds had drifted back over the city and drizzled once more. Her driver said something about the never-ending rain, but Julia ignored him.

All she heard was the white noise of panic filling her ears.

Instinctively, she reached into her pocket and retrieved her phone. She scrolled through her list of contacts with a shaky hand. When the screen displayed James's face and phone number, she paused.

It was midday. He'd be working, no doubt with frantic issues of his own. Nobody rested in the hedge fund business. Especially James. However, he might have already seen something about her disastrous morning online. If that were the case, he'd most assuredly expect her to call.

And she should phone him. Shouldn't she?

Julia stared a second longer. For some reason, she was unable to make her finger hit the call button. Thinking of how James might react, visualizing his concern morphing into potential disappointment, she felt a kind of hollowness move in and take up residence just behind her heart. Glumly, she swiped past his name and kept going.

The next name she landed on was the one she chose. It wasn't planned, but it felt right. Like coming across a beloved blanket that had been tucked away in a closet for far too long. Instinctually, she yearned to retrieve it now. Julia hesitated for only a fraction of an instant before she dialed the number. As it rang, she calculated the time difference in Arizona. But she also didn't care.

She just needed to talk to her sister.

CHAPTER THREE
GINNY

Ginny stood under a small shade tent and scrutinized a display of heirloom tomatoes. Inhaling, she caught the fragrant aroma of ripe fruit just off the vine. Her eyes fluttered closed. Sometimes there was nothing better than fresh produce.

Thanks to an unwanted phone call, she'd gotten up early enough to catch the outdoor market just after it opened. Being there was both an indulgence and a necessity. If anything, it took her mind off the call she'd ignored from her younger sister. It had been three years since they'd really talked, and the last thing Ginny wanted to do was pick up where they'd left off. No, she was more interested in spending her free time seeking out the perfect ingredients for her menu.

There wasn't any room for unwelcome distractions.

The variety in the growing season would normally be limited this time of year. But today, during the weekday market, she was in luck. A rainbow of vegetables was spread out before her: deep yellows, rich and traditional reds, tucked in with vivid greens and oranges. Each tomato boasted a different size and shape. The lumpy ones were the best; they added more texture and interest to the plate. They made each dish unique.

Unique was what Ginny was after.

Bloodred and still covered with a thin veil of dusty earth, the assortment at this stand appeared to be the best selection at the farmers' market. She'd come often enough to know which vendors to skip over entirely. Some had handwritten signs propped up, requesting that customers not handle the produce before buying. That wasn't for her. She supposed she understood a farmer's need to protect inventory from overzealous shoppers who fondled the food too roughly. But Ginny wanted to get up close and personal with everything before it made its way into her basket.

She wholeheartedly believed it was important to study her ingredients before adding them to a recipe. In many ways, her work was as much science as it was art. To both crafts, she was equally devoted.

Plucking a tomato that she recognized as a Brandywine variety, Ginny delicately rolled it in her fingers. Next she tipped it over. She tended to judge value by the level of darkness that lay on the underside. Glancing into the distance, she paused to recall the requirements of a specific recipe. In the process, a nearby bin from another vendor caught her eye. It was loaded with squash the color of butter. She made a mental note to grab those next.

"How much, Andy?" Ginny asked, holding out the tomato and leaning over to catch the farmer's attention. Having been a local now for three years, she'd become friendly with the growers in the region. She frequented the farmers' markets often, sometimes spending whole weekends hunting for the perfect produce.

A young man strolled over. "For you, Ginny? Three ninety-nine per pound."

Ginny let out a low whistle. "Geez, they've gone up. Haven't they?" She had the urge to haggle; this wasn't the answer she'd wanted. If she'd been back in New York, with her usual bunch of tough vendors, her ruthless side would have quickly emerged. But this wasn't the city. It was a close-knit community. Andy had a family to feed back home, so she refrained.

Andy pushed a worn trucker's hat back against his head of damp curls. He dragged a checkered shirtsleeve across his forehead. Ginny felt sorry for him, standing there for hours with the sun at his back. The Arizona heat was full-on that morning. It had been an unnaturally warm winter so far, and they were all feeling the effects.

Andy replaced his hat and shrugged. "End of the season. We're planting more in the greenhouse, but you know how it goes. These are good, though. I promise."

Ginny stuck a hand into her jeans pocket and touched a thin fold of bills. She hesitated. A pebble of doubt materialized in her gut. Money was running low this month. It was a luxury, and possibly even a risk, to spend so much on a single produce item. But she needed the ingredients for a certain recipe. The prudent thing would be to make a compromise.

Ginny did a lot of things well, but compromising wasn't one of them.

"Okay. If you promise . . ." She met Andy's eye and paid in cash.

As her change was counted out, Ginny's mind skipped to the credit card she'd hidden in the freezer the night before. Somewhere tucked behind the box of frozen peas was her maxed-out Visa, secured neatly in a plastic bag. It was necessary to keep it out of easy access, and frozen peas were just about the last thing she'd reach for in her kitchen, reserved for stubbed toes and twisted ankles only. She couldn't afford to rack up any more debt. Things were just too tight.

She hoped Olive wouldn't discover what she'd done. Additional tension between the two of them was the last thing she needed, and she didn't want to argue over money.

With the tomatoes secured in her basket, she made for the group of squash displayed next door. Squash was a great winter vegetable, a versatile starch that added color to the plate. A puree came to mind as she moved toward them.

Easing around a confused-looking woman, Ginny reached for one that caught her eye.

"How do you know which one to pick?" the woman asked as she turned to Ginny with a face full of curiosity. Ginny's gaze flicked momentarily to the sequined sandals and pale legs sticking out from under a pair of excessively bright Bermuda shorts.

Tourist, Ginny thought.

Her eyes went up to the large-brimmed straw hat that was almost the size of a small umbrella. *East Coast, most likely.* "Snowbirds" were what the locals called them, the droves of travelers renting high-priced vacation homes in order to escape frigid temperatures and dry out for the winter.

Ginny didn't blame the woman. Trading East Coast weather for the Sonoran Desert was understandable. She'd done the same thing. Never mind that it hadn't exactly been a vacation, or planned for that matter.

There was so much more that came with Arizona besides the weather. It took Ginny a long while to recognize this, considering the cross-country move home hadn't been her choice. Her return had been out of obligation, and along with it had come deep grief and anger. Arizona wasn't where she'd planned to wind up, but over time this sentiment had begun to fade, and she'd come to terms with the hand that she'd been dealt. Had come to enjoy this place and the serenity it offered, if she was honest.

The desert offered a certain sense of tranquility. All that natural beauty she'd forgotten about—the way the evenings magically morphed into stunning sorbet-colored sunsets and how spectacular shadows traversed the mountainous landscape during a storm. Looking back, Ginny supposed she'd been too jaded when she'd first arrived home. Her unease over relocating had made her unable to take in the raw beauty and the vastness of the landscape. Slowly, as things began to settle, the atmosphere eventually offered Ginny a certain level of peace. She'd never experienced anything like it in the city. And now that she was here, despite some unwanted hardships, she appreciated her environment. Mostly.

"Well," Ginny said, addressing the waiting woman, "first, you've got to handle it. That's right," she urged as the woman tentatively took one into her grasp.

"Okay."

"It should be heavy for its size. We don't want lightweights here." Ginny gestured with her chin. "Then you've got to check it all over. Are there pockmarks, signs of frostbite, or punctures? Does it have a sound, glossy exterior? You see, the ones in the supermarkets are sorted; the ugly or odd get rejected, so as consumers, we're used to only seeing displays of the conventional and uniform."

"Oh. I see."

"Here," Ginny said, waving her arm, "when you're sourcing food directly from the growers, you need to be discerning. Get in there and push your nose around. Smell it and imagine what it might taste like. Go on."

The woman's mouth popped open. Ginny worried she'd gone too far. Not everyone felt the way she did about vegetables.

"Did that make sense?" Ginny asked.

The woman smiled nervously. "Um, wow. You sure know a lot about your produce. You a gardener or something?"

"A chef."

The woman brightened. "Impressive! I guess you have to know these things, then."

"I guess I do." Ginny felt the familiar self-consciousness bloom. It was one thing she'd never gotten used to as a high-profile chef in New York City. All that attention. The fierce competition and the amplified focus of her every move behind the scenes. She'd put 150 percent of herself into a coveted career she'd always dreamed of obtaining. But she'd rather the spotlight be aimed away from her and on the food. That's where it belonged. That's what she was proud of.

Not wanting to be delayed, she wished the woman good luck and continued down the line. A box of dark, round zucchini tempted her from yet another booth. This sparked an idea for a lovely stuffed starter course. Thinking twice, she worried about the time. Squash picking would have to wait until tomorrow.

While she could've hung around the market to discuss vegetables all day, Ginny had to keep moving or she'd never get out of there. A lengthy to-do list waited back at home. Plus, Olive would (finally) be returning to work, and Ginny wanted to get the girl prepping as soon as possible. It was a veritable relief knowing she didn't have to work solo anymore.

Frankly, she wasn't sure how much more of Olive's flitting around she could take. The business was demanding, and having her singular employee constantly coming and going was less than ideal. But so was the thought of having to train someone else.

Thankfully, the holiday season was over. It had been good to Ginny in one way but taxing in others. The dining room had been full, and work had never been better. Her calendar had been booked solid from November through New Year's, as she'd juggled to accommodate last-minute celebrations and out-of-town guests. But as usual she'd pushed herself too far, running on an average of five hours of sleep a night, tossing and turning over the business. What choice did she have? Too many details required her attention, from the painstaking menu planning right down to making creative table arrangements. With a minuscule staff of one, she'd had to make do.

But Ginny had also let her ego drive her decisions. She'd wanted to impress her guests—and maybe even prove to herself that she still "had it"—by ordering high-priced specialty items and exotic ingredients. For the most part, it had been worth it.

Regular guests had claimed she'd outdone herself with such creations as her Aberdeen Angus grass-fed rib eye with mushroom puree and beef tea; they'd gushed over her sea bass with prawn tortellini accompanied by fennel and a white wine sauce; and the crowd favorite always received lots of compliments, a chocolate orange mousse with fruit brioche. Ginny had spent many backbreaking hours bent over the tiled kitchen counter, testing recipes and perfecting sauces until they satisfied her foodie palate.

She was hard on herself—this she knew—but it was her name and face attached to those dishes, so they had to be perfect.

If at least one guest per night didn't jump up to snatch his or her smartphone and post food photos to a social media account, she considered her presentation a failure. It was the oohing and aahing, people moaning in ecstasy with their eyes closed, cheeks pink with passion as the fork exited their lips, that she loved. To Ginny, there was no better high.

It was the closest thing to pure happiness she knew how to achieve.

People spent an evening with her for an experience they couldn't get anywhere else. Ginny took this seriously. Her lifestyle and her location might have changed since her years in the big city, but not her work ethic or desire to push herself creatively.

The kitchen was her church, sacred and holy. And at forty-two years old, after withstanding losses of all kinds, she required the spiritual fulfillment that cooking offered. It was one thing that remained constant.

Such a level of satisfaction came with a high price tag, though. The visitors who'd arrived over the recent holidays had been of the big-spender variety, so Ginny had had to rise to the occasion and make their experience extraordinary. As a result, she'd wound up depleting her bank account. The season may have stretched her reputation to new clientele, but it had also stretched her funds too far.

Now it was January and bills required payment. The problem was, she didn't have enough to cover them.

And she really didn't want Olive to find out.

CHAPTER FOUR
JULIA

Julia drooped on the sofa as James paced in front of the coffee maker. With each turn of his heels, she felt her dread deepen. James was preparing to leave for the day, which meant she'd be home alone with nothing but her thoughts to keep her company. Unless she counted the growing onslaught of jabs sent her way on social media.

"Could this thing be any slower?" James asked. He was trying to be kind and bring her a dose of caffeine before heading out, but his patience was wearing thin. His slacks pulled at the knees, the dark fabric creeping up his calves as he bent over the narrow kitchen counter. Julia watched him peer repeatedly at the digital readout on the decade-old drip machine. "Why don't you retire this relic and finally use my espresso maker? It takes, like, twenty minutes to brew. How does that not drive you crazy?"

Julia sighed inwardly and rolled over to look out the window. The sky was a light ash gray. She'd been wallowing there, in her bathrobe, since before the sun had peeked out from the horizon. The idea of moving had just felt like too much.

"Julia?" James strode into the living room.

"Huh?" She turned to face him. His clean-shaven face dropped a little; his voice was edged in worry. He held an empty cup at his side and waited. Julia knew he'd never really witnessed her act this vulnerable, this defeated, before. She suspected it scared him.

"Are you going to be okay?" he asked. "I'd love to stay, but you know I can't. Still—"

"I'm fine," she managed to respond, a crack in her voice betraying her words. It was unkind to drag him down into the muck of despair with her. He hadn't done anything wrong, after all. In fact, by all accounts, he'd done everything a partner should do the night before. He'd watched snippets of her show, realized something catastrophic had happened, made phone calls, and finally returned home with an expression twisted with confusion after she'd failed to respond. He'd held her and expressed genuine concern. For this, she was grateful.

James came in close and searched her face. His breath smelled of toasted bagels and toothpaste. She offered a thin smile when her stomach growled. Julia realized she hadn't bothered to eat anything of real substance since her pizza binge two days earlier. If James had noticed her lack of appetite, he hadn't said anything. He'd been around enough to know she was constantly watching her calories for the cameras. Perhaps he hadn't made her a bagel when he'd prepared his that morning because he'd suspected she'd refuse it anyway. They'd been together long enough for him to know her morning meals usually consisted of green liquid from a juicer.

When she didn't say anything more, he leaned in closer, seemingly to scrutinize her thoughts. Impulsively, she grabbed a throw pillow and hugged it to her chest. She felt as if the moment required a kind of barrier, a way to shield her crumbling spirit from the man she loved. He'd seen too much already.

Two steady blue eyes connected with hers as James dipped his head. There was a flash of pity. "There's another way to look at this, you know," he said, using his free hand to push back a lock of her unbrushed hair.

Julia suddenly wondered if she'd even bothered to wash the bleeding mascara from under her stinging eyes. She pulled back a little. "Oh yeah? What's that?"

"You could turn this situation around," he said, standing taller. His words took on the air of a pep talk. "Get showered and dressed and march right back into the office and state your case. Demand the network give you time to prove your story wasn't made up. Get corroborating evidence."

"You mean fix my 'fake news' story? I think it's a little late for that."

"Why?"

"Because there are memes out there, James. Of me. And they're *trending*!" She felt her face contorting and tried to hold back the rising taste of salt at the back of her throat. Her arms hugged the pillow tighter. "There are really awful depictions of me floating around, and they're being retweeted on the hour."

It all felt so unfair. True, she'd made a professional miscalculation and had been irresponsible. She knew better than to broadcast a story that she hadn't fully vetted, let alone discussed with her producer. But it was the way in which the fans of the network had turned so quickly on her. As had her colleagues. No one had bothered to ask her side of the story.

Julia dragged her attention back to his face. She realized he'd given up on her coffee and was moving for the apartment door.

"I really have to go," he said. "You'll figure it out. But don't let those internet stories deter you. What you need is to get back on your feet and take control. Create your own narrative! Dust yourself off and get back out there."

"I'll think about it," she grumbled. Perhaps it was better that he was leaving.

"I hope you do. There's always a way, if you want it bad enough." He waved a hand and was out the door.

Julia pressed backward into the cushions again. James's words echoed in her brain. *Do I want it bad enough?* she wondered. The answer, up until now, had always been a resounding yes.

But now she wasn't so sure.

From under the folds of her terrycloth robe, she retrieved her phone. The temptation to google herself was great, but she resisted. She'd done that too much already, and her discovery had only sunk her deeper into depression. Glancing at the screen, her finger hovered above the list of outgoing calls. Earlier, when James was in the shower, she'd snuck another call to her sister. Only she still hadn't gotten through.

Sitting there, with the apartment empty and her thoughts swirling, she debated. What would be her next move?

And then, all at once, as if her body had made the decision for her, she knew. No, she wouldn't sit there and wallow in self-pity. She would skip town.

Her bag was packed with quick resolution. James would surely understand. It was only going to be a temporary escape.

The question of where she'd go had lingered for only a minute. It needed to be somewhere in the States, in case she was summoned back by the network, which expected her to remain available. She was wise enough not to shake off all her responsibilities. But she also fantasized about escaping somewhere remote enough that the paparazzi and the bulk of GBN viewers and Rossetti loyalists wouldn't recognize her. Somewhere she could have a little breathing room. Somewhere the world had once made sense.

Ginny could ignore Julia's calls, but she couldn't refuse her if she was standing in her doorway.

At least she hoped not.

CHAPTER FIVE
GINNY

Ginny stood in the center of the dining room and fumed. With a mechanical motion, she yanked fistfuls of dry-cleaning bags from wire hangers, retrieving pristine, cream-colored table linens before casting them into a haphazard pile. This was not how she'd wanted her morning to go. But here she was anyway, bedraggled and half-dressed despite the late morning hour, frantically doing Olive's job rather than attend to the food prep that should have begun an hour ago.

Everything had to be started from scratch in Ginny's kitchen, no matter if yesterday's ingredients still tasted good. That rule was non-negotiable. It had held in her restaurant days in New York and it held in Arizona. Always.

Her hopes plummeted as she tossed a mournful glance toward the vacant kitchen. On the front counter lay an unopened box with her name on the label. Her grip on a hanger tightened. There were too many things to do, and she was going to run out of time.

Ginny had planned to spend her morning testing out her newly purchased piece of equipment: a sous vide immersion circulator designed to heat water and circulate it around a pot to maintain precise cooking temperatures. Her last one had broken, and now it was imperative to make sure the replacement product was up to par. The success of the evening depended on it. She needed to spend time confirming everything in the kitchen was just right before the onslaught of guests arrived for the dinner service. She was anticipating a full house. Perfection was expected.

The table linens should've been the least of her worries.

"Where is that damn girl?" she griped aloud, her voice echoing off the dining room's stucco walls. Table setting was Olive's responsibility. Among other things. Ginny desperately needed to be in the kitchen. But Olive—big surprise—was nowhere to be found. And because of this, Ginny began to panic.

Her fingers moved with haste as she folded napkins. With each crease, she carefully inspected them for stains. Whenever she came across a harsh smear of a woman's lipstick or unforgiving dribble of chocolate sauce, she cursed the naive decision to purchase light-colored linens. Originally, she'd believed the color palette would brighten the space and complement the sprawling, dark wood tables. After dozens of services, however, coupled with Olive's unwanted scoffing, Ginny realized she'd been wrong.

And she didn't like to be wrong. About anything.

But Ginny wasn't in a position to replace more items. Her dwindling bank account had been slowly ratcheting up her anxiety level. It felt as if every detail of the business demanded resources she simply didn't have. No matter how hard she worked, the circumstances seemed stacked against her.

Hovering over the rectangular table, Ginny became aware she'd been holding her breath. She had the sensation of something tugging at her, like a strong current threatening to pull her under if she wasn't careful. She understood there was more riding on Olive's absence than just the job. And yet, at the same time, the job was everything. It was what tied the two of them together in a complex knot, forcing them to confront one another on a daily basis and figure out how to untangle their situation. They'd both been at this place before. But somehow, this time felt different.

Ginny didn't want to think about that. Not yet, anyway. She couldn't afford to waste a single minute. With a hasty motion, the thought and the pile of napkins were brushed aside.

Her gaze flicked across the room, taking in the remaining list of chores. A small piece of her softened. The main area, with its traditional southwestern kiva-style fireplace and rounded hearth, was just the type of traditional design she'd been seeking when she was house hunting. The clean white plaster fascia encased everything like a layer of firm frosting on a cake and matched the region's adobe architecture. Woven Navajo patterned rugs were artfully positioned on the mission-style terra-cotta floors. The color palette of earthy clays and brick reds made Ginny feel as if this space was somehow rooted in the earth, at one with the land. Farther out, in the surrounding rooms, simple overstuffed sofas and chairs dressed in twill slipcovers of muted tones were what Ginny hoped gave her guests a sense of peace.

She wanted people to feel comfortable in the space, to be at liberty to sink down into the cushions, enjoying a specialty cocktail while the warmth of a wood-burning fire nipped pleasantly at their cheeks. She'd put a great deal of effort into the arrangement of the furnishings, careful to create an inviting southwestern environment that appeared lived-in but also fresh and new at the same time. Like a chic hotel with a touch of luxury but not an ounce of pretentiousness. It had been a difficult balance to achieve, and she was proud of what she'd accomplished out here in the desert.

As Ginny moved past her musings, her brows knit back together. A sound caused her ears to prick up. Was her phone ringing from another room? She brightened at the thought. Perhaps it was Olive, calling with an apology and an explanation. Maybe Ginny had been too hasty in jumping to conclusions before giving Olive a chance to share her side.

Her mind went backward. Where had she last left that damn phone? She rarely kept it on her person. She knew this aged her—far beyond her forty-two years—but cell phones had never been her thing. She loathed having to carry around something in her pocket that made her accessible to anyone and everyone all the time. One of the reasons she'd become a chef in the first place was the alluring sense of seclusion in the confines of a kitchen. A chance to exist behind the scenes, not at the front of the house, where one had to constantly chat people up and make sure a smile never dropped. That type of socialization was more suited to someone like Olive. The girl had an uncanny ease around strangers. Ginny admired her for this. She only wished Olive had the same sense of responsibility.

The idea that Olive was trying to reach her now, however, propelled Ginny to rush around in search of her phone. She darted from room to room, retracing her steps with urgency. Perhaps this day was savable after all.

At last, she located it on the bathroom vanity. As she reached for it, the illuminated screen darkened. Two missed calls.

Snatching it up, she read the incoming numbers. Seeing that neither call was from Olive, her optimism evaporated. One was from a vendor she knew. The other, earlier caller, she also recognized.

The identity of the first caller unsettled her. Two attempts from Julia over the past twenty-four hours. *What could she possibly want?*

Tucking the phone into her back pocket, she sighed. She and her sister hadn't parted on the best of terms, and their last encounter had been messy.

Her fingers froze with indecision over whether or not to call back. She pondered the various possibilities while staring at her distraught reflection in the bathroom mirror. A worry took hold. The lines around her almond-shaped eyes sank inward. She let her shoulders fall forward.

How had she become this person? This woman with worry lines and hardened edges? She once was so unflinchingly close to the important people in her life, but she had drifted so depressingly far away. Had it been all her fault?

The sudden thudding of the front door, followed by footsteps, stole her focus from the mirror and directed it down the hallway. She only hoped this signaled the arrival of Olive.

"Hello?" a young female voice called out.

Finally!

Ginny rushed toward the entryway, wiping her palms down the length of her sides with a mixture of disapproval and relief flooding her chest. She was familiar with this reaction to Olive's impromptu comings and goings in her life. It was a maddening merry-go-round of hope and angst that Ginny very much wanted to exit. Yet she simply couldn't let go.

"Oh, thank god!" she said, planting her hands on her hips in the entryway. "You're finally here. What took so long? I didn't read about a flight delay. I was expecting you back hours ago! Don't you realize how much there is to do?"

The young woman standing in front of her in a long skirt and cropped top released an army-green duffel bag from her delicate shoulder and scowled. "Hello to you, too, Mother. I'm fine; thanks for asking."

The sharp response cut into Ginny like a wound. A familiar shame rose up and enflamed her face. This twenty-one-year-old daughter of hers had a distinct manner of swooping in and making her feel like a failure. Every time.

Ginny knew responding to her daughter with anger was what normally got her tangled up in an ugly exchange, yet she couldn't help herself. Olive had left her high and dry once again. Plus, her emotions ran hot when it came to her only child. This was the kid she'd cared for even when her ex, the absentee parent, had bowed out at the height of their family troubles. He'd chosen himself over everything else. Despite this, Olive still—maddeningly—ran to her father whenever she managed to scrounge up enough time and money.

It was the one act of defiance that hurt Ginny the most.

There had been other things Olive undoubtedly did to get a rise out of her mother: the tattoos, the nose ring, the monthlong stint of blue hair that she very well knew would put off the uptight, rich, conservative clientele to whom Ginny catered. Whenever Ginny protested, Olive complained about all the injustices she faced. And each argument ended with a final twist of a dagger, the barbed comment that her dad thought it was "cool."

Will, or "Wild Wild Will," as their circle of friends had jokingly referred to Ginny's ex-boyfriend, was nothing more than a failed writer who refused to grow up and accept what it meant to be a partner and a father. Of course he *would* think Olive's little acts of rebellion were cool. His whole life centered on that very concept.

When he left, there'd been no explanation, just a mailbox full of overdue bills and a teenage girl who'd blamed the fractured family unit on the one adult who'd chosen to stick around: Ginny.

Ginny had worked her fingers to the bone. But none of it seemed to matter. Olive's empathy had swung in another direction. Since the breakup, their mother-daughter relationship had been turbulent.

"Olive, you're really late. I was worried about you." Ginny stepped forward hesitantly. She wanted to reach out and run a hand over Olive's bare arm. A faint whiff of lavender oil could be detected. How Ginny wanted to pull her daughter in just once, like old times, and feel the weight of the girl in her arms.

Olive sidestepped her. She didn't like to be hugged, at least not by her mother.

"Olive—"

Her daughter's tanned face scrunched, the soft freckles caving in around her eyes. Olive flipped her newly highlighted, waist-length hair behind the frame of her slender back. "I'm fine," she responded in an acrid tone. "But you weren't really worried about me. Let's be honest. You were worried about tonight's service."

This time, it was Ginny who winced.

Olive parted two chapped lips and sighed. "It's fine, Mom. I've lived with you long enough to know the drill. I said I'd be back in time to work tonight's shift and here I am. Reporting for duty. Dad says hello, by the way. In case you cared."

Ginny was still burning when Olive picked up her bag and brushed past her toward the back rooms.

Emotions always got the best of Ginny, especially anger. And, as always, she regretted her quick mouth. But Olive left her no choice. The girl knew how to push every single one of her buttons. She'd been doing it for years.

Bringing up Will, who the girl believed could do no wrong, was a usual tactic for Olive. Her daughter thought the man had hung the moon, with his weird poetry and existential novel ideas. Ginny's ex could have fallen into depression because his literary work wasn't resonating with an audience. He hadn't yet been able to obtain the career he'd wanted. But Will's inflated ego always prevented him from accepting a "layman's job" to make a living. Nevertheless, Olive still adored and admired him. Ginny supposed this was because her daughter, being more like her creative father, always felt understood by Will in ways that Ginny often dismissed.

"Dad gets what it means to be free," she'd once said. "He works to live. Not lives to work, like other people I know."

The statement had broken Ginny's heart. If only her daughter knew the sacrifices Ginny had made. How the scales of responsibility had been tipped so unevenly. How, for so many years, Ginny had been the breadwinner because her partner simply couldn't be bothered. Ginny had been forced to set aside her thriving career to attend to family obligations. There'd been years of pain because of it. But she'd remained quiet and soldiered on.

She prayed Olive would one day come to her senses and realize Will wasn't as amazing and free as she believed him to be. The reality was that the New York publishing scene had wanted no part of his experimental literature once he veered off the path of relatable essays and short stories and into the self-righteous and obscure. At the first signs of failure, Will had slunk away with his tail between his legs and left a damaged family in his wake. Ginny was just glad they'd never gotten married. They'd lived together for years before they'd broken up, but she'd be forever tied to him because of Olive.

"Thanks for coming back," Ginny mumbled as she watched her daughter saunter away.

"Uh-huh. Don't I always?" A door slammed and Ginny deflated.

Olive had returned for now. Ginny had a sinking feeling, however, that if things continued to deteriorate between the two of them, it might be the last time.

CHAPTER SIX

JULIA

Maneuvering out of town later that afternoon went surprisingly swiftly. It dawned on Julia just how easily it all came together. The packing, booking the ticket, the ride to the airport. In the absence of extra time, she didn't have a chance to second-guess her decision.

Before she left her apartment, she sent an email to Peter with the scant details surrounding her side of the story. She needed him to know that she hadn't just pulled the Rossetti story from thin air. Not entirely, at least. The whole fiasco was born from overhearing what she believed to be a legitimate source gossiping about someone in public office committing a crime. What she didn't tell Peter was that the act of scooping a secret conversation (while she hid behind a bathroom door, no less) kept her from reaching out to that source now that the damage was done. In the aftermath, she found she didn't have the courage to ring up the state attorney's office and admit that she was desperate.

She also made a point to phone James. Naturally he didn't pick up, which she expected. While he always had his phone on him, James wasn't one to return personal calls during business hours. He'd explained to her once before that his days were so overloaded with meetings and client lunches that he didn't have time for pleasantries. It was bad form to talk to his girlfriend while trying to close a deal. She supposed she understood.

Despite knowing this, Julia had hoped to connect, to hear her partner's voice before committing to leaving. A small part of her thought that if she just caught the calm, confident tone of his voice, then maybe she wouldn't follow through on her wild plan. If James picked up, it might be a sign she shouldn't go.

But he didn't.

"James," she breathed softly into the receiver, leaning against the stone-colored wall of their shared bedroom. She closed her eyes and pictured his caring face from earlier that morning. Leaving the comfort of his steadfast security wasn't easy, but something stronger pulled at her core. "It's me. I was hoping to reach you before I go. I'm . . . I'm sorry. I just need some time to figure things out. Away from the city. This thing with work is making me crazy. I wish you could come with me, but maybe it's best you don't. It might be good for me to sort this mess out on my own. At least for a couple of days. I'm headed to my sister's. I'll call once I get there. I love you. Bye." With a swift motion, she hit "End" and turned her phone off.

No use going back now that she'd said it out loud. She really wasn't sure how James would take the news. She only hoped he would understand.

Ginny, however, had not been forewarned with any such message. After considering whether or not to call her sister for a third time and give her a heads-up, Julia decided against it. What if Ginny wouldn't see her? They hadn't spoken in so long that it was possible Ginny wouldn't open the door to her. If that was the case, then where would Julia hide out? Sure, she could check into some obscure hotel somewhere and lick her wounds with the help of a minibar and a movie channel. But being alone wasn't particularly her strong suit. Julia didn't like to be isolated.

She wanted to be *left alone*, not lonely.

There was a big difference between the two. The latter frightened Julia more than she cared to admit. Maybe it was because her childhood, and even early adulthood, had always included the constant company of Ginny and her protective older friends.

Maybe it was because when, many years earlier, Julia had moved to New York and landed her first job in broadcasting, she'd suddenly found herself surrounded by more activity than she'd ever experienced growing up in the Southwest. At work there was always a cameraman or assistant producer in tow. Nights were filled with drinks around large, loud tables of colleagues swapping work-related woes.

And then there were the back rooms of Ginny's Manhattan restaurants, the steaming kitchens buzzing with frenetic energy, the beating pulse of nightlife. Ginny could always be counted on to invite Julia through the back door of whichever restaurant she worked for and plate her something heavenly and rich.

But that was a long time ago.

A female ticketing agent at the airport smiled and scanned the boarding pass on Julia's phone before ushering her through the gate. The departure terminal was busy that time of day, and bodies were pressed together with the frenzied energy that only harried travelers possessed. Everything smelled of a cloying mix of stale air, fast-food grease, and body odor. There was little room for personal space, let alone concealing one's identity.

Julia thought the woman behind the ticket desk threw her a double glance, a pair of pink frosted lips parting ever so slightly with recognition. A flash of heat rose to her cheeks. Hastily, Julia dropped her head and focused on the mottled carpeting as she continued past the woman and down the ramp. A pit developed low in her gut. Maybe she should open her purse and retrieve her dark sunglasses.

She had the last seat in first class, up against the window. Small miracles. At least it wasn't the aisle. With any luck the person next to her wouldn't show up. Relieved to find a landing spot, she flung her jacket down and slumped in her chair. Quickly, she fumbled through her purse and slipped on her metallic aviators. The remainder of the passengers filed past, some casting half-interested glances her way, others too harried to notice. When the door finally latched and the seat next to her remained open, Julia let out a shaky breath.

Thank you, she said silently. And in no time, they were airborne.

~

Five and a half hours later, Julia was jolted awake by the captain's scratchy announcements echoing through the cabin. She had just fallen asleep and now gingerly uncoiled herself from her bent-over position. She squinted at the golden light pouring through her small window and ran a lazy hand through her hair. Flight attendants scurried by, collecting trash and instructing everyone to put their seat backs and tray tables into the upright position. But Julia couldn't help but stare outside.

She'd forgotten about the time difference. Of course the sun had yet to set over the Arizona desert. It was two whole hours behind East Coast time. Somewhere down there, Ginny was likely just sitting down to dinner. And oblivious to the fact that her estranged sister was dropping by for a visit.

How would she explain herself? Julia wondered. And how would Ginny respond?

While her brain tried to fast-forward and imagine all the possibilities, she couldn't help but be mesmerized by the fantastic sight below. It had been too long, but the familiar scene now flooded her memory. Pinks and browns and vivid patches of greens caught her eye, nearly taking her breath away. The expanse of the desert captivated her. In the absence of buildings were low mountains and jagged rocks, colorful houses and muted landscape. It was a curious yet startlingly familiar sight, and one so opposite of the city.

This wasn't going to be easy, to face her present demons in the shadow of her past.

Ready or not, big sister, she thought, *here I come.*

CHAPTER SEVEN

GINNY

Friday nights were always busy, and this one was no exception. There would be two dinner shifts: one table of eight at six o'clock and one table of ten at eight o'clock. She'd assumed with the holidays behind them, she and Olive would be down to only one serving per evening, back to the simple Friday-, Saturday-, and Sunday-night meals that the slower season usually entailed, leaving the weekdays for prep work and free time. However, it appeared the Arizona snowbirds had largely remained in town and were seeking entertainment.

It was times like these, when her patience ran thin and Olive's support even thinner, that Ginny toyed with the idea of opening a legitimate space in a real restaurant, one with a long, silvery bank of reliable commercial-grade equipment, a professionally trained waitstaff, and an eager team of dishwashers and sous chefs grateful for their jobs. Like the old days, only smaller. Much smaller.

But that was not how her vision was playing out here in the desert. When she'd arrived, she'd never imagined she would remain, let alone buy a house and start a business.

Ginny's trajectory in New York had been on the rise. The awards and accolades were beginning to collect. Her status as a celebrity chef was growing. Other restaurants were attempting to poach her because of her winning reputation.

But then, in the midst of it all, her parents died.

Suddenly there were multiple fires to put out back home in Arizona, such as selling off her parents' belongings and outdated house. There were bank accounts to close, burials to arrange, and debts to pay down. All of which required a heavy commitment on her end. And then there was the agonizing weight of grieving that quickly settled in.

Julia, who had all too easily shed her Arizona roots in search of greener pastures, was too wrapped up in her skyrocketing news career to help. Her sister was hungry for the limelight, and once she got a taste, there was no looking back. Arizona, Julia claimed, had nothing more to offer her. With no other siblings or close family to call on, the burden fell on Ginny, the firstborn, to pack up her daughter and life in New York City and head out west. No matter the cost.

In one fell swoop, Ginny was forced to make a serious pivot from her culinary career in Manhattan. There was simply too much to handle for her to return to her job. Handling the affairs associated with her parents' deaths took over for far longer than she'd ever expected. Her circumstances also put considerable strain on her relationship with Will, and in the end, he didn't care enough to stick around and wait.

Thus, Ginny's homecoming visit turned into a permanent stay.

Since then, she had done a lot of research and profound soul-searching to figure out the best way to utilize her talents. There were the tight parameters of having to work within her means as well. It was at that point that everything changed.

So there she was, in a quieter location with quieter clientele. Ginny had launched a boutique business. A larger operation would have required more start-up capital than she could comfortably dole out; she also needed to keep a low profile so that reservations didn't hit a critical mass. Through trial and error, she'd finally figured out how to stay connected to her cooking roots, be her own boss, and also earn some sort of income.

A secret supper club.

Emphasis on "secret."

Before coming to Arizona, underground supper clubs—hidden speakeasies for well-heeled foodies and dinner club enthusiasts—were a concept of which she was only vaguely aware. While Ginny was working for well-known establishments in the city, the kind that had months-long reservation lists and whose regulars ordered thousand-dollar bottles of wine, the idea that some other mysterious chef was carving away a piece of her clientele with a makeshift kitchen in some clandestine apartment-size dining room had seemed farcical. Those rogue chefs had no staff, no regimented health codes, and no premier window tables to offer. How could they try to compete?

Plus, if they got caught, there was a hefty fine to pay and they'd be run out of business, if not out of town.

How ironic that after Ginny sorted out all her viable options, such a scenario became her reality. Running a business out of her dining room was about all she'd been able to handle, given her new circumstances.

Before she knew it, three years had gone by and the supper club had taken over her entire life.

Running her own business, Ginny now found herself sleep deprived, stressed out, overweight, and out of joy. She'd given every part of herself to getting her supper club off the ground and now to keeping it at a low boil, popular enough to drum up regular business but secretive enough to operate under the radar. On top of this, her daughter was pulling away even further.

Ginny wasn't sure if she'd find happiness again. At least, not the kind of happiness that she'd known in New York.

She could say the same for Olive. Her daughter was resentful of the work Ginny asked of her. Perhaps even resentful of their life altogether.

Now, as Ginny glanced at the clock, she noticed it was five thirty in the evening. The first guests of the weekend shift would be arriving soon. Olive had shown herself only once since returning, ambling to the refrigerator in her sweatpants to retrieve a mineral water and a package of pretzels and then sleepwalking herself back to her room.

Ginny stood in the center of the kitchen and seethed. She was sure her willful child was aggravating her on purpose, failing to hustle around and prepare the house the way she should before an onslaught of customers. Olive was waiting until the last possible minute to "show up" for work, and Ginny realized her daughter was making a statement by doing so. Olive wanted out of the family business. That much was clear. And she was possibly even unhappy that she'd had to leave her father's carefree lifestyle and return to her mother's, where the theme was work.

There was no avoiding the fact that they both needed the money and Ginny needed the staff.

She frantically scrubbed counters and mixed sauces, counting the minutes until her hostess / server / sommelier decided to grace the room with her presence.

A timer dinged, and Ginny snapped back into focus. The planned starter course of heirloom tomatoes and butter lettuce salad had been prepped. But she still had to clean dozens of scallops and mince green onions for the second course.

Her current roadblock, however, was that the white truffle sauce she'd been whisking wasn't cooperating. She'd envisioned a thicker version of what currently frothed in a bowl. The color wasn't right either. She dove a jittery index finger into the creamy liquid and then touched it to her tongue. The flavor wasn't bad, but it would never fly in a professional kitchen. She pushed the bowl back with a sigh. It would have to do.

She was running out of time, and Olive was leaving her little choice but to cut corners and make concessions.

Thankfully, the carrot-and-ginger puree had already been made, and the main course of salmon would require only a quick searing. Sometimes seafood felt less complicated to Ginny. Tonight, she was grateful for the menu she'd planned. The guests hadn't reported a shellfish allergy when they'd made the reservation, but there wasn't time for alternatives anyway. Not tonight.

"Olive!" she yelled. "Can you come help, please?" She could hear a scuffling around in the back bedroom, then a door opening.

"I'm still getting dressed. Have you seen my black pants?" Olive hollered back.

"Did you check the laundry room?" Ginny rolled her eyes. They had this kind of exchange weekly. Olive was always missing some important article of clothing and passive-aggressively blaming Ginny for its disappearance.

"Yep, checked in there." Olive was getting on Ginny's last nerve.

"Well, I don't know where they are, but you better get your butt out here soon. I'm drowning with prep work and you still haven't put together the cheese platter or uncorked the wine!" Fury boiled beneath Ginny's skin as she waited for Olive to get her act together. People would be knocking on the front door soon, expecting someone to take their coats and their drink orders. Olive was responsible for the front of the house. She had to be. Ginny couldn't tear herself away from the stove. Otherwise, all it took was one talkative guest and the whole schedule would fall behind.

"Olive! Do you hear me? Let's go!"

"Don't yell at me—it only makes me go slower!" Olive waltzed down the hallway on her way back from another room. Her hair was now up in a messy bun and she was only half-dressed. She knew how important Ginny thought it was to be presentable to guests. White shirt, black pants, piercings out, tattoos covered. It was as simple as that. The same standards would've held in any high-end establishment in New York. But Olive never made it simple. She always had to push things to the limit. "I'm getting ready as fast as I can."

"Well, go faster!" Ginny glared in her direction.

Feet slapped down the hallway. The door slammed. *Here we go again,* Ginny thought. Not even twenty-four hours back from her father's and the fighting had already begun. *Perfect.*

Five minutes later, the doorbell rang. And just as Ginny's pulse spiked, heat rising under the collar of her white chef's coat, Olive appeared, dressed and polished. Ginny watched in shock as her daughter breezed down the hallway to the foyer, hair glossy and brushed, lips colored ever so slightly. At the last second, Olive adjusted her blouse and pressed a button on her smartphone to start a low hum of music through the home's speaker system. Her face broke into a warm smile and she flung the door open.

All right on time.

It was a miracle.

"Hello! Come in! Welcome to Mesquite," Olive could be overheard saying in a singsong voice. Ginny released a whoosh of breath, grateful that in front of the guests, Olive set aside whatever animosity existed between the two of them. Her daughter had turned friendly and cheery, giving off an inviting vibe as she announced the restaurant's name.

Ginny had named her supper club after the prominent mesquite tree that shaded the home's picturesque front garden. She adored these deciduous trees—native to Arizona—with their soft, ferny canopies that dotted the desert landscape. The species of velvet mesquite on her property routinely produced fragrant spikes of yellow flowers in April and sometimes again in August after it rained. The blossoms reminded Ginny of random bursts of sunshine. She hoped all who saw them took them as a good omen, just as she had upon discovering the house.

When she'd first chosen the name, Olive had even sketched out a logo, complete with a whimsical, twiggy tree. She'd enthusiastically suggested Ginny get cocktail napkins printed up to match. The gesture had warmed Ginny. Olive was very creative and could be generous with her ideas when she wanted to be. When Ginny wasn't "pressuring her," according to Olive. They'd had fun picking out the restaurant's colors and the logo's font together. Ginny smiled every time her eyes landed on the logo now, despite everything. She liked to think many of the supper club ideas had been mother-daughter collaborations. Whether Olive wanted to stay and be a part of it was another question entirely.

Ginny listened as Olive directed the guests and then assumed her position behind the width of the eggshell-colored counter. She'd learned by now it was best to remain busy, only greeting the guests temporarily as she chopped and sautéed away.

When people entered her home for the first time, they usually had lots of questions. Many came because a friend suggested Mesquite, or they had read up on Ginny's career—her Michelin star–rated food and her prominence in the New York food scene—and they were curious about what had brought her out west and whether she would live up to her reputation. Ginny was polite and did her best to be transparent. Most of her repeat customers were now considered friends; they came so often and settled themselves so easily into her home that she'd developed relationships with them.

Tonight, however, the first service was filled with newcomers. Ginny could tell by the curious lilt of their voices and the way Olive toured them through the house. She assumed this group must be mostly stragglers who remained in town after the holidays. There were always one or two local hotel concierges to thank for this new business. Ginny would have to remember to send over treats to the employees as a way of saying thank you.

"Feel free to come in and warm yourself by one of our three kivas— that's what we call our traditional adobe-style wood-burning fireplaces," Olive was saying to the cluster of elderly people who trailed behind her into the living room. "Dinner will be served in here." Ginny peeked out around the corner and spied her daughter waving a hand toward the set table. "But feel free to make yourselves at home while I get drink orders going."

Half a dozen men and women, all smartly dressed and sporting silver hair, nodded and smiled approvingly as their eyes took in Ginny's home. Several began helping themselves to the overstuffed chairs in the adjacent living room, which was part of the open-concept space. Ginny watched them from her spot, then flagged Olive when they weren't looking.

"We don't have time for them to lounge in there tonight," she hissed under her breath. "And where are the rest of them? I show we have a booking for eight people. I only see six." She anxiously twisted her hands into a rag and waited for Olive to get on her level.

"I dunno," Olive replied. "Why can't they hang out while I handle their drinks? Just calm down for a second and let them chill."

Ugh. Ginny loathed that word. Olive told her to "chill" on a regular basis. It usually had the opposite effect. Why couldn't Olive see that this business was important to Ginny? Would it kill the girl to take things a little more seriously?

"Olive, I swear," she said. The rag was tossed to the side. "Don't start with me tonight. We have two bookings, back to back. Need I remind you? So can you please just seat these people and get a move on?"

A look filled with daggers shot in Ginny's direction. "For your information, I left what I was doing at Dad's just to come here and help you out. Which, I might add, you never bothered asking me to do. You just demanded. Like always. Like I have no life beyond your kitchen. And here I am, the dutiful daughter taking orders. But instead of saying thank you, all you've done since I got here is point out your disappointment."

Ginny frowned and craned her neck. She quickly checked to see if the others were within earshot of Olive's rising tantrum. After ensuring that the group was still chatting among themselves, she fixed her gaze on Olive.

"For your information, missy, I do take you into consideration. Why do you think I gave you all that time off to go be with your dad for the holidays? Do you know how I busted my butt doing this job alone while you were on vacation? And you might be back," she said, her finger jutting out and shaking in Olive's direction, "but you're not *really* back. You've got your head in the clouds, and you don't seem to care how your thoughtlessness is affecting my business."

"Ha!" Olive laughed a little too loudly, the whites of her molars flashing as she tilted back her head. Ginny's eyes darted to the other room. "That's a laugh. How could I have my head in the clouds when you're constantly yanking me back down to earth?"

"I don't—"

"Save it." Olive shot a hand up. "I don't have time to hear whatever you're about to say. We've got guests. Remember?"

Ginny's jaw tightened. She loathed the snark. "Yes, of course I realize that."

"Well, we know you'll blame me for running behind schedule if our guests don't get seated ASAP." The sneer on her lips lingered as Olive spun away, her flaxen hair splaying across her shoulders. Ginny watched her back as she snatched an open wine bottle from the sideboard and tromped into the living room.

My daughter hates me, Ginny thought. She stood, dumbfounded, as Olive briskly went about seating people and pouring the wine. Not once did she look back in Ginny's direction. They'd fought plenty before, but something about the way her daughter's words were so barbed sent a shiver of worry down her spine. Then, a second and even more unsettling thought occurred. *She's going to leave me.*

Ginny tore her gaze away and went back to plating the first course. Olive would be back any second, expecting food, and Ginny needed to keep on schedule. She cursed herself and the restaurant for getting in the way. She wanted to pull Olive aside so they could sit down and hash out their feud. But there wasn't any time. People were waiting. And Ginny needed to get paid.

Hastily, she shoved handfuls of salad onto plates. She cursed when her jittery hand nearly knocked over the container of dressing. What was going through Olive's head out there as she fake smiled and then poured waters? The girl was detaching herself. That much was clear. Ginny had a feeling something terrible was about to happen. She only wondered how to stop it.

CHAPTER EIGHT

JULIA

The wheels touched down, and Julia put her plan into motion. She wanted to get on the road and head toward her sister's neighborhood as soon as possible. Her feet carried her through the airport's baggage claim and then on to secure a rental car. The frugal side of her kicked in when she stepped up to the rental counter.

"I'll take the smallest car you've got," she announced, handing over her credit card. Keeping her sunglasses nearby, she scouted the area for onlookers but saw none.

A young kid hunted and pecked at a computer keyboard at a snail's pace. Julia huffed and wondered whether she had enough savings to float her salary for a while. If things got bad and she couldn't find gainful employment after her debacle, that apartment of hers might not be so easy to swing anymore.

Of course, James had money. Because of this, she and her fiancé lived quite comfortably, and then some. James's job was solid, and he brought in enough to cover both of them. But Julia didn't like the idea of having to rely on him. Not yet, anyway. That would perhaps come later—if they ever actually sat down and planned a wedding. For some reason, there never seemed to be time for it. At present, it still meant something to be someone on her own.

There she was, however, ordering an economy-size car and uneasily counting the bills in her wallet. Her shoulders sagged. How did she get to this point? She couldn't think about it. Otherwise she might curl into a ball.

Once through the parking garage and inside her compact vehicle, she had a distinct feeling of déjà vu. She knew this car, or its type anyway. It was the lack of decent legroom and the faded velour upholstery reeking of another woman's perfume that sparked her memory. Julia was instantly reminded of her rookie reporter days.

Back in her twenties, she'd traveled regularly in cars just like this one, holding on to a shaky wheel and navigating with paper maps through small towns. There was never any fancy news van, like those seen in movies. Oftentimes she'd go it alone, setting up a camera and writing a short script all by herself. But those were the demands of the job. She'd had to prove her tenacity to get noticed.

As a general news reporter, she was forever en route to log a story. When she wasn't working, she was brushing up on law, city codes, and environmental studies. She had to at least sound like she knew what she was talking about.

Early on, the stories assigned to her didn't have much girth. The local station that employed her wasn't big on taking risks with newbies. This was understood from the start. She and her equally green cameraman, once he was hired, were usually stuck covering town hall meetings or contentious disputes between a local business and some kind of city parking ordinance or what have you. Nothing sexy, and usually dry as dirt.

There were other times when the story assigned was so remote and away from creature comforts that not a bathroom was in sight. On one particular occasion, she had to hike into the trees—knit dress, patent leather pumps, and all—in order to relieve herself. When she came back out, her legs were crawling with fire ants. That was one of the grimmer memories.

Those stories, however difficult, nonetheless helped her build her portfolio. She cut her teeth on city councilmen interviews and ten-second monologues. It was all in a day's work, and back then, she'd loved every minute of it.

Not having driven for a long time, Julia now welcomed the chance to get behind the wheel of the rental car and hit the open road. Even if it was a congested Phoenix interstate. Lately, most of her commuting had taken place in the back seat of an Uber. And she was ashamed to realize that during those rides, she'd hardly peeled her gaze away from her devices long enough to appreciate the view.

But out here, where the air was a little easier to breathe, Julia consciously took in the backdrop.

Starting her journey, she briefly considered checking into a hotel. Perhaps waiting things out for a bit longer would be the wise decision. After a good night's sleep, she could rise and strategically drive out to Ginny's address. But when exactly was the right time to show up on an estranged sibling's doorstep? she debated.

After coffee?

On a weekend?

Or while she still had the courage?

Speeding along the interstate toward the foothills, she opted for the latter. *Best to seize the moment,* she thought. A little surge of adrenaline coursed through her veins, making her giddy and nervous all at the same time. There was no telling what Ginny's reaction might be. There was also no telling what kind of condition she'd find her sister in. Would she be a total couch potato, having folded up her career? Or would she be a hardened product of the Arizona sun, tucked away on some ranch, growing produce and hiding from society? It was impossible to know, considering Ginny didn't subscribe to any form of social media. Julia's half-hearted research had never turned up much.

And then there was Olive to consider. Where on earth was her niece? The last Ginny had heard, Olive was still yo-yoing between her mother and her father. That much probably hadn't changed. She knew the girl held an affinity for her artsy father but also kept a somewhat forced loyalty to Ginny. It had been a hard situation to watch while they still lived in New York. Julia had tried, years ago, to be present in Olive's life. But so much had changed.

A twinge of guilt came over her as she thought about it. She should have tried harder to reach Olive via text or email or something over the past few years. Despite the widening gap between Julia and her sister, Olive should have been better looked after. Instead, Julia had let work consume her schedule and her dear niece slip from her life too easily.

It was a shame that had clung to the shadows of Julia's mind for too long.

Gripping the wheel tighter, she tried to bring up an image of Olive's young face. The wide-eyed little girl who used to fall into fits of contagious laughter and had the ability to fill any dull room with joy. Julia loved that girl. She needed to find her now and tell her she was sorry. That she'd do better, no matter what her relationship was with her sister. An aunt should be someone to be relied upon. It was a precious role Julia had been given, but she'd fallen short in her duties. She'd make up for it somehow.

She just needed to get to Ginny's. Before she lost her nerve.

~

Thirty minutes later, after snaking over highways and onto a quieter road that pointed toward the mouth of the foothills, Julia neared Ginny's listed address (thank goodness for the online white pages). She checked the time and wondered what her sister might be doing at seven thirty in the evening on a Friday night.

Her thoughts drifted.

The western sun lingered overhead, despite the dinner hour. After being away for so long, Julia had nearly forgotten about the Arizona skies. Witnessing her surroundings now, a powerful nostalgia welled up. Images of her mother in the backyard, picking lemons from a row of citrus trees, her father tipping back his hat under the summer sun, and Ginny's bright face during their childhood games of hide-and-seek among the saguaros all came rushing back. These were memories she carried from a simpler time, and that time was now gone.

Julia craned her neck to peer upward through the bug-pitted windshield. A pinkish glow radiated overhead. Peaked mountaintops stood silhouetted in the distance, large shadows against the changing light. A thin ribbon of blue remained at the crest of the skyline, and a few bright stars could be seen as evening morphed into night. The beauty that greeted her was overwhelming.

She was starting to recall a bit of the appeal, why her sister returned home and then stayed there. But only a bit.

Easing her foot off the gas, she scanned the area. The homes, which were popping up more frequently now, mirrored the color palette of the sky.

Ginger-hued adobe buildings rose up from the brown earth, colorful and warm. Some were clustered together and modest in stature; others were situated on swaths of cactus-dotted land with gated driveways, outdoor decks, and visible swimming pools. The modernized pueblo-style architecture of the homes was impressive.

She'd passed a couple of swanky resorts just north of downtown, luxurious-looking ones that had soothing names and most likely equally soothing spa services. She'd made a mental note of their locations, just in case this surprise visit with Ginny didn't go well and she needed a place to stay. Not that she could afford to splurge too much, but still. The idea of a deep-tissue massage followed by an aromatherapy steam shower was rather tempting. She might very well require that type of rescue from her current predicament back home.

What awaited her now was anyone's guess.

The automated voice on the navigation app announced she'd reached her destination. Julia sucked in her breath and looked around. *So this is Ginny's street.* Instinctively, she stopped. Maybe this was a bad idea. Now that she was here, a matter of feet from her sister's house, she wondered if she was running the risk of disaster.

Don't back out now, she told herself. It was important to be brave. And why couldn't she be? After all, she'd taken all kinds of chances as a reporter over the years, overstepping boundaries and pushing a microphone into people's faces. What was her problem now?

She knew what it was. She'd lost her nerve.

Before she could fully pull over to the curb and gather up a bit of bravery, bright lights sliced through the darkened neighborhood and a car unexpectedly peeled down a gravel drive. It barreled out in her direction. Julia swerved, narrowly avoiding the headlights on an oncoming Jeep as dust and debris kicked up into the air. The Jeep's windshield was partially obscured, but for a half second she thought she recognized the driver. A young woman with a flurry of highlighted hair sped past her, nearly causing a collision.

"What on earth?" Julia removed her jittery hands from the wheel and then let them drop into her lap. Relieved she'd avoided an accident, she exhaled the breath she'd been holding.

And then she started, the cogs in her brain still spinning. That wasn't just any girl. That was Olive.

A flag of worry flickered. If that really was Olive flying out of there, then Julia suspected trouble. And now here she was, about to walk into it.

She hesitated for a minute longer, calculating.

The Jeep had come from a narrow driveway just a few yards ahead. Julia glanced in both directions and realized there were hardly any other residences around. This tucked-away neighborhood had a remote feel to it, with scrubs and spindly trees occupying the empty space. It was almost like another planet.

Was her sister living like a hermit?

Shifting the car carefully back into gear, Julia eased parallel to the curb until she reached the still-dusty driveway. Putting the car back into park, she stared.

Dusk had just fallen, and it would have been difficult to see save for the twinkle of lights at the top of a small rise. Julia climbed out of the driver's side and squinted. A front patio was strung with tiny white party lights, and more light poured from the windows of a single-level adobe home.

Curiosity tugged at her. Snatching her purse, she trudged up the gravel drive. It wasn't terribly steep, but her footing was off due to the loose rocks. She cursed herself for wearing shoes with a heel. They were impractical for travel, but then again, her head hadn't been fully clear when she'd fled town.

Closer now, she was able to make out the front of the property. A scattering of outdoor lights lit the way. It was charming, really. The gravel entrance led to a circular drive with an umbrella-like tree right in the center. A kind of rustic gate fashioned from wooden sticks was unlatched, and it swung onto a footpath leading to a bright-blue door. The house itself was a cream-colored stucco in a style similar to the adobe houses Julia had seen along her drive. This one had a kind of historic feel to it, with arched entries and sunken windows. There was even a part of the roof that appeared thatched. Glimpsing to her right, she noticed a small fountain gurgling near the front door.

Julia's breath caught as she came to stand closer still, now on the front path's row of brick-colored pavers. Her feet ached from the trek up the driveway. Seeing the smooth, warm pavers, she had a sudden—if not inexplicable—urge to slip out of her shoes and spread her bare toes on their surface. The whole path felt oddly reassuring somehow, as if she was welcome even though unexpected.

"Huh," she murmured to herself. This wasn't at all what she'd imagined. But then again, she wasn't sure what she'd expected to find. Certainly, Ginny had always had good taste, with an eye for all things comfortably elegant. But when Julia had heard that her sister had sold their childhood home and bought a place in the desert, she'd envisioned something more rustic.

The exterior of Ginny's attractive home indicated her sister hadn't fully gone off the deep end. But just to be sure, she needed to get inside and lay her eyes on the place. And on Ginny.

Approaching the front door, Julia heard a trickle of laughter float through an open window. She froze.

Both male and female voices could be overheard, joining in the low din of lively conversation. She started again, her finger hovering over the doorbell. She hadn't expected Ginny to be entertaining. Was she about to crash a party? Her finger hung in midair a second longer as she debated. Creating a scene was the last thing she wanted.

Now or never, Julia.

On impulse, she pressed the doorbell. Fast footsteps could be heard on the other side of the door. Julia's leg twitched; she forced herself not to turn away. If she embarrassed herself, so be it. At this point she had little left to lose.

The door flung open. "Olive?" Ginny's expectant eyes looked out, searching, and then bulged. The gleam of a white chef's coat pulled across her shoulders. Ginny recoiled. Her face was red, and Julia noticed small beads of perspiration gathered at her temples. A deep line of worry hung above her brow. They both stood there a beat longer as a mixture of disappointment and shock crossed over Ginny's face. Julia was not at all whom she was expecting.

"Oh!" Ginny gasped. A bit of color drained from her face. "It's you."

"Hello, Ginny." Julia attempted a smile and waited for her appearance to sink in. She wondered why her sister was wearing a work outfit. Was she catering something? At her own house? She'd assumed Ginny had given up being a chef when she left New York. This didn't make any sense. "Is this a bad time?"

By the stunned expression on Ginny's face, she was sure it was.

CHAPTER NINE

GINNY

The words caught in Ginny's throat. Discovering her younger sister in her doorway had kicked up an unexpected tornado of grief and anxiety that swirled wildly inside her. Standing speechless, she tried to unscramble the bizarre turn of events. First, Olive had stormed out. In her place, astoundingly, was her little sister, whom she hadn't seen or heard from in years.

Three long years of tension and resentment. And silence.

What exactly was going on?

Her eyes searched Julia with disbelief. There was her sister, looking like she hadn't aged a bit, all polished and put together and expectant. This was real. It just made no sense.

A burst of laughter, followed by the clinking of stemware, trailed out from the dining room. Ginny cringed and then threw an uneasy glimpse over her shoulder toward her waiting guests. Hastily, she whipped her focus back to her sister.

"Aren't you going to invite me inside?"

"What are you doing here?" Ginny's inquiry was delivered with an edge of accusation. She opened her mouth to ask another question but then snapped it shut. She hadn't meant it to sound that way, but this was the worst possible timing for an unannounced visit. Especially one that could be volatile. She and her sister hadn't exactly parted on the best of terms.

And now she didn't know how to feel. Or what Julia wanted.

"I came to see you. And Olive." Julia's voice croaked, and she offered a timid smile. "Surprise."

"Yeah, surprise is right." Ginny ran a hand over the back of her neck, her level of discomfort rising.

Julia waited with blinking eyes.

"I thought you might be Olive."

"I think I saw her driving away," Julia said. A manicured hand waved in the direction of the road. "Does she have a Jeep?"

That was her. Ginny deflated. She swiped the tea towel she was wearing at her forehead and then let it drop to her side. "Damn. I can't believe she took off like that."

She scanned the distance beyond Julia's shoulder. Fresh anxiety bubbled up. What was she going to do now? There was an entire evening's worth of dinner guests to wait on and no one around to help. Ginny couldn't afford to send anyone away. There was too much riding on the evening.

Julia shifted, clearly uncomfortable. "Oh! Well, hopefully she'll be back soon?"

"I don't know." Ginny felt the hope draining out of her. She studied Julia. "This is quite a surprise. But it's kind of a, um . . ." She wavered. One part of her wanted to grab Julia by the shoulders and pull her close, to pepper her with questions about why she had come. To find out if Julia was sorry and if she'd finally come to make amends.

But the other part of her, the practical and responsible side, needed to send Julia away before more damage could be done. There was an entire roomful of customers—paying customers—waiting on her. Food was likely burning on the stove at that very moment. Sauces would be curdled, vegetables would go limp.

Ginny had her daughter to blame. Olive had gotten too angry and left her mother in the lurch, right in the middle of preparing the main course. Because of this, there was now no one to serve. And time was not on Ginny's side.

The evening was already running terribly behind, thanks to Olive's antics, and another shift of diners was expected to arrive shortly. On top of all this, Ginny's only sibling had shockingly appeared out of nowhere and landed on her doorstep with a heavy look of expectation. What in the hell was Ginny supposed to do?

Julia faltered in the doorway, the points of her high heels balancing just over the threshold. Her voice rose into a tight question. "I could come back if you want. Tomorrow?"

What was she to say? Ginny's mind raced. Her eyes darted to her wristwatch. *Damn!* She was so far behind. Plus, she was worn out. Between fighting with Olive and trying to keep up with a demanding double shift, her limbs were weary and her head ached. A layer of sticky sweat had settled just underneath her chef's coat. All she wanted to do was find a soft spot and collapse. But there was no time for that. Not if she wanted to keep Mesquite's reputation and get paid.

She summoned up a bit of energy and then studied Julia. "You for sure saw Olive take off in her Jeep?"

Julia pumped her head. "Yeah, she looked like she was in kind of a hurry."

Ginny snorted. "You could say that."

"Anything I can do to help?"

Help? She did need assistance. Preferably from Olive. Ginny's mouth twisted; she was ready to decline Julia's offer. It was absurd to involve her sister. Mesquite wasn't for everyone, and Ginny preferred to keep it that way.

Besides, Julia surely didn't realize what she was asking. And she wasn't normally one to be relied on for help. Not really. But still, should Ginny accept? She really didn't want to. The rational side of her brain knew doing so would turn out disastrous. How could it not? Yet Ginny's present circumstance felt equally absurd. She was overextended in every sense of the word.

Gathering herself up, Ginny prepared to eat crow.

She gave her sister a once-over, taking in the done-up hair and perfectly applied makeup. Julia's bird-thin torso was sheathed in an expensive-looking silk blouse that revealed faint semicircles of sweat under her arms. Ginny wondered how long Julia'd been traveling. The hike up the rocky driveway would have been treacherous in those ridiculous heels. Her sister looked out of place. This wasn't the city. Julia's polished, metropolitan ensemble looked as if she might have just walked off the set of *Daybreak*.

Ginny knew some of Julia's present life. Julia was a cohost for a morning show with a major news organization. She only half-heartedly followed her sister's career online and tuned into the show occasionally. While she'd wanted to learn of Julia's success, sometimes it hurt too much to witness it. Ginny was always left with a bitterness that was difficult to ignore. That and regret.

A memory of their last time together dislodged itself and began to play back in her mind. She recalled an argument fraught with grief and misunderstanding. A room full of moving boxes and hurtful words. The image of her sister's rigid back as she stormed away.

"Ginny?"

Ginny shook herself from the recollection. Precious minutes were being wasted. "Your timing is kind of lousy," Ginny admitted. "I don't really know what brought you here. And I'm sure whatever it is requires a lengthy discussion. But if you're really offering to help, I could use it."

Julia stepped forward, her white teeth gleaming. "Yes. Anything! What do you need?"

"What I need is no questions asked. Not tonight, anyway. I just need help. Do you think you can agree to that?" Ginny scrutinized her sister's face and tried to press back her mounting anxiety as she waited for an answer.

"Okay. Agreed."

"Come on, then." She waved Julia inside and instructed her to follow as quickly and quietly as possible. Scurrying through the living room and into the kitchen's side entrance, they were able to avoid being seen. Ginny hastily checked the still-simmering pots, lifting the metal lids and sticking her nose down for close inspection. She then switched off all four burners. Luckily, none of the delicate sauces had been scorched.

She could feel Julia's wide eyes on her as she flung open drawers to produce clean utensils. Her kitchen was much messier than she normally kept it. And there were strangers waiting in the next room. There would be judgment, Ginny was sure of it. Julia was good at that part. But she was willing to deal with those repercussions tomorrow. Tonight, she needed to cook.

"Here," she urged under her breath. Julia appeared frightened by her curt tone. "Wash your hands and put this apron on. You remember how to serve, don't you? Like when we used to work at Manny's together?"

Julia's well-defined brows shot up. "I'm serving? Food? To those people in the other room?" A lacquered nail pointed. Ginny could tell by her sister's alarmed expression that the statement had thrown her off-balance.

"Yes, just pretend you're in high school again. Seriously, this is a big deal to me. I promised I would explain tomorrow, and I will. But for right now I've got six hungry people in there." She angled her head toward the adjacent dining room. "Another ten are coming thirty minutes from now. I'm behind schedule and understaffed. This is you, helping. And this is me, accepting. So tie that apron around your waist and start taking out plates once I've placed them on the counter. As fast as you can. *Comprende?*"

Ginny inhaled and looked Julia hard in the eye.

"*Comprende,*" Julia stammered back. She understood. It was an old inside joke they had, to answer in the affirmative using a Spanish word. They'd learned it from their former boss at a local eatery back home. Recalling Manny's was sentimental for Ginny. It was the place where she'd fallen in love with being in the kitchen. Manny had opened her eyes to the possibilities of food. She also believed it was where her sister had fallen in love with listening to other people's stories. In a way, Manny's Restaurant had sent them each on the course toward their future.

It had been a long time since Ginny had reflected on that part of her life. Manny's represented a time when the two sisters had been so close. Ginny and Julia used to playfully mock Old Man Manuel behind his back, shuffling around and yelling, "*Comprende, girls? Comprende?*" Ginny would hold up an open hand and shake it in the air. It had always brought them to fits of laughter.

But tonight, it held the potential to bring on another kind of emotion entirely.

The fact that Julia repeated the phrase now meant that she'd heard her sister. Despite the giant chasm of guilt and pain that lingered between them, Julia's response connected them momentarily. Ginny believed Julia would play along. For now, anyway.

She knew there'd almost assuredly be consequences later.

Once Julia had tied a crisp white apron around the waist of her size-zero slacks, Ginny got focused. Her hands flew over dishes and made quick work of sautéing the fish and spooning the sauces. A puree was spread onto plates first and then topped with the main course. After an ultrafine sliver of ginger was placed as the final garnish, she turned and nodded to a dumbfounded Julia.

"Go!" she whispered.

Julia used both hands to scoop up the white dishes, her painted nails curving over the rims. Then she stopped.

"What is it?" Ginny asked.

"Serve from the right, take from the left?" Julia inquired. Her head was cocked, her blonde hair cascading to one side. It occurred to Ginny that she suddenly looked very young.

Ginny nodded. "Yes. See? You remember. It's just like riding a bike. Get going before anything goes cold!" She shooed her sister from the room with a face full of encouragement.

Julia strode from the kitchen, her heels clicking on the tile floor. Ginny overheard a burst of voices as people welcomed the long-awaited delivery of hot food. Men and women chattered eagerly, their volume traveling to the kitchen. She couldn't make out what they were saying, but she could tell by their tones it was all positive.

As Ginny went for the freezer and began the preparations for the frozen dessert, something dawned on her. She realized that in all her haste, she'd overlooked one thing: Julia, with her sparkling eyes and impressively blown-out hair, might very well be recognized. If that were to happen, what would be the reaction? What would the guests say about a high-profile news anchor appearing out of nowhere to pour their waters and bus their dirty plates? What would Ginny—or Julia, for that matter—offer as an explanation?

Her mind ran through the possibilities. After setting aside a bowl of freshly whipped cream, she cleaned her hands on a towel and did her best to wipe the fear from her face. She raised her chin and strode purposefully toward the dining room.

Well, she told herself, *there's only one way to find out.* Bracing for what might prove an awkward encounter, she went in to greet her guests.

CHAPTER TEN

JULIA

Julia's mouth watered as she placed the final plate of food down on a long wooden table. The setting spread out before her was quite stunning, really. The table's surface, adorned with flickering votive candles and metallic containers cradling miniature geometric succulents, had a kind of rustic elegance with a natural edge and rich finish. She noticed fine white linens had been tucked onto people's laps and polished sterling-silver serving pieces were lined up on each end. Faint notes of acoustic guitar music trailed into the room from a sound system somewhere in the house, and a low fire crackled in a corner fireplace.

Julia also observed that the high-backed chairs were filled with chattering, well-dressed men and women sipping pinot noir and sinking their forks into artfully assembled plates of ginger and fish. The lighting was soft and the mood was festive. A flavorful, buttery aroma encircled the room. At first glance, it appeared to be a dinner party full of happy acquaintances.

But why were these people here in Ginny's dining room while her sister was hidden, toiling away in the kitchen? And why had Julia been made to serve them without so much as an explanation? Perhaps this was one of those dinners offered at a charity auction, the kind that promised a personal chef to cater to the winner's dinner party? She'd seen that sort of event publicized before. But still, why were these people in Ginny's house and not someone else's?

She glanced around the table once more. It was baffling. No one there appeared to be the type of friend Ginny usually kept. It was nothing like her diverse, eclectic New York scene of fellow chefs and colorful artists.

Something felt off.

Julia's empty stomach grumbled loudly as she continued to gawk, causing an elderly woman to swivel around in her seat. The woman's milky-blue eyes drifted upward and then settled on Julia with a hard squint. Her lips pushed out with stern concentration.

Instinctually, Julia understood what would come next. She was going to be recognized.

"I've seen you before," the woman said. Her quizzical stare indicated she was slowly connecting the dots in her head.

"Possibly." Julia stiffened. She sensed the unwanted rush of heat creeping along her skin. She'd experienced that brand of suspicious scrutiny many times before. Strangers would often stop her on the city streets and peer into her face, gauging whether she was famous. She hadn't been on GBN long enough to become a household name— not like the lineup of well-known evening anchors—but she'd been on enough television screens to be recognized by many people. At least in New York.

In Arizona, she had no idea.

This woman's blatant inspection, especially in such close proximity, caused Julia to squirm. Casting about for a place to hide, she stumbled sideways with a burst of clumsiness. Her heel caught and created an unfortunate scraping sound along the colorful Mexican tile. More heads popped up now and curious faces landed on her. The older woman narrowed her eyes. Julia kept her lips tight and forced a restrained smile.

She'd hoped to back out of the room quietly, avoiding the need to engage.

The entire evening had taken the most bizarre turn. In all the scenarios Julia had imagined, this was definitely not one of them. Showing up at her long-lost sister's house only to have an apron and water pitcher shoved into her hands had been shocking. Being recognized, especially after her very public snafu, while serving a bunch of strangers in some remote Arizona dining room, was just plain demoralizing. She'd gone from a high-paid television personality to waitstaff in only a matter of hours.

Perhaps that's exactly what Ginny wanted. Humiliation. If that was the case, coming here had been a big mistake.

"Where do I know you from?" The prying woman twisted farther in her chair midbite, a little fleck of food clinging to the corner of her mouth. Julia had the urge to offer a napkin and walk away. But she didn't want to be rude. The rest of the table paused in their chewing and waited for Julia to respond.

"Oh!" she exclaimed in a well-practiced breathy tone. "You might know me. I may have shown up in your home on occasion." It was a playful line she'd tossed out many times before. One she deployed to suggest she wasn't vain enough—unlike Miller, who relished these types of encounters—to outright announce her GBN status, but that was coy enough to indicate onlookers might be familiar with her show. This reserved answer was apparently not good enough for this crowd, however. Because they all scowled in unison as if she'd said something crazy.

And at the moment, Julia felt a little crazy.

"This is my younger sister, Julia," Ginny announced suddenly, barging into the room with swift authority. The dark-blonde roots of her wavy, cropped hair were damp with perspiration. The effects of working over a hot stove had transformed the fair skin of her exposed neck to a gummy pink. Julia noticed her face was one full shade darker, flushed from hard work.

A tingle of nostalgia ran through Julia. Her sister looked just as she used to in her old Manhattan restaurant days, when she'd labored for hours at a bank of steaming equipment. Only now, she appeared older and perhaps a tinge wearier. It was unsettling and reassuring at the same time.

Ginny dipped her head ever so slightly as she caught Julia's disoriented gaze. It was a signal that the situation would be handled. Julia was to move on.

She retreated gratefully, heading to the sideboard to clutch an icy water pitcher in her mildly shaky hands. She watched as Ginny hiked up the long white sleeves of her coat and smiled at the group. "Julia has come for a visit and kindly offered to help out. This is her first night, so I know we'll all go easy on her."

There was a wink and then a rumbling of understanding.

"Ah." A few of them nodded and murmured to one another before looking back at Ginny.

Julia's eyes darted away and then back to the inquisitive woman, who, unlike the others, still appeared unconvinced.

"Well," the woman began, "I don't see the resemblance. But there is something familiar about you I just can't put my finger on." Julia held her breath as the tip of a semignarled index finger wagged in her direction. She felt as if a fortune-teller were suddenly uncovering an unwelcome truth.

Julia froze and swallowed awkwardly. It would have been so nice to avoid people altogether that day. But no such luck. This woman was suddenly a dog with a bone. Julia realized a better explanation was in order. Or perhaps a white lie.

Her lips parted, but nothing came out. She cast Ginny a pleading look.

"Julia works in the media," Ginny said. "She's on vacation from New York. Coming for a bit of sun. Just like most of you. Am I right?"

Ginny chuckled a little too loudly, her throat undulating. "Who here is from out of state? I'd love to know where my guests hail from!" Her eyebrows arched as she made her way to the head of the table, smoothing down her coat and offering a handshake to a couple seated near the end.

"Oh, my wife and I are from the East Coast," offered one man in a neatly pressed linen shirt.

Then another woman perked up. "I'm from Connecticut! And I ate at one of your restaurants when you worked in New York."

"Really?" Ginny asked. Her smile deepened. She placed a hand over her heart. "And you found your way to my private dining room. I'm flattered." The guests bobbed their heads enthusiastically. "Tell me what you think of your salmon this evening. I tried something new."

A multitude of voices chimed in at once.

And just like that, Ginny was able to steer the conversation swiftly away from Julia and any potential scandal. The room thankfully switched gears, and guests expounded on Ginny's specialty menu. Eager diners doled out equal amounts of praise and enthusiasm and agreed they'd be back.

Julia slipped from the room, stunned.

Despite whatever hard feelings her sister might harbor, despite the purposeful distance between the two of them, Ginny apparently still held on to her role as protective older sister. It was quite astounding, really.

A small patch of warmth bloomed in Julia's chest, filling a place that had been empty for so long.

She tilted her hip against the kitchen counter and waited for Ginny to return. At present, the kitchen was quiet. It was the first moment she'd had to fully observe the space. The interior of the home had a definite southwestern feel, with brightly patterned woven rugs, slipcovered furniture, and authentic-looking tile. A charming fireplace stood in the corner of the breakfast nook, with a smooth, rounded hearth. Its broad base and narrow top included a little recessed shelf notched into the white plaster, which housed miniature bits of Mexican art.

A set of glass doors led out onto a patio, and beyond that was a view of the mountains. It was dark out now, so it was difficult to see, but she could make out that much from where she stood. On all accounts, the house seemed to offer a cozy, lived-in vibe with a wide-open outdoor space. It was rather welcoming. Like a meditative retreat of some sort.

Listening to the hum of conversation in the next room, Julia allowed herself to relax slightly. She eased her sore and swollen feet from her shoes and rested them on the cool tile. Leaning back on her elbows, she surveyed the kitchen. The first thing she spied was a nearby bowl of fluffy whipped cream, and she wondered if she might steal a quick spoonful. Next to this she noticed a thick cutting board piled high with beautiful arcs of dark chocolate shavings. The temptation of sugar lured her closer. Slowly, she reached out and placed a few fragments of sweetness on her hungry tongue.

Julia closed her eyes and sighed. The reward was immediate. Velvety heaven melted in her mouth. Oh, how she'd missed desserts.

Maybe coming here wasn't such a terrible idea after all. As long as she could keep up the pretense, that was. Julia wasn't ready to disclose the details of her epic career failure to Ginny just yet. The humiliation was still raw. She also didn't know if Ginny could be trusted with her feelings. Though she was willing to find out.

Just as Julia's weary limbs began to go slack, Ginny came rushing back into the kitchen. The friendly face from the other room had vanished. Julia tensed. Hopefully there wasn't any chocolate on her mouth that would give her away.

"No time for standing around," Ginny said. She clapped her hands together as if to jolt Julia from her stupor. With quick movements, she strode past Julia's sagging pose and began retrieving things from the freezer.

"What do you mean?" Julia asked, perplexed. At this point in the evening, with a long day of travel and the time difference catching up to her, she was more than ready to go somewhere quiet to lay her head. Surely Ginny didn't expect her to keep working.

She pointed toward the other room. "It looks like the dinner's winding down and all your guests out there are happy." She watched Ginny embellish ice cream with swirls of crisp meringue, chocolate shavings, and berries. After sticking a sprig of mint into the side of each one, Ginny shoved the icy bowls in Julia's direction.

"What I mean is we have to get these people through dessert, pronto. I've got another group coming very soon. If we don't get this first group out of here by the time the others arrive, I'm screwed."

She can't be serious.

Julia looked on, dumbfounded. Glistening bowls of ice cream were lined up and waiting to be served. "Wait a minute. What? I thought you were kidding. We're playing this game all over again? What exactly is going on here, Ginny? Who are these people? And why are more of them coming?"

Ginny swatted at the air. "Never mind all that. We had an agreement, remember? You promised to help with no questions asked. I don't have time for this. If you want to stay, then stay. If not, I've got work to do!" Ginny's voice escalated and the pink color returned to her neck.

"But—"

Ginny halted. "But nothing. You're the one who came here unannounced. Not me. Remember? So either get your bag and go, or get out there and deliver those desserts!"

Julia bit her lip and deliberated. It was a negotiation. As a reporter who often had to pry more information out of people than they wanted to reveal, she recognized that. And normally Julia would have used some sort of leverage to glean more details before moving forward. But at the moment, with a frantic-faced sister and a clock ticking against her, she didn't see that she had much choice in the matter.

With wounded pride, she shook off her mounting exhaustion. She slipped her swollen and tender feet back into her abandoned shoes. The dessert bowls were snatched up, and she trudged back toward the dining room with reluctance.

Something told Julia it was going to be a long night.

CHAPTER ELEVEN
JULIA

The next morning, Julia found herself alone and upright in a strange bed. She smacked her dry lips. It was as if all the moisture had been sucked from the air overnight. Her hands skimmed across the length of a textured quilt that was not her own. Early-morning light cast shadows on the wall. She cocked an ear. The staccato song of once-familiar caws and chirps traveled in from the desert landscape just beyond her window. She knew these sounds.

A flash of remorse shot through her.

These were the distant echoes of her childhood, of growing up in the comfort of her parents' Arizona home. So much had been lost, and here was a sudden reminder of the grief she'd so carefully locked away.

Rubbing her eyes, she readjusted. It was too hard to dwell on that now. The heartache over her parents' deaths might swallow her whole if she wasn't careful. And that wasn't why she was here.

Instead, she turned her focus to Ginny. The decor of her sister's house was curious—the wrought-iron daybed and its floral printed bedcovers, the punched-tin wall mirror with a brightly patterned inlay, and the tobacco-colored Mexican leather and twig chair standing in the corner. From the looks of the decor, Ginny had embraced her move back to Arizona.

What a strange twenty-four hours it had been.

After the last guest had finally headed out the door just before midnight and the candles had melted down into flattened puddles of wax, Ginny had claimed she was too tired to talk. The lights were turned off and the appliances shut down.

Julia stood in the kitchen in stunned silence as her sister muttered, "Good night." A stack of bedsheets was deposited into Julia's arms, and she was pointed toward the guest room. Julia watched her sister shuffle off down a darkened hallway before she herself collapsed into the guest bed and drifted off to sleep.

She hoped to learn more today, but it was still too early to play detective. Julia turned her attention to her phone instead. Out of habit, she began scrolling. Her home screen filled her with concern. A glaring list of red notifications cascaded downward, announcing half a dozen missed calls and unanswered texts. No doubt James was upset.

A pang of guilt shot through her. Pushing up on her hands, she sat a little straighter in bed. With a hasty motion, she pressed the first message and listened.

"Julia, it's me. What happened? I'm worried. I don't understand why you'd run off like this. We need to talk. Please call me." James's speech sounded broken and far away. She detected concern but also traces of frustration. She'd disappeared, and she'd let him down.

Quickly, she punched out a text. Hi, hon. Sorry I missed your calls. I'm taking the weekend to be with my sister. Don't worry about me. I'm okay. I won't be gone long. I'll try and call soon. She hit "Send" and hugged the phone to her chest.

What she'd wanted to say but hadn't was that she needed space. She wanted to know what it felt like to be quiet enough to hear her own voice rather than everyone else's. But she knew admitting such a thing would only hurt James. He considered them a pair, a dynamic duo that made decisions together. And this was a decision he hadn't endorsed.

How could she tell him otherwise?

A vibration in her hand drew her attention back to the phone. The headline of an online news alert popped up. Months ago, after she'd been hired at GBN, she'd signed up to receive notifications any time her name appeared online. It was an app she'd learned about from Miller. He claimed it was important for them to know what was being said regarding their morning show. How viewers perceived them. Miller loved counting how many times his name was mentioned each week. Julia only partially warmed to the idea, but she played along anyway.

Instinctually, she located her laptop, which lay next to the bed, and brought it to life. Checking the clock, she saw she had just enough time to catch the last ten minutes of the weekend news. She was curious to see if GBN's producers had been keeping a tighter rein on the network's content since her debacle. That would surely have ruffled Miller's preened feathers.

Opening the "Live" link from the GBN website, she waited for it to load. Suddenly her screen changed, and the weekend anchor's face appeared. It felt strange to see this from such a distance. Almost as if she were no longer a part of the staff, or even a part of that world.

Julia pressed the volume button and watched. The anchor offered some friendly comments about the craziness of the local winter weather, a car commercial ran, and then there was a brief wrap-up of the headlines before the show ended.

Julia slumped backward. That could've been her just yesterday behind that desk, reading the news and encouraging viewers to have a good day before signing off. But it wasn't. And the blow this sent to her ego bordered on catastrophic.

Rather than stew in this dangerous sentiment, she decided it was best to occupy her thoughts by clicking on another news site. Perhaps there would be headlines of interest somewhere else. Something to take her mind away from the fear of losing her job.

However, all it took was a singular mention of Rossetti's name linked to hers in an online article for the computer to tumble from her lap. A trickle of panic moved in. She realized that while she might be miles away from the turmoil, it was still out there, looming.

She remained in bed a few seconds longer, contemplating her next move. Sunny daylight had begun to stream in through a large window, and as it did, the bird chirps outside rose by degrees. The usual orchestra of city noises to which she'd become accustomed no longer existed. She found herself missing the sound of life crashing into itself on the streets below. With only the dull hush of silence punctuated by waking wildlife, Julia found herself rather unnerved.

The quiet, she realized, had the acute ability to make her feel alone.

What she needed—or rather, what she was comfortably used to— was a quick jaunt to a nearby Starbucks, where the buzzing of other human life ran abundant. She craved getting dressed up and heading into town for a morning of shopping. Anything that let her hide among the busyness of other people. Julia missed the bustle of her own city. The desert was too uninhabited, too expansive, and too vacant.

Perhaps her spontaneous visit had been a serious mistake. Yet there were still things she wanted to know. For that reason, she was going to have to manage.

Like any good reporter, Julia knew that if she wanted to uncover more about Ginny's new life, she was going to have to get up and walk around. Some sleuthing was in order. It hadn't been so long since her stringer days that her journalistic instincts had completely vanished. There were certain things she needed to understand about her estranged sibling and missing niece. Things she needed to look into.

The urge sent her to her feet. She shrugged on a tunic-length cashmere sweater from the depths of her luggage, wrapped her arms around her middle, and crept barefoot along the cool floor. Julia shivered and cursed herself for packing such thin pajamas.

Truthfully, she hadn't put much thought into her packing at all. Back in New York, she hadn't had any idea what her days might look like if she weren't in the office each morning, researching stories, weighing in during pitch meetings, or taping the news. Even on her days off, she usually found herself at the studio, putting in time. Now, without work, she felt adrift.

She needed to attach herself to something secure. Whether this was her sister remained to be seen.

~

Wandering down a narrow hallway, Julia passed a guest bathroom and a closed bedroom. Hesitantly, she placed her ear against the door and then nudged it back with her toe. She froze when it emitted an ear-splitting creak. Her pulse quickened. The last thing she wanted was to be caught snooping. But she was doing it anyway.

After making sure no one was coming, she let out her breath and edged farther into the darkened space. The soles of her feet left the hard floors and moved over the threshold to connect with a patch of cushioned carpet. Her nostrils tickled at the remnants of a vanilla-scented candle and floral-smelling body lotion.

Pausing, Julia splayed her toes and waited for her eyes to adjust. After a moment she could see an unmade bed resting against the far wall. Quilts and covers were heaped to form a small mountain near the footboard. An adjacent nightstand held a turquoise glass lamp and some dirty dishes. A drooping flower hung forlornly over the side of a mason jar, a few fallen petals at its base.

Julia moved farther into the center of the room, taking mental notes of the space. At the opposite end of the room, away from the messy bed, was a desk littered with lotions, compacts, and a box full of makeup brushes. Along the floor, just in front of a mirrored closet, lay a haphazard pile of a young woman's laundry.

Instantly, Julia recognized this as Olive's room.

Julia walked over and ran a single finger along the edge of the desk. She stared into the distance and tried to recall the details of the previous night. She saw the image of her now-grown niece careening away from the house in a car. The trailing honey-colored hair, the determined hands planted on the wheel. It had been for only a flash, but from what Julia had witnessed, she understood Olive to be very angry. It was all so baffling.

Sweet, shy Olive, who used to take up her crayons and color for hours on end as she sat huddled in a restaurant booth. Then, later, she'd developed into a creative and thoughtful teen. This innocent girl was now, allegedly, an unpredictable—and messy—young woman whom she no longer knew. How had this happened?

A darkness eclipsed Julia's heart. It saddened her to think of the ways she'd failed Olive. When Ginny had still lived in the city and the two of them had been on good terms, Julia had still been too consumed by work to give Olive much attention.

What's worse, Julia knew the girl could have used a confidant. She reportedly had trouble connecting with peers in school, and Will was a failed and jaded creative who encouraged her retreat from society. Ginny was of course killing herself at the restaurant, working late hours and under pressure to perform. Somehow Olive just trailed along, quietly existing in the background.

Julia always planned to do more, to take her niece to Broadway shows and on shopping sprees. She naively assumed there'd be a free weekend here or there to offer up her time. But then she got the job at a start-up network. Her broadcast-news career took off at breakneck pace, just around the time her and Ginny's parents were unexpectedly killed. The sisters clashed over how to handle the affairs, and their relationship fractured. Julia's decision to stay had eventually landed her a dream position at GBN. Ginny's decision to go had cost her her own career.

Life had sent them all splintering into chaos.

Through it all, Julia had always hoped she'd find a way to catch up with Olive. But a grueling work schedule and a new romance hadn't left room for much else. And now here she was, standing alone in Olive's empty bedroom, filled with immeasurable regret.

There was little she could do until Olive returned, which she hoped would be soon.

Exiting, Julia stepped back into the dim hallway and debated. Where to next? There was one door left, but it was shut tight. No light spilled out from the cracks. She could only assume this was Ginny's room. It was perhaps still too early to wake her sister, even though there'd been a late-night promise to rise early and offer explanations. Deciding it was best to wait, Julia pivoted and went in the direction from which she'd come.

Arriving in the galley-style kitchen, she began peering into cupboards and drawers in search of ground coffee. Everything had its place. The utensils and cooking tools were neatly organized by type and size: the metal whisks and silicone spatulas had been separated from the larger ladles and tongs, and so forth. Julia knew her sister well enough to understand that, just like her restaurants, Ginny's home kitchen required a certain level of disciplined perfection. God help the poor soul who accidentally put a confusing boning knife away in the wrong drawer.

Julia had been on the receiving end of that kind of flip-out first-hand. And it cut worse than the knife could.

Reflecting, she shook her head. The memory of a slick-haired sous chef bubbled up. She recalled a young man shrinking in the corner of Ginny's former kitchen after the poor kid had neglected to properly wash and return a mandoline he'd borrowed for a batch of julienned vegetables. He'd been new and hadn't yet been warned of Chef's sometimes-merciless behavior. Or maybe the staff had neglected to do this on purpose. Ginny used to tell Julia tales of secret alliances and backstabbing among her workers, just so they could rise to the top of their highly competitive industry.

The result of the sous chef's error, Julia remembered, had been Ginny's thunderous affront followed by the young man being covered in a tidal wave of carrot shavings. Line cooks and dishwashers had all taken a collective gasp right along with a visiting Julia. The offender had been fired on the spot, and the episode had provided gossip fodder for days. Ginny Frank could sometimes be unforgiving.

People in the restaurant industry respected Ginny for her strength and talent, but it was always a fierce competition nonetheless. In the end, however, something stronger had taken her down.

Julia believed Ginny had given the job everything she had, but it had apparently been too much. This, coupled with her sister's onset of grief over their parents' deaths and overwhelming sense of responsibility to clean up the aftermath, had consumed Ginny. It was difficult to understand why her sister—her well-accomplished, grounded sister—had permanently left New York. Beyond that, Julia was angered by the act of abandonment that had accompanied Ginny's dramatic departure. She'd been left in her wake with very little explanation.

Admittedly, Julia's anger was still looming.

Moving around the kitchen, she brightened a little. It was amusing that, just like her, Ginny had refused to update to the trendy pod coffee makers and instead stuck with an older, slow-drip system.

She chuckled.

There was something about that full pot of dark liquid that Julia looked forward to each morning. Plus, you couldn't stick your nose into a plastic pod and inhale freshly ground beans the way you could with a brown bag. It was the ritual she adored. And she'd learned it from Ginny.

She wondered just what else she might still have in common with Ginny. *Still* being the operative word.

Ginny had made it clear when she'd fled New York three years earlier that she'd intended to retreat. She'd let the lease go on her town house, collected her teenage daughter, and left. Julia had balked at the time. Didn't Ginny know how important it was to keep a tight grip on all that had been built? Doors had finally begun to open for both of them. And while Julia was striding confidently through them, Ginny let them swing shut.

As far as Julia was concerned, Ginny had given up. She'd abandoned her.

Julia recalled the two of them fighting on one particular night, three years earlier. It had been the argument that wedged them apart with cruel finality. She could still see the image of a red-eyed Ginny thrashing about, packing her things, and informing her sister why she couldn't possibly understand.

But she hadn't really even been given the chance. That stung the most.

"You're up early," a voice said behind her. Julia startled and whirled around. A robe-clad Ginny stood before her, wiping at her droopy eyes and making her way toward the coffee maker. "You came a long way. We had a late night. I figured you'd still be in bed."

Julia glanced from her sister to the clock on the wall. It read seven fifteen. "I couldn't sleep," she stammered. She only hoped Ginny hadn't heard her snooping. "Plus, I'm still on East Coast time. Two hours ahead."

"Ah," Ginny said. She nodded and busied herself with pouring the coffee. "Thanks for starting the machine."

"Sure." Julia wavered. She was uncertain what to do next. Ginny wasn't much for words at the moment. Perhaps she resented Julia being there. A shift in energy filled the hollow space between them. The earlier awkwardness of Julia's unannounced arrival had returned.

Julia realized she'd been a fool for thinking this would be easy. It was anything but. The two of them might have figured out a way to come together the previous evening, for the sake of a crisis, but any spirit of teamwork had apparently dissipated overnight.

Ginny sipped at an oversize mug and shuffled in slippered feet over to a small breakfast nook. Wordlessly, Julia followed, unsure if that was what Ginny wanted. She hung back slightly, waiting for an invitation to sit down.

It was ironic, really. Back in the city she had a host of interns and staffers eager to rush around and fetch her coffee and cold-pressed juice. But not here. Julia's status carried little weight in Ginny's world. That much was glaringly clear.

A round glass table and a pair of wicker chairs sat tucked against the wall opposite a fireplace. Ginny pulled out a seat and plunked down. Her shoulders rounded as she placed her elbows onto the table and stared into her coffee.

A fragment of tucked-away grief wriggled free inside Julia.

Seeing Ginny like that, hunched over the kitchen table, was reminiscent of their father, who also used to stoop in a similar fashion. Ginny had aged in the past several years, Julia could tell. Pushing into her forties, her sister had become so much more like their father—the way she carried herself, the shape of her body, the pinched lines at the corners of her mouth.

Of their two parents, Ginny had always been closer to him. He was commanding and strong and as determined as a bull. He and Ginny shared a type of work ethic that had the ability to push them to the very brink of health if they allowed it. This was perhaps something Ginny had recognized about herself back in New York. Perhaps it was partially what made her leave it all behind. No matter the cost to her career.

The grief lingered a bit longer as Julia stood there. She wondered if her sister missed their parents every day. Or maybe Ginny had locked her feelings somewhere dark and far away. Just as Julia had done.

But being back here, in Arizona and with Ginny, was beginning to remind her of how things used to be. And all the time she'd lost by staying away.

Julia shifted. Ginny appeared lost in thought as she slowly blew on her drink and then sipped. It was surreal to see her there, back in their home state, in a house so removed from their lives in the city. An adobe affair set back against the foothills of a faraway desert land.

It wasn't that it was so bad. It was quite charming, actually. Just different. Julia tried to imagine Ginny and Olive spending time in that cozy nook, waking up each morning to share conversation over breakfast, planning the events of their days.

But where was Olive? Julia frowned. She still had no idea where her niece had gone. Clearly the girl hadn't bothered to come home the night before.

"Mind if I sit?" she finally asked.

Ginny thrust out the empty chair with the tip of her foot but didn't bother to make eye contact. She shrugged. "Go ahead."

Julia eased into the seat and cradled her half-empty mug. Starting a conversation had never felt so hard. "So, um, where's Olive? Doesn't she live here?"

Ginny grunted. Her head lifted slowly, as if burdened with thought. "Olive? Yeah, sometimes."

"Oh." Julia paused. "What exactly does that mean?"

A long sigh passed across the table. Ginny met her curious gaze. "She hates me, if you want to know the truth."

"I see." Julia leaned back, choosing her words. From what she remembered, Olive had always favored her dad. Ironically, just as Ginny had always favored their own father, though for opposite reasons. Will was reckless and free, and she supposed that would appeal to a girl with a creative spirit. But it had been sad to witness Ginny work so hard over the years with little connection to her daughter. The two just seemed to exist together, but not relate to each other. There wasn't that tight bond some parents and children have. Julia had never quite understood it. But then again, she'd been too wrapped up in her own life for so much of the time. And if she thought about it now, so had Ginny. They both could have done better.

"From what I remember, Olive always had a soft spot for Will."

Ginny shrugged, a look of defeat passing behind her eyes. "Yeah, that's true. But now that we're over two thousand miles away from him, she's taken a clear preference. It's like he's some kind of mythical creature she can't get enough of. Which is fine, I guess. He is her dad. But she keeps flitting off and leaving me in the lurch. As you can tell by last night's performance, I need her here to help out."

Julia raised an eyebrow. "About that . . . Help with what, exactly? What we did last night, is that a regular thing? Do people pay you to come here?" The entire concept was madly confusing. Hadn't Ginny moved away from New York to escape the restaurant scene? Wasn't she done cooking for other people? Especially rich, uptight ones like the group from last night?

Ginny cast her a sidelong glance. She straightened slowly, as if being propped up with sore muscles. Julia watched as she dug the knuckles of her right hand into the small of her back. A little groan escaped. "If you must know, yes. It's a regular thing. I invite people into my home on the weekends and they pay me to cook for them."

"Strangers come into your home? Every weekend?" A flag of concern popped up. It sounded rather bizarre, and maybe even slightly illegitimate. "Is this, like, a business?"

Ginny rolled her eyes. "Yes, Julia. It's like a business. It's called underground dining, if you must know. It's a thing. Big cities have it, small cities have it. And you can stop your snobby judgment right there. I already know what you're thinking. It's not illegal, per se. Well, I suppose a little bit, if the health inspector gets wind of it. But it's a trend that I'm happy to jump on if it pays my mortgage. I don't have to worry about a big overhead at a commercial space, I don't have to commute, and, most importantly, I don't have to answer to anyone but myself." She paused, narrowing her eyes. "And that includes you. Remember, you were the one who wrote me off when I moved away. You don't get to come in here and lay on your self-righteous criticism. Not anymore."

That stung. Ginny was acting as if she'd been innocent in the whole thing. Well, she hadn't. And Julia planned to get to that. But first, she needed to know more.

This was not at all what she'd expected from Ginny. Underground dining? She'd never heard of such a thing. Before she could think, the reporter in her blurted out the next question. "How do people find you? Aren't you afraid of weirdos coming in here? Invading the space where you *live*?"

Ginny huffed. Julia was clearly annoying her. "They find me by word of mouth. And to answer your question about whether I'm worried about strangers busting in on me, no, not really. Unless you count yourself . . . Otherwise, did you see any weird people here last night?"

"Wow, Ginny, thanks for that." She rolled her eyes. "I just think it's a questionable decision. But then again, it wouldn't be the first time you did something bizarre."

"Look, Julia, I invite people into my house to give them a different experience." She paused a minute, swallowing as if she had a bad taste in her mouth. Then she continued. "These people come exclusively for the food. To indulge with others in their collective love of culinary fare. They don't care about all the other trappings. They come for the unique menu only I can provide. And they come for community. And I get to give that to them."

This was so much more than Julia could process. How strange her sister's new life had become.

"Wow," Julia uttered. Never in a million years would she have suspected that this was what her sister would wind up doing. Running a speakeasy in her own house. "I guess I'm pretty surprised."

Ginny smirked. "Well, you can be whatever you want," she said. "But unfortunately, you'll have to do it elsewhere. I've got too much going on right now. I have to prepare for more people coming again later tonight. And as you noticed, I've got difficulties with Olive. So while you may have come to talk, or rehash old history, or I don't know what, I need to get back to work. I'm sorry, but you need to go."

Julia's heart sank. She could tell Ginny was quickly retreating. She recognized the old, familiar pulling away. And her opportunity to hide out from her looming problems was going with it. She needed to think fast.

"Wait."

Ginny sighed. "What?"

"I was, uh, kind of hoping I could stay. Not for long, just for a short bit while some things at home have a chance to quiet down. I know I didn't exactly give you notice, but I've come all this way." She searched Ginny's face for a sign of compassion.

Ginny tilted her head. "What do you mean, 'quiet down'? Is this about a man? Are you in the middle of a breakup or some early midlife crisis or something?" It came out flat, and Julia couldn't tell if it was meant as an accusation or not.

"Yes. I'm going through some personal relationship stuff." Julia felt herself shrinking with the lie. But Ginny was so smug sitting there, Julia couldn't imagine opening up just yet. It was better to avoid the truth for now. Until she could gain back some even footing.

"Julia." Ginny pursed her lips. It was evident by her shift in tone that she was debating something. "If you seriously want to stay, fine. I'm not sure why you want to be here, but I'm not going to force you out if you have nowhere else to go. However, you need to understand what you're walking into. Things around here are different. *I'm* different. If you can handle that, well then, I guess it's okay. Temporarily."

"Yes, of course. Temporarily."

"I'm not finished," Ginny said, her tone strengthening. "Another thing is, you're going to have to work if that's the case. The truth is, I'm short-staffed; I have no idea when Olive is coming back and there are no other employees. I've got too much to do without a houseguest getting in the way. Sorry to be blunt, but that's the truth. If you're willing to suit up and repeat what you did last night, that's the offer. Take it or leave it. I don't care, but I don't have time to stand around and wait."

Julia felt a flop in her stomach. What was she supposed to say? She desperately wanted a place to hide, and also the chance to patch things up with both Ginny and Olive. But this was preposterous. Help run some secret restaurant? She hadn't shown up here, after all this time, just to be her bossy sister's lackey.

"Well . . ." Julia waffled. She wanted more time to ask questions. But she could tell by Ginny's tightening face that her sister was rapidly losing patience. "Okay, fine."

Ginny eyed her suspiciously. "Fine, what?"

"Fine, I'll stay and be your secret supper club helper. Or whatever it's called. Temporarily."

"It's called Mesquite, for your information," Ginny retorted.

"What is?"

"My supper club. Named for the tree out front."

"Ah." Julia nodded, not entirely understanding but not wanting to sound like a clueless city snob.

Ginny rose. "Get dressed in something other than silk and meet me back here in fifteen minutes. You've got potatoes to peel."

And just like that, it was settled. Julia would stay another day.

CHAPTER TWELVE

GINNY

As soon as she heard the crash of glass stemware breaking, followed by a high-pitched yelp, Ginny understood involving her sister had been a mistake. That evening's table of dinner guests had been seated for no more than five minutes before Julia had a chance to screw things up. And of course, in typical maddening fashion, Olive had yet to materialize.

"Oh, for god's sake. I'm coming," Ginny grumbled, more to herself than anyone else. Pivoting from her place at the stove, she yanked a towel from its hook and groused, "What now?" Her first instinct was to reprimand her jumpy sister. But she knew she couldn't. At least not in front of company.

Julia had been a bundle of nerves all afternoon as Ginny walked her through the serving process. It really shouldn't have been difficult: set the table, serve the guests, try not to spill anything. Was that so much to ask?

But Julia was on another planet. Whatever had happened back in the city was taking over Julia's ability to concentrate. Ginny didn't say anything when her sister appeared in her kitchen, ready for work, wearing some pricey-looking romper that seemed better suited for a nightclub. She only raised an eyebrow in disbelief.

"What?" Julia cocked her head in confusion. "You said no silk. This was the only other nice thing I had. I didn't exactly plan on being your scullery maid when I arrived."

"Seriously?"

Julia only shrugged and turned away with a wounded look.

Ginny also held her tongue the numerous times she caught Julia in the corner, scrolling through her phone for news alerts and text messages. But after the potato peeler was discovered in the garbage, rather than the sink, Ginny knew it was time to snap her distracted sister back into focus.

"It's Saturday," Ginny snipped. "Let the broadcast news world go for now. And please, Julia, pay attention. This is important. Your phone will still be there in a few hours, I promise."

Julia succumbed, begrudgingly. The device slid into her back pocket, where it vibrated at regular intervals. Both women had pretended not to notice the thick tension in the air as they went about prepping for dinner.

It wasn't that Ginny was insensitive to her sister's plight. She understood all too well the constant pressures of life in New York. It was a city of "see and be seen." Stay out of the fray too long and run the risk of being forgotten. And she also understood what a big deal GBN was. Her sister was likely worried about taking time away from work. Or maybe it was something more.

Julia's habitual nail biting alone had told her all she needed to know for the moment. Ginny, however, was under stress too. Couldn't her sister appreciate that? She'd made her situation clear. If Julia didn't plan on cooperating, she would simply have to hide out and nurse her ego elsewhere.

Especially if it meant sending Ginny's business into chaos.

Arriving in the packed dining room, Ginny slowed her gait and plastered on a thick smile. "Hello, everyone! Sounds like it's quite lively in here tonight!" It took all her restraint to stop and make eye contact with the roomful of expectant faces before sending her gaze swiftly in Julia's direction. The guests appeared a bit startled but smiled back, murmuring their hellos. Ginny recognized many of them. Tonight was an evening of regulars, thankfully. They would hopefully be sympathetic.

"Hi, George. Hi, Maddie! Nice to see you both back again!" She beamed at the couple and then zeroed in on a pile of broken glass on the sideboard. A waterfall of iced tea poured over the side and onto the floor, creating little splashing sounds. Next to it was a dazed and flushed Julia, who was attempting to pluck up the sharp pieces with her bare hands.

"Oh dear, I'll get a mop. Sorry, everyone! I've put my poor sister to work tonight. She's new, obviously. I hope no one got hurt!" She grinned through gritted teeth before sending Julia a look of disapproval.

"No harm," said a gentleman in a sport coat. Ginny recognized him and relaxed.

"Thanks, Roger. So glad you're here tonight."

Her friend beamed in her direction. "How nice you have a sister! What a surprise! Sandy used to say she wanted a sibling. It was something she asked about constantly as a small child. You two must have some fun stories!"

Ginny smiled, doing her best to cover up her sadness for Roger. Roger and his wife had lost their only child, Sandy, to leukemia many years earlier. While Ginny had met the couple long after their teenager had succumbed to the disease, her heart went out to them. They talked of Sandy often, as though trying to keep her spirit alive. Ginny always made time to listen. There was so much life in the stories of Sandy. So much love. Perhaps because he no longer had a child of his own, Roger treated Ginny like a daughter of sorts, calling on her, checking up on the progress of her business, and even offering a tone of parental concern from time to time. Because of this, Ginny felt a particular bond with him.

Turning now, she shook off the familiar grief she felt for her friend. It was best to lighten the mood. "Oh, my sister and I have stories. That's for sure! We used to work in a yummy little taqueria together back in high school. I chopped vegetables and Julia bused tables. It seems Julia needs to knock a bit of rust off tonight, though."

The sisters locked eyes and Ginny narrowed her gaze.

"Yeah, right," Julia muttered.

"Well, good for you, Julia!" Roger cast bright approval across the room, catching Julia midstoop. She quickly gathered up a large shard of glass with her shaky fingers. "Would you like us to help with that?"

"No!" Ginny's dismissal came out harsher than she'd intended. Julia was throwing everything off-kilter. But she couldn't let her guests know that. Smoothing the front of her coat, she relaxed her features. "You just sit and enjoy. My sister's got this under control, I'm sure."

Roger started to protest. The other guests looked on dumbly. Spilled dishes and broken glass were not normally part of the evening at Mesquite.

"Wait until you taste the steak tartare," Ginny continued. "I sourced that farm you turned me on to, Roger. I'm so impressed with their product." She was grateful the menu she'd prepared was a showstopper tonight, hopefully enough to overshadow any of Julia's calamities.

"Wonderful! I'm looking forward!" Roger, with his ruddy nose and big grin, nodded enthusiastically. A local retiree, Roger had been frequenting Mesquite from the start. Ginny considered him to be one of her best customers. He'd been a surprising informant regarding up-and-coming boutique farms. Plus, he had quite the foodie palate to boot. If only all her customers could be like Roger: willing and generous. Ginny made a mental note to pull out the good wine for him tonight.

"Julia, dear," Ginny said, still keeping her smile. "Let's go get you something helpful for that spill. Shall we?"

Julia straightened from her crouched position, disbelief clouding her expression. Ginny never spoke to her in such a saccharine tone. If anything, they were used to barking at one another. But Julia followed along anyway, scurrying into the kitchen behind her.

Ginny spun around once they were out of earshot. "What the hell is the matter with you?" she hissed. "Julia, you've got to get your head in the game. These are big paying customers tonight."

Julia recoiled. A smattering of iced tea stained the front of her romper.

"Sorry." Ginny sent energy into a balled fist down by her side and reminded herself to keep calm. Her voice lowered. "I'm under just as much stress as you. I'm sure you didn't mean it, but come on. You've got to be more careful. Why don't you take five minutes to collect yourself and go change? You do have more clothes in that bag of yours, don't you?"

Julia nodded wordlessly, a faint tremor in her chin. Ginny softened. She wondered if her sister was more fragile than she'd realized. It dawned on her that there could be more to Julia's visit than just running away from a bad romance.

Julia had, after all, never visited before. She'd never really reached out before either. Ever since Ginny moved away, the two had stopped confiding in one another. Wiping her sweaty palms on her coat, Ginny felt a momentary surge of guilt. In all her haste, she hadn't bothered to find out more about Julia's situation. But then again, the current demands of Mesquite, coupled with Olive's abrupt abandonment, had been about as much as she could handle. Ginny would get to Julia's troubles soon, just not now.

"Okay, then. Sorry again for snapping. See you back here in five."

"Okay," Julia mumbled. Ginny watched her sister's narrow back disappear as she slunk away.

The sound of animated conversation trailing in from the other room brought Ginny back into focus. She'd have to get back to cooking if she was to stay on schedule. At least tonight was made up of mostly regulars, which eased her stress level slightly. Diners like Roger, George, and Maddie were known for enjoying long, leisurely meals as they relaxed at her dinner table. They'd be in no rush. Ginny only hoped Julia's graceless accident hadn't put anyone off.

Waiting for Julia to return—hopefully dressed in something more practical—she busied herself chopping a medley of shallots, chives, and parsley for her steak tartare. That evening's recipe, which was typically summer fare, would include a healthy dose of brandy and Tabasco, to give the dish a punch. She liked to mix things up, change seasonal items around and serve them when unexpected. Plus, she'd come across such a high grade of beef, thanks to Roger's source, that she couldn't help herself. The flavors needed to be shown off. And this would be a fun way to do it.

She was just preparing the final element to the tartare course, cracking perfectly shaped raw egg yolks onto the center of the patties, when Julia appeared, even more flustered, bumping her way back into the kitchen.

"Watch it!" Ginny barked. The first yolk broke in half, oozing a creamy yellow down over her knuckles and in between her fingers. She sniffed and tossed the mess into the sink.

"Sorry," Julia said. "Ew, what is that?" She wrinkled her nose at the pink, doughy strands of uncooked beef.

Ginny sighed and continued plating, careful to add a drizzle of sauce and arrange toasted sourdough spears artfully around the appetizer. "Really? Haven't you been in my kitchens enough over the years to know better?"

"Sorry," Julia said again. "It's been a while."

"Uh-huh." Ginny snatched up a plate and held it out in front of her. "So I hope you're feeling steady. This egg, see here?" She pointed with her free hand. "This beautiful, sunny little thing cannot lose its shape. So maybe you should just carry one at a time. Gently! Please, go slow and don't bump into anything."

A hesitant hand reached for the plate. Ginny fixed her gaze on Julia's unsure expression. "Okay?"

"Yes, got it. Don't mess up your precious egg." She took the appetizer plate in both hands and walked toward the dining room methodically, as if she were marching in a wedding procession. Ginny scoffed. Julia was pissing her off. She needed real help. Where in the hell was Olive when she needed her?

But her irritation toward her daughter was now morphing into real concern. She'd checked her phone for responses to texts she'd sent Olive the night before. No answer. A text to Will had been fruitless as well. The only thing keeping her from calling the authorities was the fact that Olive had done this kind of disappearing act before. Whenever the two of them had a particularly bad argument, Olive would stay at a friend's. Which friend, Ginny was never quite sure, since her daughter kept her mostly in the dark about the people she hung out with. There was a kid who worked for one of the cheese vendors, a Logan Something-or-other, who sometimes hung around after deliveries. She knew he and Olive had struck up a friendship, or possibly something more, she wasn't really sure. Maybe Olive was with this kid now, drinking beers and swapping complaints about their lame jobs. Maybe they were doing something she didn't even want to consider.

What Ginny did know was that if her daughter didn't surface soon, Mesquite would be without a decent server, because Julia was proving to be a piss-poor substitute. Maybe she had been wrong to expect anything more.

CHAPTER THIRTEEN
JULIA

While the house was still, Julia stood outside on the back patio and soaked in the warming rays of the rising sun. Now that it was Sunday, she assumed everyone would finally sleep in. It had rained overnight, a little pitter-patter of drops playing on her window sometime just after midnight. The storm had moved in and washed over the dusty outcroppings of Ginny's property. Everything was left with a dewy sense of renewal.

The ground was still damp but oddly warm against Julia's bare toes. A veil of steam floated up from the stone pavers, giving everything a mystical feel. She remembered these kinds of mornings. The recollection comforted her. Closing her eyes, she inhaled. Fresh air filled her lungs. She liked the sweet, organic smell that touched at the back of her throat and hinted of sage. Probably the rains had been responsible for releasing such an ethereal aroma. The desert was often like that in January. Little by little, the land she once knew was becoming less of a mystery.

Despite Julia's difficulty falling asleep the night before, starting upright at the howls of a distant coyote and hooting of a large owl, she was beginning to recognize certain elements of the wild.

Yet she also longed for the city, with the constant humming of action that only New York could provide. She deeply missed the fulfilling rush of heading into work and getting caught up in the business of breaking news stories, the excitement of the jam-packed editorial pitch meetings, and the electric-charged energy of the harried support staff on the newsroom floor.

Out of habit she'd been up early, checking email and skimming the weekend news. She'd glanced at social media for any mention of her name on GBN's site. There were several posts that included a brief retraction—all terribly dry and legal sounding in Julia's opinion—but no explanation of why *Daybreak* was down a cohost at the end of the week. It maddened her to think how easily she'd been cast off. Peter still had explaining to do.

Her email included a terse directive from Peter not to come in on Monday morning. Another day Julia wouldn't be on the show. Hang tight until we sort this thing out, his message read. The execs don't want you coming back to the show quite yet. More from legal soon. Peter. No word on what was being done. No inquiry as to Julia's side of the story. Just a continuance of her punishment.

Julia sulked. She wondered how long this could go on.

"I see you're up early again," Ginny's voice called, breaking the silence. Her sister pushed the double doors wide and stepped out onto the patio. An oversize pair of what looked like men's tailored pajamas were buttoned and rolled up at the sleeves. Even in her sleep, Ginny looked like she was ready to get down to business. Julia stifled a grin.

"Yeah, still on East Coast time, I'm afraid."

Ginny yawned and rubbed at her face. Little sleep lines ran down one cheek. In that light, Julia noticed how her sister's features had aged. The soft skin at her neck had begun to be drawn down by gravity, and the edges of her hairline revealed a thinning that didn't used to be there. If she looked hard enough, Julia could detect threads of gray weaving their way into the blonde. Despite this, Ginny appeared healthy in other ways. The strong desert sun had given her skin a golden hue that wasn't there before. And there was an element of brightness in her eyes. Overworked or not, Ginny seemed to be thriving in her new environment.

Despite the grueling pace of having to feed people in her own home, her sister seemed to enjoy herself. She'd caught Ginny on several occasions laughing with guests and puffing out her chest slightly as she offered details on each dish and its specialty ingredients. Watching her was like witnessing a flash of the old Ginny, the one whose artful menus had earned her awards and garnered the big bucks from important restaurant owners.

It was kind of touching, really. Albeit still strange.

Julia held on to a healthy dose of skepticism about the whole affair. Her sister had left it all behind—the glitz, the glamour, the adoration—for a modest adobe house tucked away in the desert. It was quite a risk. Julia worried. It all felt so tenuous. Her sister and her niece were just one phone call away from being out of a job.

True, Julia still harbored a grudge toward Ginny over certain events from the past, but that didn't mean she wasn't concerned. This was family, after all. The only family Julia had left.

"You're staring," Ginny said dryly.

Julia shook her head, embarrassed. They'd never felt so awkward around each other in the old days. "Sorry. Didn't mean to. It's just that . . ."

"That we haven't seen one another for three years? Yeah, I know." Her words were edged with remorse.

"It's kind of strange, isn't it?"

"Strange that you popped up out of nowhere after you accused me of foolishly giving up? Um, yeah. You could say so." A fresh bitterness coated Ginny's words. She'd set her anger aside for the past few days, but clearly it had existed all this time.

Julia winced at the memory of their harsh exchange. It had been such a difficult time, for both of them. The grief over losing their parents to a freak car accident had gutted them equally, but the sisters' reactions had been altogether different.

Unable to explain how something so cruel and random could happen to her family, Julia had chosen to throw herself into her work as a kind of escape from the pain of her shattered heart. She loved her parents and secretly held on to guilt over not seeing them as often as she should have. Then, suddenly, they were gone. Her time was up. There was nothing she could do other than press on. If she didn't, Julia feared she might slip into an abyss of sadness that had the potential to swallow her whole.

Ginny, on the other hand, had let the grief entirely overcome her. Her reaction was to step back into some kind of free fall, to let go of nearly everything she'd once had such a firm grasp on: the restaurant, her friends, the notoriety, and even Julia. It was maddening and confusing, and Julia hadn't taken the separation well.

But then again, neither had Ginny.

Yes, Julia could admit she'd said some ugly things at the time of Ginny's abrupt departure from the city. She'd been so consumed with anger and sadness at being abandoned in the wake of their parents' deaths. Even now, she could feel the ripple of resentment running through her. She still didn't understand her sister's choices. More than that, she'd been stung by them.

It was as if Ginny had morphed into someone she no longer knew, and she hadn't bothered to inform Julia of her life-altering plans. They'd both been in pain over the loss of their parents, but Julia had expected Ginny to stick around and weather the storm right alongside her. When Ginny announced that she'd quit her job and would stay in Arizona with Olive, it hurt.

Julia couldn't help but feel betrayed by her sister's actions. Blindsided, even. Now, reflecting, she felt a hint of regret for how she had behaved. Her wants might have been selfish. Despite this admission, she was also irritated with Ginny for acting the martyr and then never really explaining herself. For acting as if Julia were some sort of stranger to whom she owed little clarification. In one fell swoop, she'd shut Julia out.

As a result, Julia's wounds, though tucked away, were still raw.

She stood facing Ginny now, reflecting. Another equally painful memory surfaced. Ginny hadn't been all that supportive of Julia's swift rise up the corporate ladder. Julia hadn't ever figured out if it was jealousy or real concern coming from Ginny, but her sister's outward disapproval had smarted.

"Don't forget," Julia said, the volume of her voice increasing. Pinpricks of anger made their way along her skin. "You accused me of selling out. Something about me losing myself to the lure of the limelight. You called me self-centered and, if I'm not mistaken, said my big head was stuck so far up my ass, it was no wonder I couldn't see anyone but myself. So I'd say you aren't exactly innocent in all this."

It felt good to get it out, to finally unleash the anger she'd suppressed all these years. It was like a cork had been popped.

Ginny tensed, her lips forming a taut line.

Julia wanted to press her further, to step forward and force an admission of her sister's wrongdoing. She'd waited three years to have this conversation.

"Our parents had just died, Julia," Ginny seethed. Her jaw clenched. It was apparent she was barely containing herself. "And instead of putting things on hold to mourn them and honor their memories, to help tie up the loose ends of their lives, you pretty much brushed the event aside and went full throttle into promoting yourself with all the subtlety of a carnival barker. I couldn't take it. You did everything you could to get the attention put back on you. It was so obvious. I mean, who doesn't take even one sick day off from work when her parents die? Who doesn't care about helping pack up their stuff or making sure the house sells after they've gone? Instead, you slapped on lipstick and high heels and trotted yourself out in front of the cameras like it was any other day. Seriously, Julia. It was embarrassing. People who knew Mom and Dad were watching. *I* was watching." Ginny's chest was heaving; whatever wrath she'd been subduing now surged like an angry red tide.

Julia guffawed, her lips curling into a sneer. "Oh, come on. Your memory is distorted. You've always been so high and mighty. You chose to take it all on, without any input from me. Remember? I did nothing wrong and you know it!"

"Ha! That's a laugh. You were so self-absorbed it was disgusting." Ginny's tone was cruel. "Not much has changed, by the looks of it."

Julia recoiled. "You make me sound like a monster. I was doing my job, Ginny," she spat. "One that I was contractually obligated to do. That's what news reporters do, they show up. No matter what. Don't blame me because I was good at my job. And just because I worked my way through that period of our lives doesn't mean it didn't affect me."

Ginny rolled her eyes. Julia was so sick of her sister's condescension. She'd had enough.

"You can be so judgmental." She jabbed her finger in Ginny's direction. "Would you rather I curl up in a fetal position and just take it all lying down? Slink away out of town because I can't face hardship? Give up a career I've worked unbelievably hard to obtain? All just for the sake of appearances? Get over yourself, Ginny!"

Ginny scoffed. "You don't know what I went through. I lost more than you did."

"That's not true!" *How could she?* Julia's eyes blurred. The rage she felt for Ginny, old rage that had been lying dormant for so long, rushed forward and felt as if it might split her wide open. If Ginny wanted a confrontation, well, she was getting one. Who the hell did she think she was, telling Julia she hadn't mourned correctly, or as much as she had? As though this was a pissing contest.

Ginny's voice cracked slightly as she dropped her arms. For a flash, Julia got the sense that her sister was giving up on her. "Julia, I lost my partner, the father of my child. My coming out here was the final nail in the coffin of our dying relationship. My parents had been ripped from my life. I gave up *everything* to return home and clean up the mess. Without hesitating. I think I deserve a little understanding. My life was turned upside down. Coming back here wasn't a choice. Someone had to do it, and I didn't dare ask you. If you couldn't see what needed to be done and step up to the plate out of a sense of duty and love, I couldn't force you to. So I don't appreciate you throwing my actions back in my face like I was some weakling. What I did took strength, whether you want to admit it or not. And I'm not going to change my perspective just because you can't wrap your head around that."

Julia folded her arms. All of her ugly emotions wound themselves into difficult knots. The anger still loomed. Yet she couldn't walk away. She'd come so far just to try to reconnect. Was it really worth it? She wasn't sure.

Part of her still wanted to try.

"I came here because I needed to escape my life, if it makes you feel any better," Julia said, more evenly now. She caught Ginny's gaze shifting. "To get a better perspective on things. Go ahead and gloat if you want to. But at least I had the courage to stick around and try." Her shoulders fell. She'd had enough. She'd been a fool to think they might have moved past all this.

So Julia had chased her broadcasting dream and allowed herself to be molded into what the job demanded of her. Was she really that terrible a person? She didn't think so. Yes, she'd gotten her hair and makeup done a certain way, changed the lilt of her voice, and put a great deal of effort into losing unwanted weight for the cameras. Those sacrifices, along with hard work, had landed her on GBN. It was one of the most powerful news networks in the world. Surely Ginny would have to give her credit for that much.

But studying Ginny's contorted face now, it was difficult to tell. Too much had been said.

Ginny's sigh was edged in weariness. "I don't need to gloat, Julia. It doesn't make me happy to see you suffering. Despite what you might think, I do have a heart, you know." Ginny's arms went back across her chest. She was insulted, but she wasn't walking away. This was new.

Julia saw this as a kind of olive branch, she supposed. Even if only a temporary one. She wondered what Ginny was thinking—if she wanted to work through their differences or if she just needed Julia to stay in order to help with her business. It was difficult to tell.

They needed one another, for reasons neither could admit.

"I know you do," Julia answered. She decided to take the first step. "That's part of why I came. I was hoping that despite our rocky past, you'd see it in your heart to let me stay for a few days. And you have. Everything else aside, I'm grateful."

Ginny's arms loosened slightly. The inflamed color of her cheeks faded some. "And I'm grateful for your help in Olive's absence."

Julia nodded. Maybe it was best to leave the rest of this conversation for another time. There had been progress. Not a lot, but she'd take it.

"Where is Olive, anyway?" Julia asked, wanting to change the conversation. "Does she make a habit out of running off whenever you two argue?" *Like mother, like daughter,* Julia thought.

Ginny shifted, her gaze floating into the distance. It appeared she was considering just how much to reveal. "Olive takes off sometimes, yes. But she always comes back. I'm guessing she's staying with one of her friends. But she doesn't usually stay away this long. So I'm a bit worried."

"Shouldn't you call or text or something to make sure she's not lying in a ditch somewhere?" Julia's pulse began to speed up once more. Had something bad happened to Olive? She wouldn't be able to forgive could lose your job." He was incredulous, his speech climbing toward a frenzied pitch.

Julia blew air through her nose. She knew James meant well; he only wanted her to keep a firm hold on her career. He also liked things to have forward momentum, steps to be continually taken toward goals. It was bad enough he couldn't get Julia to commit to a wedding date. The state of limbo this caused drove him crazy, but she'd had her job to consider. Up until now, she hadn't been willing to take time off. Now that she'd been forced to take a leave, though, James wasn't happy about it.

His urgent reasoning, in the form of fearmongering, certainly wasn't helping. If anything, it was making her more sickened than she already was.

Running back to New York to get beaten down again in the form of public humiliation was the least appealing option. Yet she was conflicted.

"I obviously can't control what the network does, or doesn't do, in my absence. They're a big company and I'm a tiny cog in the wheel. Peter has made it pretty clear I made a costly mistake, and they want me to stay away until it's sorted out."

"But did you make a mistake? Are you sure there isn't any validity to the Rossetti story?"

"I don't know."

"And why did you have to go all the way to Arizona to visit a sister whom you literally never talk about? I don't understand. I'm the one who actually cares, and you ran away from me."

Julia sank down on the edge of the daybed, folding over to cradle her achy head in her hands. Poor James. He had a point. She hadn't mentioned her sister much over the past year. James knew the basics about her parents' deaths and the famous older sister who'd abruptly crumbled under her grief and given up her culinary career for a quieter life. And he knew that there'd been some kind of blowup between the

herself for not stopping her when she'd had the chance the other night. But how could she have known?

"She's fine," Ginny said. "I have been texting her. Olive likes to keep me hanging by only responding with one-word texts. But she confirmed she's still mad at me and she confirmed she's safe."

"Huh." Julia didn't know what to make of it. Ginny seemed somewhat resigned to the fact that her daughter liked to keep things vague. A part of her understood that this might be a young person's desire to strike out on her own. To push against the confines of a small town and yearn for something bigger. It was what Julia had done when she'd first left Arizona, after all. Perhaps her niece was feeling the same way. "So, if you don't mind me asking, why not hire someone else to take her place? I mean, you must be pretty desperate if you had me fill in. We all know I'm more than rusty when it comes to service."

"Ha! You've got that right. But yeah, you could say I'm desperate."

"So?"

"So, I can't afford to hire new help. I'm strapped as it is." The arms were back across her chest. The invisible wall was up.

Julia frowned. This wasn't necessarily the answer she'd expected. Surely life out here in the desert had only a fraction of the high cost of living in New York. Didn't it? And Ginny had established a business. If you could call it that.

"Can't you use whatever it is you pay Olive for a new person?"

"No." It came out in almost a whisper.

"No?"

"I don't exactly pay Olive in a consistent manner," Ginny said, her gaze drifting to the ground. Julia detected the shame in her sister's response. "I don't have the money for that. Not now, anyway. Olive gets free room and board in exchange. And some cash on the side. That's pretty good for a twenty-one-year-old. She gets to eat and sleep here for free."

Julia laughed out loud. She couldn't help herself. Her sister could be pragmatic to a fault. "Well, that explains a lot! Oh my god, Ginny. No wonder she's pissed. Come on, let's go inside and make some coffee and you can tell me when your next group of diners is expected. Because I now have a million more questions."

"Okay." Ginny dropped her arms in concession. Julia sensed a crack in the wall her sister had built. Perhaps there was hope for the weekend after all. The future was a whole different matter.

CHAPTER FOURTEEN

JULIA

Julia pressed the phone to her ear and paced the tiny guest room. After talking things over with Ginny, she'd realized she was overdue for a phone call with James. No doubt he'd be worried about her well-being, and she wanted to assure him she was fine. Only, at the moment, she wasn't able to get a word in edgewise. Her fiancé was too busy listing all the reasons why she should jump on the next plane home and begin the arduous task of repairing her damaged career.

"But the network specifically asked me—ordered me, actually—to steer clear. They don't want me coming in to work just yet." Her voice sounded whiny and she hated herself for it. James was making her feel incompetent.

"But I just told you a retraction was read during Friday night's evening news. Actually, they're calling it a correction, and it's been blasted all over GBN's social media accounts all weekend. Haven't you seen any of this? They're making it sound like it was a statement from you and hinted that a formal apology to Rossetti might be coming next. What's more, Rossetti is on Twitter calling for your immediate firing. Doesn't that bother you? Don't you want to speak up for yourself? You

two of them, causing Julia to brush him off whenever he'd pressed her for more information. But he also was an only child and didn't fully understand the pull of another sibling, so to him, it seemed easy to cut out a person who didn't serve a purpose. Just another business transaction dealt with.

"I know this doesn't make much sense to you, but I needed to get away. Far away. My sister's place seemed like a good spot to clear my head and sort things out. So here I am."

"Far away, huh? From work or from me?" His tone was pained.

"Oh, James. Not from you." Her voice softened. She wasn't being a very good fiancée. "None of this has to do with me needing a break from you. I just didn't want to be where people could see me, you know? To be under intense scrutiny because of the show."

"But people see *me*, Julia. Don't you get that? Friends and colleagues are asking me what happened. They're wondering if there's any truth to your story. It's not been easy for me. Especially when I didn't even know where you'd gone. It was pretty selfish of you to just take off and leave me to take the brunt of it."

Now it was Julia who felt hurt. Somehow the whole thing had gotten twisted around and she was to blame not only for her sloppy news reporting but now also for James's being inconvenienced.

"That's not fair."

"It's not? Then tell me what is, Julia. Because I'm at a loss."

She sighed and let her eyes drift across the room to her overflowing luggage. Shoes littered the floor; wrinkled blouses spilled over the edge. There hadn't exactly been time to unpack, but Julia hadn't kept herself travel ready either. Should she gather up her belongings now, say goodbye to Ginny, and catch the next flight home? Part of her knew returning to face the fire was inevitable. But the other, more fragile part yearned to stay hidden away at Ginny's for a little while longer.

She was just about to respond when the sound of the front door slamming, followed by female voices, echoed down the hallway.

Distracted, Julia strained to listen. The two voices quickly escalated. She recognized one as Ginny's and the other as belonging to a young woman.

Her heart skipped. Olive was home.

"James, I'm going to have to call you back. I've got to go take care of something urgent." The need to get off the phone was overpowering the desire to soothe his wounded feelings. She wanted to see Olive.

"Something urgent has come up? What does that mean?"

"Someone's here and I have to go." She was already on her feet and heading for the door. "Sorry. I'll call soon, I swear. Bye!"

A brief shard of guilt pierced her lifting mood. Olive had returned, and that could only mean good news for everyone. Ginny would have her daughter and helper back. Julia could catch up with her niece. And the three women would finally have the chance to reunite properly. James was upset, but she promised herself she'd patch things up with him as soon as she could.

For now, she trotted eagerly down the hallway in search of the others.

The scene she discovered, however, wasn't what she'd hoped to find. Not exactly. Ginny and Olive were, thankfully, both facing each other in the front entry. Olive appeared to be in one piece, a bit tousled in baggy sweats and windblown hair, but back home where she belonged. Yet neither of them looked pleased to see the other. And Julia's breathless arrival in the center of what appeared to be a family feud suddenly felt awkward and intrusive.

"Aunt Julia?" Olive's angry expression dropped into one of reserved surprise. "What are you doing here?"

Julia stepped forward with trepidation, praying her wide smile might lighten the room's toxic energy. "Hi, Olive. I came for a visit. I was hoping to see you before I had to leave." She moved in closer still, reaching out for a hug. Olive, with her day-old mascara smudged under her lashes and tangle of dirty hair, responded with a half embrace. The kind you give someone you might not fully trust. Julia held on a beat longer to offer a form of reassurance. A whiff of something resembling incense or marijuana floated through the air.

Julia frowned. A crack in her heart deepened. This grown-up version of her niece was unhinged and irresponsible. It was either all an act to piss off her controlling mother or a cry for attention. Either way, Julia was concerned.

"Huh." Olive pulled away. "You're kind of the last person I expected to see. If I would've known you were coming I would've—"

"You would have what?" Ginny cut her off. "You would have shown up? Stuck around? Answered my umpteen million texts, perhaps?" Ginny sank her teeth into the last question and glared. Anger radiated off her tense shoulders and filled the room.

Reflexively, both Julia and Olive backed up a step.

Olive's expression tightened. Bending at the knees, she reached down and grabbed a canvas duffel bag and then hoisted it over one shoulder. "Well, I need to take a long, hot shower."

Julia nodded, uncertain of what to say. "I should be here when you get out. Come and find me?"

Olive only half nodded in response and then wandered off down the hall. Julia deflated further. It seemed her only niece was holding a grudge just as immovable as her mother's.

Both women watched her disappear into the back bedroom. Olive's arrival had caused a knot in Julia's stomach. Ginny's family was full of even more discontent than she'd imagined. How had those two tolerated working together? From what she could gather, they could barely stand being in the same room. And Julia's reception hadn't been any better. It was clear Ginny had left some things out of their earlier conversation.

"Why didn't you tell me it was this bad?" Julia turned and asked. To her surprise, Ginny's eyes were shiny with emotion.

"I don't know. I just feel like things are impossible now. I had hoped Olive would've had time to cool off and that she'd come home more mellow. But as you can see, she's one big ball of anger. I swear Will is partially to blame. He probably filled her head with all kinds of crap during her latest visit. He always does that. Tells her she should be on the road, traveling and finding herself. It's all a bunch of visionary BS, of course, and it usually takes a few days for his influence to slough off. But not this time. She thinks everything is all my fault."

Or mine, Julia thought.

There was the sound of a door slamming, followed by the heavy pulse of a shower. Julia watched her sister flinch. The next thing she knew, Ginny's brave face had crumpled. A mournful sob escaped, and Ginny's hands flew to cover her stricken face. Julia went to her side.

"Oh, Ginny." Her palm gently rubbed her sister's back. It felt strange to be comforting her, but Julia could see it was necessary. "I'm so sorry. There's got to be a way for you two to come to an understanding. You're the only mother she has. Surely, deep down inside, she loves you. And I know you love her right back."

Ginny shuddered as another wave of soft sobs racked her body. "I only wish you were right."

"I am. You'll see." But the truth was, Julia wasn't so sure. Ever since her arrival in Arizona, everything she'd blindly assumed had been proven wrong. It had all been a shock, from Ginny's secret business to James's unwarranted anger and Olive's ugly rebellion. So far, she'd only made her problems worse by piling on more of them.

And all of it broke her heart.

"Julia," Ginny croaked. "I know we still have stuff we don't agree on, but do you think you might hang around? I'm sure this isn't what you want. But honestly, it would be a favor to me—another favor—if you could maybe try and reach Olive. I feel like I'm at my wit's end. I just don't know how to get through to her anymore."

Julia wavered. Ginny looked so vulnerable just then, as if a fissure was deepening.

Julia had come for an escape, but it was clear that her family needed her. If she left now, too many loose pieces would be left hanging. Again. Julia would only be leaving one problem for another. Although she'd promised herself, and James, that her return would be speedy, Julia worried that she couldn't turn her back on people who needed her.

"I, uh . . ." What was she supposed to say? Her job and everything that went with it were hanging in the balance. Her whole life. She shifted.

Ginny continued to hold her gaze, watery and broken.

"I'll see what I can do." Julia sighed. She really had no idea what this meant. But she felt she just couldn't say no.

"Thank you." Ginny sniffed.

Julia would stay in Arizona for a while longer. Her troubles back home weren't going anywhere, but they would have to wait.

CHAPTER FIFTEEN
GINNY

Ginny was relieved Julia had agreed to stay beyond the weekend. Sure, there was still a lot more to discuss—and their first attempt at repairing their broken relationship hadn't gone great—but the idea that Julia would act as a kind of buffer between her and Olive gave her a faint sense of relief. Plus, Ginny believed Julia owed her. Her sister had much to make up for after her behavior when their parents died. She could be bothered to make a small sacrifice for her own family for once.

"So, your next set of guests has dinner reservations tomorrow night?" Julia asked. "I thought you said you only did this supper club thing on weekends." They were both hunched over the glass table just off the kitchen, nibbling on a plate of scones and locally made jam that Ginny had set out. The hum of a hair dryer could be heard coming from a bathroom.

"Yes and no. I usually only cook for people on weekends. But sometimes customers ask for a midweek seating; you know, if there's a birthday or special occasion or something. If that's the case, I tend to make exceptions." Ginny's front teeth bit down on a marionberry scone. A swath of purple jam clung to her lower lip.

Julia pushed a paper napkin across the table and nodded. "Okay, so Monday night is unusual."

"Yes. Tomorrow night I have reservations booked for a table of twelve. That's a big group, which means a big check. I couldn't say no." Ginny pressed her lips together to refrain from saying more. Julia was aware money was tight, but she didn't need to know *how* tight.

"Ah." Julia narrowed her eyes and rubbed her chin, as if she understood the appeal of a potential payout.

"So what exactly needs to be done between now and then?" Julia asked.

"A lot, actually. Today is Sunday, which means a visit to the farmers' market. And Olive needs to go with me to pick out the flowers." *Which unfortunately means spending more money.* Ginny knew they needed to prep for a big night at Mesquite, but she couldn't ignore the tightness in her chest that accompanied having to dip further into her dwindling bank account in order to do so. She'd never not been able to plate food for a seating. But that might change.

This anxiety, however, was not something she was yet willing to share with Julia. Or her daughter, for that matter.

Julia lifted her head midbite. "Olive does the flowers? I wouldn't exactly take her for the bright, cheerful type."

Ginny snapped back into focus, masking her concern. "Yep. She does. That girl may be bratty and unpredictable, but she's also got talent. You should see these floral displays she puts together. It would blow your mind. She's kind of got a natural gift. Sometimes, if the mood strikes her, she'll be out on the back patio for the better part of a day, just repotting succulents and grasses and perennials with this kind of dreamy expression on her face. And wait until you see her table centerpieces, not like the simple one I threw together in the dining room."

"Wow." Julia chewed slowly, as if she was taking it all in. "That's amazing."

"Yeah, it is. Of course, if I push her to do more of it, she only scoffs. Like I couldn't possibly know what I'm talking about." Ginny felt herself bristle.

"I'd like to see what she can do."

"You will. But the three of us better get dressed and head into town. I don't want all the booths to be picked over before we get there." *And I need the leverage of being able to haggle while inventory is still high,* she thought. "Sundays have some of the best vendors." Ginny had big plans for the party of twelve she was expecting. She wanted to try a new seasonal dish, but first she had to get to the market and see what she was dealing with. Seeing as it was nearly midday, they needed to hustle.

Lately, every day felt to Ginny as if she were losing time.

"Wait, *we?* As in all three of us are going? Together?" Julia leaned back in her chair, her eyebrows hovering in high arches.

"Well, I sort of assumed so." Ginny felt the color rushing to her cheeks. She'd just figured that when Julia said she'd stay for a few more days, it meant she planned to help out with Mesquite. She certainly wasn't a great server, but she was a warm body nonetheless.

"You're buying the food and Olive is allegedly picking out flowers. What do you need me to do? I would hardly be able to identify a shallot from a scallion. Won't I just be in the way?"

Ginny relaxed a little and chuckled. "Yeah, you always used to love eating my food but never bothered to learn much about it, did you?"

Julia shrugged. "I suppose not."

A wave of Ginny's hand brushed off the worry. "Don't worry. I mostly just need you there for moral support."

"Okay."

Ginny knew her sister considered this a big ask. After all, she was proposing Julia forgo her own set of problems only to take on hers. On top of this, neither of them had made much progress in admitting fault in the big fight that had occurred the day Ginny left town. Insults and accusations still loomed. But somehow both sisters had pushed the tension into the background. For the time being, anyway.

~

Forty-five minutes later, all three of them climbed out of Ginny's car and scattered onto the grounds of the outdoor market. The midwinter air was crisp and dry; fingers of sunlight bled through a streak of white clouds, highlighting the open courtyard. Ginny loved days like this. Out in the desert, Mother Nature had a way of painting a beautiful picture that never failed to impress. She peered over at her sister and wondered if Julia might appreciate some of the beauty of Arizona they had both missed for so many years. Judging by the wistful smile on Julia's face, she suspected the answer was yes.

All around them tents and tarps had been erected, sheltering displays of fresh produce, organic meats, and colorful blooms from the sun. Shoppers filed into the available spaces, eagerly chatting with vendors and stuffing their reusable bags with produce.

With a shopping list in hand, Ginny directed Julia to follow her as she aimed for the butcher first. Olive, armed with a yellow wicker basket and wearing a bohemian wide-brimmed straw hat, blandly said goodbye to run her own errands. She made a sharp turn toward the flower stalls and disappeared. Ginny's heart caught at the sight of her daughter walking away, a single braid running down the back of her tank top, a long, flowing skirt swishing breezily around her tanned legs. Olive had so much beauty to share, if only she'd knock that giant chip off her shoulder. She worried for her daughter's future.

She worried for them both.

Catching herself still lost in thought, she directed her focus back to the task at hand. The three of them had agreed to meet back at the car in an hour, which wouldn't give her much time to gather all the ingredients needed for the party expected the next night. Plenty needed to be done in anticipation of such a large group.

But at the moment, it seemed her sister was struck with awe.

"Wow, this is cool," Julia murmured, her eyes wide. "Do you really buy all your food here?" Her gaze remained fixed on the row of tents as if mesmerized.

Ginny pushed her sunglasses up the bridge of her nose and grinned.

"Yeah. I try to source as many local ingredients as possible," she said, slowing her stride as Julia rubbernecked around. A little flutter filled her chest. She recognized that look in Julia's eyes. It was easy to recall that same feeling of pure glee she'd had the day she'd first discovered the market. Seeing it through someone else's eyes now brought up that familiar sensation.

Julia started walking faster now, drawn to the sweet aroma in the air. Ginny could tell her sister was taking it all in with a renewed sense of wonder. It made her chuckle when Julia broke off only to duck into a booth to press her nose into a display of homemade lavender soaps.

"Did you smell these?" she asked, holding a bar of soap in the air before bringing it back to her nose.

"Nice, huh?" Ginny came to her side.

"Amazing."

"Okay, well, we kind of have to keep going. You can come back when we're done." Ginny had to laugh at how her thirty-eight-year-old citified sister had suddenly turned into a wide-eyed child. It was sweet, and Ginny was glad to see some of the gloom Julia carried from New York slip away for a while. She knew, however, a quiet distress bubbled just under the surface. Her sister had more troubles than she was letting on.

Julia was hiding out. Plus, she wasn't talking much about that oversize engagement ring on her finger. Ginny had asked earlier but had been promptly shut down. Did Julia not trust her enough to share her relationship problems? Something was obviously going on. Ginny wasn't naive, but for now she was content not to probe and merely let Julia enjoy the day. They both deserved a little happy distraction.

All of their problems would still be there tomorrow.

Over the next hour, the pair hopped from vendor to vendor, purchasing cuts of grass-fed beef, sampling organic fruits and artisan cheeses, and asking lots of questions. It was fun to introduce Julia to the flavors of specialty items, like locally made honey infused with rosemary and rich, buttery Arizona pecans. Julia was a willing participant, trying anything Ginny pointed out.

A flash of nostalgia shot through Ginny as she thought of the old days, when Julia would sneak through the back door of her restaurant, eager to taste new flavors. That was also when Julia wasn't so stick thin, as she was now, and was careless about the calories Ginny's food might contain. It was back in the days when the sisters trusted one another fully. Before the fighting and hurt feelings. Spending time in the market with Julia that Sunday provided a small slice of that old camaraderie, and for that, Ginny was grateful.

When their hour of shopping was up, Ginny came away inspired. She was excited to get back to her kitchen and start experimenting with her newly purchased ingredients. There was a moment, when she'd pulled out her nearly maxed-out credit card, when she fretted over the price. The previous week's dinners had provided the smallest of cushions to her finances, but that wouldn't last for long.

Knowing she now had two helpers, however, friction with Olive aside, soothed her nerves. However momentarily.

Julia had announced she would stay until midweek. She claimed it was in order to spend time with her niece, but the way her sister avoided eye contact when she said this made Ginny suspect that Julia was actually avoiding whatever awaited her back home. Surely GBN required her at some point. Didn't her sister have a show to host? And what about her personal life? There was something looming behind Julia's eyes that made her seem fragile. It was best not to push.

Ginny mused on how the two of them could pick up where they left off yet strategically avoid the bigger, more volatile topics that simmered just below the surface. Ginny believed they'd have to broach those topics eventually. Certain things still needed to be said.

At present, she was just happy for the additional help with Mesquite. Driving back home, with her daughter and her sister together in one car, she felt a warmth spread over her. She wanted to hold on to this feeling. It was the closest thing to family togetherness she'd experienced in a long while.

The question was, how long would it last?

CHAPTER SIXTEEN

JULIA

The incessant buzzing on her bedside table woke Julia with a start. Squinting, she cast about in the dark and attempted to focus. Three a.m. She groaned. *Brutal.* Especially when she'd not been able to silence the noise in her head until nearly one. And now someone was trying to reach her at an ungodly hour. She immediately thought of James.

Propping herself on her elbows, she reached for the glowing device. A New York number popped up. *Peter.* Julia frowned. She should have known that her boss would call first thing on Monday morning.

With a heavy hand, she grabbed the phone and hit "Answer." "Hello?" A slumber-induced hoarseness coated her voice.

"Julia?" Peter's voice boomed. He sounded too alert, as if he'd already had too many cups of that blackened espresso he was always drinking.

She cleared her throat and sat up against a lump of pillows. "Hi, Peter."

"What's the matter with you? Are you sick?" His tone was not one of concern but rather had the clipped irritation Julia was all too familiar with. Peter did not like to be inconvenienced. Especially by his staff.

She sprang up. "No, I'm fine." She wanted to explain that while it might have been 5:00 a.m. and the start of his Monday in New York, she was two hours behind and nowhere near a normal caffeine-drinking hour. But no doubt the madness of Monday had hit GBN and Peter wanted to discuss strategy.

"Well, we need to hash this Rossetti thing out. Thankfully we've been able to keep his legal team at bay with a retraction."

You don't have to tell me, she thought, bringing her fingers to pinch the bridge of her nose. She'd seen the updates Peter was talking about one too many times.

Her boss didn't wait for a response. "We've promised we're looking into crafting a meaningful explanation and apology. But the mayor is still livid. You can't imagine all the fires I've had to put out over the weekend because of that interview. Thankfully, Miller is soldiering on, carrying the show with a new stand-in for now."

A stand-in.

Julia's heart sank. She'd already been replaced. And this time it was more than just one of her colleagues filling her chair. "Who is doing the show with Miller today?" Her eyes squeezed shut, steeling herself against the blow that was coming.

"A gal named Hannah O'Brian. Brought her up from one of the local stations. Today's her first day on air, but I believe she'll fill your spot nicely."

"Fill my spot?" Was he serious? Panic fired on all cylinders. Had she officially been replaced? So soon?

Peter coughed and then readjusted his tone. "Well, at least temporarily. Just until we can sort this thing out. You know we can't put you back on the air yet. The network is balancing on the edge of possible litigation. That's the most important thing right now, protecting the network. Rossetti's people need to think you're being reprimanded for what you did. That's why I'm calling. The network has decided to formally suspend you for a period of four weeks."

Four weeks. That was an eternity in the media world. Enough time for her to become obsolete. She was already taking a big risk by being away for days. But this was different. An uncomfortable lump wedged in her throat. It was suddenly difficult to breathe. Gripping the phone, she willed herself to calm down. "I'm being suspended?"

"Yes. What you did calls for consequences, Julia."

"Peter," Julia began, shoring up her nerve. "You do realize all I did was report something I got from a source. This whole 'fake news' angle the AP ran last week—or maybe that was Rossetti's PR team dishing it out—wasn't entirely true. Granted, I didn't run the bit past you for approval, but I didn't just make it up."

"That may be so, but the fact remains that you didn't do your due diligence on this one, Julia. There was no fact-checking or cross-referencing. You went rogue. When it comes down to it, you were in the wrong. And because of it, there must be repercussions. Rossetti could sue for defamation of character or slander, or worse. You've got to fall on your sword for this one."

"I see." A stifling weight settled around Julia's shoulders. Peter was simply not going to save her.

"What I can't seem to understand," Peter continued, his impatience waning a bit, "is why you did it. It's rather out of character for you to have such an outburst on air, especially one of this magnitude. You've always been content to leave the theatrics to Miller. Is there more to this whole thing than you're telling me?"

Yes, I was afraid of losing my job, of the ratings slip and the ridiculous pressure from the execs. I panicked and went for the Hail Mary, all without thinking it through. Julia sucked in her breath and debated whether to share the truth with him. This was a possible way out, her route to clemency. Peter was offering a rare chance to defend her actions, but for some reason she couldn't bring herself to speak up. It was as if her courage had rooted down too deep and was now unable to dislodge from its hiding place and reach the light.

"I suppose I just got caught up in the moment." She slumped forward. She hated herself for being so weak. In truth, she'd foolishly hoped the whole affair would blow over and she could get on with her job. Clearly, that wasn't going to happen.

"Well, you leave me no choice but to put you on extended leave. The network will issue a statement, and we'll send an official apology—one you'll willingly sign—over to the mayor's office today. We've let this thing go for an entire weekend, but we can't afford to sidestep it any longer. I need to meet with legal, but let's talk again this afternoon, once we have something in writing for Rossetti."

"Fine."

"And Julia . . ." Peter paused.

"Yes?"

"If any other detail comes to mind regarding what you heard, let me know. We're going to need all the ammunition we can get our hands on if this thing gets any uglier."

Isn't it already ugly enough? Julia wanted to ask, but she held her tongue. Peter was giving her one final chance to clear her reputation. Maybe if she had something more concrete on the Rossetti story, some shred of evidence, she could return to her job and undo the damage done to the network. She needed to look further into it.

It was that *maybe* that planted a small seed of hope inside Julia as she said goodbye and hung up with Peter.

～

Much later that morning, after a stock of hearty winter vegetables had been chopped—and rechopped with excruciating precision to meet Ginny's consistent-knife-cut requirements—the long table had been set.

Julia's mind was still buzzing with Peter's announcement. Four weeks of punishment. It was too awful to think about. If she allowed herself to dwell on the consequences, she might find herself curling into the fetal position right there on her sister's floor.

In an effort to avoid her spiraling doom, she aimed her focus in the direction of another gnawing concern. Her niece hadn't resurfaced, yet again. This was a bad sign. And it was having an effect on her sister.

Ginny silently fumed as she worked, banging stainless-steel pots around at great volume. Julia assumed this was for Olive's benefit: Ginny's raucous commotion was her means of jolting the slumbering girl from her bed. When Olive still hadn't materialized and the majority of prep work had been completed, Ginny uttered something under her breath and stalked off to take a shower. The master bedroom door slammed on its hinges, causing Julia to jump.

Between the call from work, James's disappointment, and the tension in her sister's house, Julia felt as if everything around her was unraveling.

And then, as if she knew her mother had left the room, Olive appeared. Emerging from the hall, the sleepy-eyed girl ambled in and made her way toward the coffee maker. Julia stopped what she was doing and turned to greet her. Her eyes took in the cotton pajama bottoms and oversize T-shirt Olive wore depicting the name and tour dates of a band Julia had never heard of. Her lightened hair was knotted high on top of her head in a messy beehive. The tanned skin of her face was washed and bare, save for a sparkling silver stud in her left nostril. Julia pushed aside a newly rinsed wineglass and blinked. She couldn't help but stare. So much had changed about Olive; it made Julia's heart ache. Did she even know this girl anymore?

Julia continued to examine Olive as the girl poured hot coffee into a mug. So many questions hovered, but Julia decided to wait until Olive was more awake. Judging by the significant droop in her niece's eyelids, this was not the time for probing conversation.

"Morning," Julia said, her tone overly cheery. The need to connect with Olive felt urgent, her time to make amends short. After three years of no communication, there was now an unfamiliar awkwardness looming between them. Julia supposed she didn't blame Olive for her obvious caution. From her niece's perspective, here was the aunt with whom she'd once been somewhat close but who had now turned into a stranger. Why else would she be so chilly and disinterested?

Olive sensed her staring and offered a puzzled frown. Her gaze went to the row of upturned red-wine glasses drying on the counter. "Hey, Aunt Julia. I see you've been added to the chain gang."

"Oh yeah. Ha! I get it. That's funny. I'm happy to help out." Julia chuckled and then cringed inwardly. She was trying too hard. Instead of giving off a casual air, she was coming across as goofy. It was pathetic how much she wanted this grown-up version of Olive to like her.

"Uh-huh." Olive brought down a container from a nearby cupboard and proceeded to spoon a hefty helping of granulated sugar into her mug. Julia watched her delicate fingers circle the spoon around, creating a miniature whirlpool in the dark liquid.

"So," Julia ventured. She squeezed out the sponge and returned it to the sink. "What's your plan today? Your mom mentioned something about flowers."

Olive cradled the mug and pushed her hipbone against the counter. She reached up to drag a lazy finger underneath a row of smudged lashes. "Yeah. All that stuff I bought yesterday has to be trimmed and arranged. Mom likes things to be just so. You know how she can be." She cocked her head. "Or maybe you don't, considering how long it's been since you've come around."

"Right." That one stung. Julia dried her hands on a towel and gulped back a response. It was important to remain friendly and not defensive. Olive needed to see she was on her side. Julia did know how Ginny could be when it came to her work, demanding and precise. And she suspected all this sleeping in and slow playing was Olive's way of giving her overbearing mother the virtual finger. "Your mom also mentioned you're quite good at it. The flower-arranging thing, I mean."

Olive raised an eyebrow. "My mom said that?"

"Yes, she did. She said you have a knack for it." Julia noticed something like suspicion flash in her eyes. It was clear that communication in this household had completely disintegrated.

Olive slurped her drink and then pulled herself from her lounged position. "Well, I'd better get to it, then. There's a bucketful of greenery and flowers out in the garage that has my name on it." She gave a faint wave and breezed out of the kitchen, trailing the aroma of fresh coffee behind her.

"Okay," Julia replied. She hung the wet towel over a hook and noted a pit returning to her gut. Reaching Olive was going to be a lot harder than she'd thought. And while a large piece of her yearned to follow the girl into the other room and figure out a way to repair the lost connection, another, more fearful part of Julia worried about how to do the same with her situation back home. Her job was in jeopardy. And she should bring James into the loop on all of this. Her personal and professional lives were currently deteriorating, and the blame was all hers.

How she was going to mend any of it remained a mystery.

CHAPTER SEVENTEEN
JULIA

After pacing Ginny's back patio with mounting worry, Julia decided to phone James. She'd been anxious ever since their disaster of a conversation the day before. She chose her timing carefully. On weekdays, he typically made a habit of ducking out of the office at lunchtime, if only for a quick stop at the food cart down the street. She also knew he took his lunch hour later in the day than most. If she wanted to reach him, now was the time. Sneaking into her room while the others went about their chores, she gently shut the door. A little privacy was required. Her intuition told her this wouldn't be the easiest conversation. As far as James knew, she was already boarding a plane for a quick return. Hearing otherwise might not go over so well.

After dialing his number, she waited. A coil of angst wrapped around her middle. Finally, James picked up.

"Hey." He sounded rushed and short of breath. The dull roar of street traffic could be heard rumbling in the background. It struck Julia how dissimilar their current environments were. There, James was full of purpose, surrounded by people and energy and noise, while Julia was a thousand miles away, floundering in a scene one might find on a nature channel. The only activity she heard at present was the shrill call of what she'd come to identify as a family of quail nesting somewhere beyond her window. That and the beating of her own quickening pulse.

Breaking the news to James was going to be tough.

"Hi," she said, trying to mask the apprehension in her voice. "Is this a good time?"

"You just caught me on my way to lunch."

"I was hoping I would," Julia said. She inhaled and eased down onto the bed. "Why are you panting?"

"Busy day. I have another meeting in ten, but if I don't get something to eat, I might chew off my arm." She pictured James out on the crowded sidewalk, his dark suit jacket and expensive tie flapping in the wind as he hustled down the block of high-rise buildings. It was unlike him to sound frazzled. He usually carried an air of confidence that unnerved most people. Julia twisted her engagement ring around on her finger. Maybe the last argument between them had bothered him more than she'd realized.

Guilt moved in. Because of her choices, the people in her life were suffering.

"Oh, well, I don't want to hold you up if it's a bad time." She swallowed, hoping he might cut her off and disagree. But James said nothing in response. "I only wanted to tell you I'm still thinking about everything you said. I know I've created a mess. And I didn't mean to leave you in the lurch. Truly. But now that I'm here at Ginny's, it's become clear she needs me. Her personal life is kind of in shambles too. Anyway, I promised to stay for a few more days. Then I can come home and we can really talk."

The rapid breathing quieted. James had apparently stopped walking and was now standing still. "You're staying longer?"

Julia pulled at a loose thread on the bedcover. "Um, yeah. Just a few days."

"Seriously?" James blurted.

She dropped the thread and stiffened.

"What about your job? I mean, surely it doesn't look good to GBN that you've taken off when your position is on the line." His speech sped up, the irritation in his voice increasing.

"It's okay. I've talked to Peter. They got someone to fill in. I'm sort of on extended leave."

"Of your own creation." This time an acrid tone edged his reply.

Julia frowned. "I'm sorry?"

"Are you on leave from work or from me, Julia? Because I'm having a hard time understanding all of this. Your life is here, in New York. Not in the middle of the desert. Why are you running away? This isn't the woman I fell in love with. You're acting like someone I don't even know right now!" Julia reared back, pulling the phone from her ear. What exactly was he accusing her of?

"James, you don't have to shout."

"Well, apparently I do. Because lately you just aren't hearing me."

And you're not hearing me either, she wanted to say. Why did he have to push her so hard? Couldn't he understand she wasn't ready to come back? To face the damage? That she needed to be somewhere quiet to recalibrate and lick her wounds? *But no,* she thought. He wouldn't. Not James. He was a big believer in a constant show of strength, in going after what you wanted in order to get ahead in the world. Julia wasn't sure she could catapult herself onto his level. Not yet, anyway.

"Hello?" Now he was just plain angry.

Julia sighed. "Yes, I'm here. I don't know what to say. I'm not like you. I can't just go charging back through the doors of the network when they've ordered me out. I'm respecting their wishes, and I'm taking some time for myself while I do that. I'm visiting my family and home state. Why is that so unreasonable?"

"Whatever, Julia. Do what you want. But if it were me, and I had an anchor position with a high-profile news show, I'd fight to keep my spot. I guess you don't care enough. And I guess you don't care about us either. Thanks for letting me know. I have to get to my meeting."

"James—"

"I have to go." The line went dead before Julia could find the words to respond. Dumbstruck, she kept the phone up to her ear and stared at the wall. Had he really just hung up on her? She hadn't even had a chance to explain how being suspended and replaced was affecting her dwindling sense of self-worth. He'd cut her off. He'd made her decisions all about him.

Slowly, Julia peeled herself from the rumpled bed. Despite the pin-pricks of stinging tears, she refused to wallow. If she stayed there, with the shades drawn in that darkened room, she might sink deeper into her funk. The thought frightened her. There was too much that required her attention. Ginny and Olive needed her. Guests would be arriving in a few hours. And Peter would, most likely, be contacting her later with documents to sign. She couldn't lose it now, not when so much was at stake.

James and his wounded feelings were going to have to once again be put on the back burner. She'd find a way to make him understand.

Smoothing her clothes, she filled her lungs with a cleansing breath and went out in search of the others. Maybe it would be better to be with people right now. Otherwise, the pull of despair might be too great.

The clock on her phone read eleven thirty. Slipping it into her back pocket, she prayed for the remainder of the day to improve. Ginny's dinner guests—all twelve of them—weren't set to arrive until five o'clock. She wondered if, now that Olive was home, all three of them would sit down and have lunch together. Maybe find a way to set all the contention aside and talk. Maybe she could even run into town to pick up sandwiches. Hearing the whir of a mixer, Julia went to find out what Ginny thought of her idea.

She found her sister in the kitchen, putting together some kind of liquid green puree, a sharp dip of concentration on her brow. Olive was also there, her bare feet planted at the sink as she filled vases with water and wrestled with a tightly wrapped bunch of stems. Both women had their backs to one another, and neither was speaking. Julia eyed the loud mixer and wondered if this was how they normally went about their days, in a carefully orchestrated dance of avoidance.

While their sibling connection had splintered, she'd always figured Ginny at least had Olive. There had been times, after their parents died and before James came along, when Julia had even fostered a mild jealousy—her sister had a family while she had no one. But it was clear now that she'd been so very wrong in that regard.

She and Ginny had both suffered from loneliness. And for this, she was deeply saddened.

"Hey." She came over to rest a hand on Ginny's shoulder, hoping not to take her by surprise. Ginny spun around and then flicked off the mixer.

"Hi. I didn't see you there."

"That's okay. I was thinking maybe I'd run into town and grab us all something to eat. Maybe we could break for lunch and catch up a little? You know, before the craziness of this evening takes over?"

Ginny glanced at Olive and then back to Julia. Her frown softened.

"Why not? I don't have time to make lunch. You know where you're going?"

Julia had an idea. She'd seen a little deli on the way to the farmers' market. "Yeah. I'll be back in a half hour." She brightened. This was good. All she had to do was get them to sit down in the same room and perhaps some of the ice would melt.

Jogging toward the driveway, she only hoped Ginny and Olive would behave themselves long enough for it to happen.

CHAPTER EIGHTEEN
GINNY

The three of them sat huddled around a teak table on the back patio in uncomfortable silence. In front of them were unfolded squares of white butcher paper, revealing artisan sandwiches on thick focaccia bread slathered in mustard and layered with peppered roast turkey, cheese, lettuce, and tomatoes. Ginny nibbled on hers and waited for Olive to deliver the blow that would surely hurt Julia's feelings.

Her daughter picked lethargically at the bread slices and scrunched up her face in a pained expression. Ginny held her breath. *Five, four, three, two, one . . .*

"No offense, Aunt Julia," Olive said with a huff. "I just don't do meat."

"Pfft." Ginny rolled her eyes and waited for Julia's response. Olive shot a white-hot glare in her direction.

Ginny looked away. Why couldn't her daughter just suck it up? Julia didn't know Olive was a vegetarian. If she even *was* one. The girl's preferences had changed so often that Ginny couldn't keep up. Olive tended to be obnoxiously picky, and nothing drove a chef crazier than a picky eater. Half the time, she believed Olive swore off a new food just to irk her.

"Oh! I'm so sorry. I didn't—" A look of dismay flashed on Julia's face.

"It's not your fault," Ginny chimed in. "One never knows what Olive's trend du jour will be these days. It changes all the time."

Julia's eyes widened. "I didn't realize—"

"*Trend du jour?* Really, Mom? That's respectful." Olive pushed her sandwich back and sulked.

"Sorry, Olive. I would have gotten you a veggie sandwich if I'd known." Julia's face colored as she offered an unsteady smile in Olive's direction.

"That's okay. Really. I'm sure my mom probably told you turkey would be fine. She tends to overlook my choices. Not your fault."

"Oh my god!" Ginny felt a surge of rage. This kid was just too damn much sometimes. Was she really going to sit there and insult her in front of Julia? Had she no shame at all? Where was the open-minded, sensitive girl that used to exist? Gone, that's where. And in her place was a spoiled bohemian brat.

"Hey, hey, you two. There's no need to get upset. It's just a silly sandwich. No harm, no foul."

Ginny threw her head back and let out a sharp cackle.

"What'd I say?"

"You said 'no fowl,'" Olive said flatly. She matched her mother's exaggerated eye roll and tipped back in her chair. Ginny and Julia both looked on as she took a long pull from her oversize bottle of kombucha with a bored expression.

"Ah." Julia turned to give Ginny a sidelong glance. She ran a hand through her hair. "Glad I can make someone around here laugh."

Ginny shook her head with disbelief and then sank a hearty bite into her bread. The truth was, she felt as if she might be coming a little unhinged. She'd only laughed in an effort not to cry. If her daughter wasn't going to send her over the edge, then her diminished bank account surely would. What the other two didn't know was that while she'd been in her bedroom, just stepping from the shower, the bank had called with an automated recording regarding her overdrawn account. Again. And Ginny had no idea when she might be able to pay it back. If both Julia and Olive abandoned her to run Mesquite alone—which they most likely would—then where would she be? It was a miracle that Julia had showed up when she did, but her support was only temporary.

And by the state of their lunch conversation, this current arrangement wasn't working out for any of them.

"So, Aunt Julia," Olive said, plucking out a leaf of lettuce from her rejected lunch, "how come you're here and not at your job? Isn't that show you do, like, on every morning?"

Ginny paused midbite and cocked her head. She was irritated by Olive's snarky tone, but she was also interested. Of course, she knew about her sister's vacation time and avoidance of her relationship troubles back home. But what about her job? She didn't seem to have a timeline in returning to it. She'd said as much on that first morning over breakfast. But Julia had also kept the details of her job sparse, acting as if the personal time away was merely a hiccup and she was overworked and conflicted about her love life. She claimed to have come to Arizona to reconnect—though she'd yet to say she'd come to apologize—and take a break from New York.

Ginny knew, however, from the way Julia would scurry off to her bedroom for hushed phone conversations behind closed doors, that it couldn't be the whole story. There had to be more to why her sister had extended her trip.

"Oh yes," Julia said. "We tape *Daybreak* every weekday morning. Early! Ha! You can't imagine how early." Her laugh was nervous and slightly forced. Olive looked on with an even expression, as if she wasn't buying Julia's flippancy any more than Ginny. For an instant, mother and daughter connected eyes as they exchanged dubious glances.

"Sounds hectic. So, today is a weekday. Why aren't you there?" Olive pressed.

Ginny glanced at Julia, who seemed to be stalling. Her sister smiled uncomfortably and took a belabored bite of her lunch. After several long seconds, she swallowed. "Right. I'm usually on the air. I'm just taking a vacation. It's rare, but if I get an opportunity, I jump on it."

Olive frowned. "So you came here? To Arizona, to be with people you haven't even spoken to in, like, three years? How'd you come up with that one?"

Ginny stiffened. "Olive!"

Olive's shoulders rose and then fell, as if to say, *Why not?*

Ginny's gaze darted over to Julia, whose expression was turning watery. *Oh great.* She understood Olive's hostility toward the once-close aunt who had appeared to lose interest in her teenage niece once she hit the big time. Olive had been dejected. And it wasn't any secret that the two of them had been forced to abruptly move their lives to another state—Ginny's home state—because Julia couldn't be bothered to help with the overwhelming family affairs. Ginny had complained a lot when they'd first arrived in Arizona. She supposed that animosity had seeped over onto her daughter. Plus, Olive regretted the permanent change of address. Why not blame Julia?

Still. Her daughter was purposely picking a fight.

"No, it's okay." Julia blinked back the dampness. "I'm sure she didn't mean anything by it."

I'm sure she did.

Olive crossed her arms over her chest in a sign of defiance. Perhaps Olive was meeting toughness in her mom with a certain brand of her own toughness. Perhaps this was all learned behavior. The thought was upsetting. Was Ginny the reason for her daughter's coldness?

Biting her lip, she held herself back from saying more.

"The truth is . . ." Julia hesitated. "The truth is, I made a mistake at work."

"Really?"

The two women looked on as she squirmed in her chair and repeatedly dabbed at her mouth with a napkin. This was certainly news. Ginny hadn't tuned in to Julia's show for a while now, so she couldn't be sure what her sister was referring to. It had to have been a major mistake if Julia had sought refuge across the country. Especially considering that hefty ring on her finger. Wouldn't she prefer the comfort of her fiancé and not an estranged sibling?

"Yes," Julia murmured.

Ginny noticed her sister's fidgety hands. The once immaculately manicured nails had now chipped and cracked as a result of heavy dishwashing. She also noticed, for the first time, that much of her sister's overdone TV makeup was absent. Gone was the application of thick foundation to conceal the beginnings of thin spiderweb lines around her mouth and eyes. Gone was the shiny lacquer of lip gloss to enhance her pout. Either the desert life or the stress was changing her. Regardless, Julia was apparently starting to let go of her flawless exterior and take on a refreshingly natural air instead.

"What do you mean, 'mistake'?" Olive prodded, suddenly straightening with interest.

"Well," Julia began, "when you're on television, there's a certain level of pressure to remain relevant. Believe it or not, being in my late thirties ages me quite a bit in my position. I'm not considered as 'current' as I could be, I suppose. My job relies on loyal viewers and ratings and approval from tightly wound people in suits. I regrettably let that pressure get to me. It caused me to act irrationally. I made an accusation on air without my boss's approval, and that mistake landed me in hot water. So I've been put on temporary leave. You could say I've been given a grown-up's version of a time-out. And I'm not proud of it."

"Wow."

"Yeah, 'wow' is right." Julia gave a sad smile.

Ginny was stunned. She certainly hadn't expected her guarded sister to open up and be so honest, especially in the face of Olive's ill-mannered inquiry. "What kind of accusation?" she asked.

"I accused the mayor of New York City of tax fraud."

Ginny gaped. "Wow. That's pretty big."

"Yeah. So now you know."

Ginny suddenly felt like a fool for dismissing Julia's problems as trivial. For not asking questions. She should've been paying more attention.

"Is it really that bad? I mean, you have a contract, don't you?" Ginny asked. Maybe there was a way to fix this.

"Yeah," Olive broke in before Julia could respond. "Don't newspapers print mistakes all the time and then just write a correction the next day? Couldn't you do something like that?"

"A retraction? Yes, we do it all the time. However, my problem is a bit larger. I made a statement about Mayor Rossetti. He's kind of a big deal. And he's not happy. At the rate things are going, I'll just be lucky to walk away without a lawsuit." Julia noticeably deflated against the back of her chair. Ginny searched her face. She saw the watery expression returning. Her sister was clearly under significant stress.

All the pieces of Julia's unexpected appearance now began to slide into place.

"Jeez, Aunt Julia. That sounds bad. I'm sorry." Olive's calcified edge softened considerably. Ginny was silently grateful that her daughter had a heart after all.

Julia brought her napkin to the corner of her eye. "Thanks, Olive. That means a lot. Guess I'm not much of a role model for you."

Ginny reached a hand across the table's surface and patted the wood. The heat was picking up and beginning to warm everything not covered by shade. Soon they'd need to go inside. "Don't worry," she said. Julia glanced up with a sad expression. "Something will work out. You've come too far in your career to be cast off by a single bad judgment call."

"I wish I had your confidence," Julia said. "Because right now I'm really not sure. About anything. Now if you'll excuse me, I think I'll go freshen up." Julia scooted back and stood. Clearing her food, she turned her face away and scurried back through the glass doors.

"Jeez. Didn't see that one coming," Olive said.

"Me neither." Ginny worried, as she stared back at her daughter, about what else she'd missed. With everything she was dealing with, she hadn't realized she wasn't the only one who needed help. Maybe it wasn't Julia who was self-absorbed. Maybe it had been her all along, and she'd been too blind to see that. Now that they were all gathered under her roof, she wondered what else she would be forced to admit.

CHAPTER NINETEEN
JULIA

That evening was a mad dash. Orders and dishes and frantic exchanges passed between the three women as they welcomed twelve excited guests into the dining room of Mesquite. Conversations from earlier that day had been put on hold for the sake of Ginny's business. Julia understood the three of them would likely revisit some difficult topics. It had been clear that Olive still harbored a fair amount of negative feelings, though they'd been tempered, and Ginny had more questions. Julia knew her sister well enough to know she wouldn't be let off the hook so easily.

The little home's kitchen swept them up into a fog of aromatic steam. Ginny tended to pan searing dozens of garlic-infused scallops with great care. The pleasing scent wafted up and into Julia's nostrils, causing her stomach to gurgle. Her sister's cooking never failed to tempt her palate. Being around such elevated fare had reawakened her otherwise-suppressed appetite. Working for GBN had caused her to give up so many food indulgences that she'd once adored. If only she could stop and sample a bite before moving into the other room.

There wasn't any time, however. Ginny urged the women to gather up a chilled first course and deliver it to the now-seated revelers.

The fabric of Julia's blouse dampened under her arms as she sailed around the dining room, making quick work of filling water glasses and then passing out plates of delicate quail egg and asparagus salads.

Olive was even quicker. She slid past Julia, their shoulders grazing, and expertly uncorked and poured the wine. Julia couldn't help but stare at the transformation her otherwise-blasé niece had undergone. Just minutes before the doorbell rang, Olive had come breezing into the foyer with her hair slicked back into a ballerina bun, wearing a starched white button-down rolled at the sleeves and tucked neatly into a slim pair of cigarette pants. Olive looked quite grown-up and beautiful. It was most likely that Ginny had instructed her to wear the polished work attire, but nonetheless, Julia was impressed with Olive's ability to pull it together seamlessly.

As wineglasses were filled, Julia had to catch herself from tipping a helping of creamy lemon aioli into a woman's lap. She was still trying to perfect her serving skills. Thankfully she righted the dish just in time, apologizing out loud as glossy buttons of black caviar wobbled atop miniature egg yolks. Olive stared down her nose but said nothing and continued to pour. Guests oohed and aahed as Julia used her practiced reporter voice to announce the first course.

"We haven't seen you before," a bald man in a jaunty bow tie exclaimed to Julia. "I see Ginny finally got our girl Olive here some extra help!" He grinned and raised his glass in a salute to a beaming Olive. Some of the other guests murmured their approval. Olive acknowledged each one of them. It was obvious this large table of diners were regulars.

Julia set down a water pitcher and addressed the room. "Hello, everyone. I'm Julia. I'll be one of your servers tonight." Olive sent a conspiratorial wink in Julia's direction. This was a good sign. Her niece was warming to her. "I hope everyone's enjoying themselves?"

"Of course!" piped up another woman. "But, Julia, I recognize you. You're on the news—isn't that right? I've watched your morning show. You're Julia Frank!"

Oh great. Here we go. A substantial stone of dread materialized in Julia's stomach. Not more than five minutes in the room and Julia had been identified. She had hoped wearing nothing more than mascara and securing her usually blown-out hair into a low ponytail would make her slightly less identifiable, but she'd been wrong.

It figured. This group was a bit more youthful than the previous guests. Estimating by their faces, she guessed the average age to be around sixty. Save for one nice-looking man in the middle, who was the least dressed-up of them all, with his checkered shirt and ruffled dark hair. He was tan and slightly scruffy, and his smile gave off an air of relaxed nonchalance, like he'd skipped shaving for a few days. Julia thought he might be closer to forty years old or thereabouts. And then, like a jolt of lightning, it dawned on her.

She knew him. *Isn't that Shane Hemsley from high school? In Ginny's living room?*

Her mouth opened to utter a greeting to the old acquaintance from so many years ago, but then Olive, unaware of Julia's surprise, interrupted.

"Aunt Julia is on the news. You're correct, Beverly," Olive said to the still-gawking woman. "But since she's family and out here on vacation, we're lucky enough to have her help for the evening." Olive delivered her explanation so easily; Julia felt a surge of gratitude.

"Well, that's a big deal! You're on GBN." Beverly tapped the table with a red nail, her eyes brightening. A dull chatter rose from the crowd.

"Yes, that's me." Julia eased away, hoping to exit the room before the conversation went any further. She felt oddly nervous.

Beverly's eyes flashed. Something like confusion followed by disappointment moved in and clouded her expression. Julia could practically see the wheels of her memory turning over. "Oh, but you had a tough time of it last week, didn't you? I saw the show. That Rossetti fellow was hard on you. Was it true what you said? Is he a criminal?"

The others all ceased their chatter and focused on her. Shane turned and met her awkward gaze. She blushed. The silence in the room was suddenly stifling. Even Olive appeared at a loss for words.

"Oh yeah. You saw that, did you?" The stone in Julia's belly flipped over and caused her to hug her middle self-consciously. "That was an unusual segment. It's all part of reporting the news, I'm afraid. But I'll let you folks get back to your salad. Enjoy!" With the last word, she curled her lips into an artificial smile and backed swiftly out of the room.

"We may have a problem," Julia whispered to Ginny as she entered the kitchen. Olive was right on her heels, carting an empty bottle of wine.

Ginny broke her concentration momentarily. "What is it?"

Julia hesitated. Should she tell her sister about Beverly or Shane first? Plus, she wasn't sure whether it was the right time to disturb Ginny. Her sister was currently stooped over the counter in concentration, making slow and methodical movements. Julia watched as she meticulously placed the second course of pan-seared scallops onto plates containing artful brushstrokes of pea puree and bacon trimmings. To Julia, it was a work of pure perfection. Ginny took plating food to a whole new level. This was a skill Julia never could master even if she tried. Ginny just had an eye for these things. She'd clearly gotten the creative gene in the family.

"Well, one of the women out there recognized me," Julia said, deciding on the potentially more obvious problem. "She saw the Rossetti interview."

Ginny straightened and drove a knuckle into her lower back. "Hmmm."

"It was Beverly Moorehead." Olive came in and leaned a hip against the counter. Casually, she popped a nearby breadstick into her mouth.

143

"Beverly, huh? I wouldn't worry too much about her. She's a local—harmless, even if she is a busybody."

Julia relaxed a bit. She supposed she didn't care much about being recognized from TV, although for the sake of appearances it didn't do much for her newscaster career to be caught busing food in a semi-legal speakeasy. The thing she feared was running into New Yorkers, especially when caught off guard. This Beverly woman was just being curious. Nothing more. If Ginny didn't worry, then Julia supposed she wouldn't either.

"And, um . . ." Julia trailed off, not sure whether to trust Ginny with her other discovery.

"What is it?" Judging by Ginny's deepening scowl, it was clear she was growing more annoyed by the minute. Ginny did not like to be knocked off her schedule.

Julia's gaze shifted to Olive and then down to the floor. She wasn't sure this was an admission she wanted everyone to hear. "Um, do you remember a guy from high school named Shane Hemsley? From the baseball team?"

"Not really. You were four grades younger. It's not like we always hung out with the same people. Why?"

Olive stopped chewing and leaned in close, clearly taking a new interest.

"Well, he's out there. At your table. That's all." Julia swallowed.

"So?" Ginny's patience had worn thin. "This is a small community, and we grew up one town over. We're bound to run into people we once knew. Is that a problem too?"

"No." Julia shook her head. Out of the corner of her eye, she saw Olive's eyebrows go up.

"Aunt Julia, did you used to hang out with him or something?"

Julia swallowed again. "Oh jeez. It was so long ago, and we barely knew each other."

"And?"

Julia groaned. "Maybe. I kind of admired him from afar, that's all. Oh god, this is so embarrassing. It's nothing. Really. I don't even know why I brought it up." Her hand swatted the air. "Just forget I even said anything. I recognized him and was taken aback, that's all. Don't worry about it."

Ginny chuckled. A trace of condescension was in the air. "We're not worried about it. Are *you*?"

"No. Seriously, let's just move on."

"Gladly." Ginny threw her a dry glance and went back to her plates. Julia grabbed one and refused to make eye contact. Why did she have to go and say anything in the first place?

"Now you two need to get back out there and see if they're ready for the next course. These puppies are hot, and I want them to stay that way." Ginny shooed the two women from their resting spots. Olive cleared crumbs from her mouth and gestured for Julia to follow.

For the remainder of the evening, Julia and Olive worked in tandem to deliver plate after plate of Ginny's creations to the enthusiastic guests. Other than a few sidelong glances, Beverly was thankfully too distracted making sure her husband, Phillip, enjoyed his birthday celebration. None of the others paid much attention to her. That is, until Shane eventually piped up. He'd obviously taken notice of Julia and waited for a quiet moment to say hello.

"So, newscaster and expert food server, huh? That's pretty impressive." He grinned as Julia bent down to retrieve an empty butter dish from the table. Julia could tell by the warmth in his voice that, unlike Beverly, he was offering friendly conversation to ease her jumpiness. He talked with an air of casual restraint.

"Right!" Julia clutched the dish and inched backward. She laughed softly, shrugging off her embarrassment. "Though I wouldn't say expert. Not by a long shot. Just helping my sister for a few days, that's all."

He tilted his head. "Well, I'm impressed all the same. Seems like you've done big things for yourself."

"Thanks."

As she turned to go, he stopped her. "It's nice to see you again, by the way."

"Yeah," she said. She was rather surprised he remembered her. They hadn't exactly been close friends, but she supposed they'd traveled in roughly the same circles as teenagers. "Nice to see you too. It's been a while."

He smiled. "You could say that."

"So, what do you do these days, Shane?" she asked. "That is, when you're not indulging in underground dining."

He chuckled. "Well, I'm a builder. Custom residential homes and such."

"Oh." She got the feeling he was being modest. She wondered if he was responsible for any of the large new southwestern-inspired homes she'd seen nearby. She was curious. "You sound impressive yourself. Have you been here since we graduated?"

"In Arizona? Yeah, mostly. I lived in California for a short stint, but the cost of living got so expensive, I relocated my business out here almost eight years ago. The market is ripe and I have no shortage of work, that's for sure. It's been a good spot for me. And my family is all here."

"I see. Well, congratulations."

He smiled.

She stood there a beat, feeling some of her tension fade away. There was an ease in talking to him. One she hadn't necessarily expected. It was almost as if they'd been friends all along. They chatted for a moment more as she continued to clear.

When she finally did slip away, Olive was right on her heels.

"You get any more questions?" Olive whispered, nudging Julia in the arm. Her niece had dropped all previous hostility and now was acting rather conspiratorial. Julia sensed her niece liked being in on the drama. They hustled into the kitchen and deposited the empty dishes near the sink.

"Not really."

With her back turned to Ginny, who was busy pulling ingredients from the refrigerator, Julia collected a set of stacked serving spoons. "Has Shane come in for dinner before?"

Olive shook her head. "Nope. Never seen him. I'm guessing he's here because he's related to Phillip somehow. Token birthday party guest."

"Ah." Julia nodded. She pressed her lips together and tried to shore up her disappointment. Oddly, she had hoped Olive could tell her more, or that he might be back.

Meanwhile Ginny thumped around behind them, releasing an armload of small Tupperware containers onto the counter. Olive took her cue to keep the dinner moving along before the next course was ready to go out. She wordlessly snatched an open bottle of wine and then strode back into the dining room. Julia suddenly felt foolish for having held things up with her probing.

"I can tell you're losing focus." Ginny paused her work at the counter and cast a suspicious eye toward Julia.

"Am I?" Julia's voice shot up an octave. Not wanting to be caught daydreaming, she smoothed her blouse and did her best to bring her thoughts back to neutral.

"Well, you were obviously off in la-la land," Ginny said. She gave her a suspicious once-over. "Are you worried about work? Or something else?"

Work. Julia sagged. She hadn't thought about Peter or the office since tonight's guests had arrived. Once again, she'd been neglectful. Ginny's probing reminded her of the missed calls she'd failed to return that afternoon. Peter had tried reaching her several times, but Julia couldn't bring herself to face what else he had to say. There were likely legal documents and mea culpas to deal with. And she assumed it all needed to be handled in a timely fashion. Yet she'd still not taken immediate action. Maybe James was right that she was running away, that she didn't want it bad enough to break down the doors and demand her job back. If she did, surely she could have been relied upon to return a basic phone call.

Regardless, she'd dragged her heels all day.

"Yeah." She dropped her gaze to the ground. "I am worried about work. I was supposed to return some calls earlier. But we got hectic around here, and now that it's two hours ahead in New York, I don't think anyone will be in the office at this time of night. I'll deal with it in the morning, I guess."

Ginny grunted and went about plating food. "Sounds like you're conflicted. I'm happy to talk things over with you tomorrow. You know, only if you want?" Her offer came out like a question.

Julia nodded, a hint of sadness pulling at the corners of her mouth. Ginny was gradually letting her in. It meant a lot. She only wondered if she'd been as open in return. Here she was in her sister's house, despite their rough past, and they'd somehow picked up much where they'd left off. Awkwardness and animosity excluded.

It would be nice to know the same could be said for when she returned to James. But Julia had a nagging feeling it wouldn't be. Tomorrow, she'd have to try to make him understand. But for now all she wanted was for the guests to leave so she could drown her guilt in a feast of leftovers. It had been too long since she'd been around Ginny's cooking, and tonight she wasn't going to waste one bit.

CHAPTER TWENTY

JULIA

The next morning, Julia decided to tick off her undesirable to-do list, starting with Peter. The fact that she'd avoided his calls the day before had put him in a bitter mood. She had failed to sign the apology letter the GBN lawyers had drafted for her, and now they were scrambling.

"This is unacceptable!" Peter seethed into the phone. Julia pulled her shoulders up around her ears and cringed. She hadn't meant to let it all go on so long. Well, maybe she'd evaded her boss just a little. Even though Julia was being pressed, something was stopping her from taking further action. She worried that once the crafted apology was signed and sent over with her name attached, her job would simultaneously vanish. Perhaps the network was just pretending she was suspended and planned to let her go once the mess was cleaned up. It was absurd to try to postpone the inevitable, but she found herself doing it anyway.

The backlash just kept coming.

"I'm so sorry, Peter. I've been thinking a lot about what you said before, about coming up with any other detail regarding the story." She found herself on the edge of the back patio, gazing into the distance. Keeping her tone low, she hoped her conversation wouldn't travel through any open windows. She scanned the vast horizon and struggled to get her bearings. A lizard darted out from under a nearby rock and zigzagged along the dirt. Overhead, a hawk screeched, loud and lonely, reminding Julia how far away from civilization she really was.

"And?" Peter asked. "Did you come up with something?"

Julia's head dropped. "No. Not really." She dragged a bare toe through a layer of desert sand and wished she could've answered differently.

"Well damn it, Julia! What the hell are you playing around for? Open your laptop and sign the document! I expect it done within the hour. You've been a good staffer in the past. I hate that it has come to this, but honestly, you leave me no choice."

She held her breath and waited for him to lower the boom. This was the moment she would be fired. She'd taken it all too far and there was no way to come back from it. *Daybreak* would keep going with Miller and some bimbo. (Not that she knew anything about her replacement, because she couldn't even bring herself to tune in and watch ever since Peter had broken the news, but she disliked this Hannah girl out of sheer spite.)

When Peter didn't say anything more, she nodded. "Okay, sorry. I'll take care of it."

"Good. Do some soul-searching over these next four weeks. Figure out what it is you really want. Because by the way you're acting, I'm not sure you know. We'll talk soon." The phone went dead and he was gone again.

With a fresh sense of dread, Julia headed back into the house. This was it. She would sign the written apology, it would be sent over to the mayor's office and likely posted online, and her career would be forever tarnished. She'd made a mistake, and now her ownership of that mistake would be cast in stone. Slipping back through the doorway, she wondered how she ever got here.

And if she would ever return to the life she used to have.

~

Later that afternoon, Julia found Ginny out back. Her sister was dressed in denim from head to toe and was bent over a charming little garden. Julia hadn't noticed this part of the property before because it was partially obscured by overgrown grasses near the side of the yard. But as she watched Ginny tend to it now, a pair of trimming shears in one hand and a little basket in the other, she marveled at its vitality.

"I can smell the rosemary from here," Julia said, approaching. Her eye went to the rectangular bed filled with tiny rows of thyme, coriander, and sage.

Ginny straightened and smiled. A sprig of the spiky green herb was clutched in her right hand. "Isn't it the best? This stuff grows wonderfully out here. It loves the desert climate."

Julia stepped closer and inhaled. "It reminds me of roasted Thanksgiving turkey. Remember how Mom used to stuff the bird with huge portions of it?" A pang of grief shot through her at the recollection. As a child, Julia had loved the big family spread their mother put on at holidays. Though it was just the four of them, the dining table would be covered in platters of comfort food, and each girl always had a favorite dish. Ginny and Julia were so close back then, blanketed in the security of their parents' love. But that was another lifetime ago. Neither Ginny nor Julia had brought up their parents much during this visit. Doing so ran the risk of touching on a kind of raw sadness.

"I remember," Ginny said softly. "Sometimes there's nothing better than cooking with rosemary."

"Hmm." They were both silent for a long moment, reflecting.

"Well," Ginny said, placing the herbs into her basket, "Olive is responsible for this little patch of heaven." Her head angled toward the raised bed.

"Really?"

"Yep. That girl smooth-talked one of her guy friends into building it, with exacting instructions that it had to be raised to keep out all the critters, and then she took it upon herself to plant the herbs. She even made these sweet little signs for each row in case I forgot what we were growing. Ha! Like I would forget."

"It's really nice." Julia peered down at the miniature rustic wooden markers with hand-painted labels and mused. They reminded her of something that might appear in the Beatrix Potter books Olive had liked as a child, with stories about Mr. McGregor's garden. Olive was such an anomaly to her, part hard and wild, the other part creative and loyal. The only difficulty was knowing which girl would show up at any given moment.

But seeing this garden now suggested Olive's willingness to connect with her mother. The two might butt heads more often than not, but Olive saw her mother and made little gestures in ways Ginny would appreciate—gardening and floral arrangements being some of them.

Julia studied Ginny now and wondered if her sister truly recognized this about her daughter. For both their sakes, Julia hoped she did. It wasn't lost on her how much time had been stolen from her own mother, how unexpectedly that relationship had been taken away by death. It was shameful now to Julia how she'd squandered time with her family, had taken off without much thought and set her sights on the gleaming lure of New York. Sure, she'd kept in touch with her parents, but not nearly enough. Now it was simply too late. This was not what she wished for Ginny and Olive. Time was precious. She understood that now, and the realization was painful.

"So, I couldn't help but overhear you on the phone early this morning. I'm guessing it was with someone in New York?" Ginny asked, her mouth twisting as if she wasn't sure whether she was crossing a line.

"Oh, you heard that? Sorry, I thought if I went outside, I wouldn't wake anyone." She worried just how much had been heard. Her mind quickly ticked back over the details of the call.

"Don't worry about it. I tend to toss and turn in the mornings lately. As soon as the sun comes up, my mind starts spinning over what needs to be done for the business."

It was strange to hear Ginny call it that. But Julia supposed that's what Mesquite was: a business. Up until then, she'd considered it a kind of project or experiment her sister was playing around with. Looking back on the past several days, though, she realized this secret supper club was a real venture with real clientele. And Julia had become a small part of it. However temporary, she'd been working right alongside her family to make it succeed.

"So." Ginny broke her contemplation. "Everything okay back home?"

"Oh. Not really." Julia figured her only option was to be honest. Because at that moment, she wanted to ask Ginny something important. "Ginny?"

"Yeah?"

"If I told you that work didn't want me around for the next four weeks, what would you say?"

Ginny paused, her eyes widening. "Really? Wow. I'd say that's a long time. And I'd say I'm sorry to hear that. I mean, if you are."

"Yeah, it's not great news for my career. And I can't say I was expecting such a dramatic leave of absence. But what I mean is, what would you say if I asked to stay here for a while? You know, to spend more time with you and Olive?" She shifted, the sensation of being set adrift filling her.

"You want to stay in Arizona?" Ginny's face contorted in surprise. "With Olive and me? Even now that you've witnessed all the chaos? Are you sure?"

Julia nodded. She wasn't totally sure, to be honest. What would James say about it? What would anybody say? But despite her reservations, something deep inside told her it might be the right idea. At least for now. She wasn't ready to leave.

"Yeah, even after everything. I think it would be good for me to unplug for a while. I haven't had a vacation in years. I'd forgotten what the rest of the world looked like. And correct me if I'm wrong, but I think my staying might help you out too. I mean, I may not be all that skilled of a server, but it's free labor. You can't say no to that, can you?"

Ginny studied her and then broke into a wide grin. "You're right. I can't say no to that. That's the only kind I can afford."

Julia's heart skipped. "So I can stay?"

"Yes, you can stay. The guest room is open. But, Julia," Ginny warned, "I'm sorry to say this isn't a complete vacation. Right now, Mesquite takes precedence. I was just about to come inside and prep for my next dinner booking. I could use the extra help, seeing as how I don't have anything planned. It's a small party, so it shouldn't be a big deal. But still, I need an extra pair of hands to wash and chop produce."

"Okay."

Ginny paused. "Are you sure you want to continue working for me?"

"Yeah, I'm sure." Julia stuck out her hand and gestured for Ginny to take it. Never in her wildest dreams had she imagined such an offer would provide her with this much relief. But it did. "It's a deal."

Ginny produced a gloved hand and clasped Julia's in return. "Then it's settled."

They both smiled.

"Let's go find Olive and get to work on tonight's menu."

Together, they went inside.

CHAPTER TWENTY-ONE
GINNY

By Friday of that week, Ginny was beginning to detect a crack of light seeping into her otherwise dim outlook. Despite her usual worrying over how to improve her finances and the unmended rift with Olive, things were looking up.

Over the past three days, since Julia's decision to stay on, the women had come together for the common goal of Mesquite. Preparations for the dinner guests had been divided and delegated among the group. It was the first time in a long while that Ginny had the sensation she had room to breathe—to test out new recipes, plan the shopping, and even catch up on a bit of sleep.

Olive had also miraculously tempered her sour attitude now that there were three of them in the house. Not entirely, but enough to be civil toward her mother. Ginny supposed this was due mostly to Julia's presence. Olive had seemed to soften toward Julia after the confession about the blunder at GBN. Olive appreciated honesty. That much was clear. She'd spent the better part of their time together asking Julia questions about life in New York, details of her job, and what it was like to have a fiancé.

One evening, after a dinner of quinoa salad and butternut squash soup, Ginny observed as the two women huddled together on the living room sofa.

Ginny hung back in the kitchen, giving them space. Olive had her feet curled under a blanket, Julia facing her only inches away. It both lightened and broke Ginny's heart in equal parts to watch them like that. Her daughter appeared to listen thoughtfully as Julia spoke about something Ginny couldn't quite hear. Their heads remained close together as a fire crackled at the hearth just beyond them, their smiles lazy. A half-full bottle of wine rested on the coffee table next to their drained glasses. At one point, she saw Julia reach out and push a stray lock of Olive's hair behind her ear and smile. It was such a tender moment that Ginny was suddenly ashamed at her prick of envy. It had been years since she and her daughter had talked so intimately. Feeling like a third wheel, she slipped away to her bedroom, leaving the women to enjoy the moment without her.

She'd wondered where this was all going—her family, the business, her future—and how she could get ahead of it so that it wouldn't get away from her.

~

Now that it was the end of the week and there were guests to prepare for, Ginny's energy shifted back into high gear. The three of them gathered back in the kitchen just after breakfast to discuss plans.

"Tonight's menu is arugula soup followed by acorn squash and stuffed quail with a saba glaze, served with grilled asparagus and polenta. We'll finish off the meal with a lemon-lavender sorbet. I've got to get started prepping now." Ginny's brow furrowed as she looked from the handwritten to-do list she was holding to the waiting women. "Olive, can I leave you to do fresh table arrangements? I also need someone to pick up the linens from the dry cleaners. Tell them I'll pay them later and to put it on my account. Oh, and I noticed we're nearly out of firewood."

"Yes. Got it." Olive cocked a hip and adjusted the strap of her denim overalls. She stuck out a thumb indicating she'd handle it. Her hair was back in its usual beehive bun, but she was awake and fresh-faced and ready to go. This in itself was an improvement as far as Ginny was concerned. "I'll take care of the flowers. We're also running low on votive candles. I need to make a run into the city." She turned. "Aunt Julia, want to hit the wholesale flower market with me? It's pretty cool."

"S-sure," Julia stammered, perhaps taken a bit by surprise at Olive's sudden uptick in enthusiasm. "I've never been to a flower market. I thought only florists and wedding coordinators could get into places like that."

Olive gave her a knowing look, her eyebrows waggling. "I've got my ways. Come on, it'll be fun if you've never been."

Ginny couldn't help but smile. There was a brightness returning to her daughter's face that had been missing as of late. The fact that she was opening up and inviting her aunt to run errands was a good sign. Normally, Olive preferred to be alone. Sure, she had a few local friends, and there was of course the draw of her father, but seeing her include Julia was something new.

"Go, you two." Ginny gestured with a wave. "I've got things handled here. It's still early, so you should have plenty of time. Guests don't arrive until six thirty tonight."

"Mom, I need your credit card if you want fresh flowers. I noticed the big orchid in the foyer is fading too," Olive said expectantly.

And just as suddenly as a rose dropping its petals, Ginny's smile faded. An uncomfortable lump formed in her throat. Of course Olive would need money. She'd been so happy to witness her daughter's brightened mood that she'd neglected to connect the dots and realize what a trip into the city would need: funds.

Ginny had been a fool to think her financial troubles had subsided.

157

She'd already made a big purchase. And her mortgage payment was dangerously late. She'd hidden the last batch of mail in a kitchen drawer so the others wouldn't see PAST DUE stamped in red ink on a recent bill. The single credit card available might now very well be declined. Nearly all the money Mesquite had brought in the previous weekend had been used to purchase an order of free-range, heritage whole quail, as well as a plentiful amount of their gorgeous speckled eggs, from a boutique farm in another state. The order of bird meat had arrived, and Ginny couldn't wait to get creative with the weekend menu. In anticipation of the meat, she'd also splurged on an order of truffles for a homemade ravioli starter course she'd planned.

It was extravagant, considering her present circumstances. But the extra help had allowed her to open up creatively, and in the end, she'd taken the risk. Plus, she knew her dinner guests would appreciate her upping her game. Regulars had reserved the next two nights. Serving up a repeat menu just wasn't an option.

On top of the food bills, there'd also been a third person to feed at every meal now that Julia was there. But the idea of admitting this to her unknowing daughter, especially in front of Julia, caused her to tense.

"Oh, I think I might give you cash today. But let's hold off on purchasing any new orchids, okay?" She smoothed her face and tried to keep her voice neutral. There was an envelope of emergency money she kept in her cupboard. It was a rainy-day fund she'd set aside a while back, just in case. Thank goodness she had it now. Mesquite had to keep going. And with two helpers now, Ginny just might come out on top.

Olive cocked her head. "Okay. Cash?" They both knew it was unlike Ginny to have extra money just lying around. Before she'd gone away to her dad's, Olive had understood funds were tight, but Ginny had never let on how bad things had become. Still, she sensed Olive's suspicious gaze boring into her as she turned in search of the money.

Five minutes later, she was pressing a fold of bills into Olive's hand and giving her instructions not to go overboard with her purchases. Olive pumped her head and said goodbye.

Ginny watched as Julia and Olive left through the front door, reusable bags in hand. It would be good for her sister to get out and shake the cobwebs of gloom away. While Julia had done her part around the house over the past few days, Ginny couldn't help but notice a heaviness hanging over her. She assumed Julia was worried about work, probably much more than she'd let on. And then there was the whole business of the fiancé, whom Julia still remained tight-lipped about. Ginny wanted to know more, but she also didn't believe in prying. At least not in this case. Julia would tell her eventually.

She slid her phone from her pocket to check the time. She didn't want the day to get away from her. A red button at the bottom of the screen indicated one missed call. *How did I miss that?* she wondered. Distracted, Ginny pressed the phone to her ear, half listening while a lengthy to-do list ran through her head.

"Hello, this is Garry calling from Winter's Gourmet Market. It appears your credit card was declined for your order of truffles. I'm sorry for the inconvenience, but we'll need another form of payment. It's a special order, so cancellations aren't accepted. Thanks."

Damn! Ginny's gut dropped. Her card was officially maxed out. She'd been counting on that order for her homemade ravioli dish. Without it, her menu would be lacking. Doing some quick mental math, she shuddered. The only emergency-fund money she kept had just walked out the door with Olive. Now what? The store would be expecting its money.

The only problem was, Ginny didn't have any.

CHAPTER TWENTY-TWO
JULIA

The first thing Julia noticed as she headed through the automatic sliding doors of the flower market was the intoxicating aroma of all things fresh and sweet. As the women drew farther into the refrigerated warehouse, Julia's senses lit on a rainbow of eye-catching colors as far as the eye could see.

A sea of stunning blooms greeted her. Each variety was organized in white buckets by shape and color. Julia felt as if she'd somehow walked onto the set of a vivid Technicolor dream. Of course she'd seen such scenes in the movies, and even had occasioned the odd outdoor market back home, but this place was unlike anywhere she'd been before.

"This way!" Olive tugged on her arm with a burst of energy. She ushered Julia through the aisles with a keen sense of direction.

"This place is amazing," Julia said, practically jogging to keep up.

"I know." A grin played on Olive's lips, a spark of something bright in her eyes. Julia suddenly had lots of questions, like how did Olive first find the place, and how often did she come here? She also wondered if everything her niece knew about flower arranging was self-taught or had been shown to her somehow. Whenever Julia purchased a bouquet from her local grocer back home, she never felt as if she were fully capable of trimming and arranging the stems the way she'd envisioned. There was an art to what Olive could do—Julia had witnessed this firsthand back at Ginny's.

"So," Olive said, leading them toward the middle of the packed warehouse, "I want to revamp the table arrangements, but I also want to do some new ones in different-size dish gardens. I got my inspiration on Pinterest, and I have an idea of how we can incorporate them into the front entry."

"Sounds cool." Julia arrived at her side. They had left the buckets of stemmed flowers and now found themselves in the center of the indoor succulent section, an array of miniature plants with whimsical names such as burro's tail and flaming katy. Olive slowed her pace, taking her time perusing metal racks of each variety. She stooped down and plucked a container of a sweet, blossom-shaped plant.

"What's that one?" Julia asked. She liked the look of its pink-edged tips, whose color reminded her of a radish.

"This guy here is called roseum. It likes the sun, so I'd have to think of a spot near a window. But it's a nice touch of color among all the green. At different times of year, it develops clusters of light-pink star-shaped flowers. I like it because it adds texture next to something like, say, that jade plant, which is more like a stocky little tree. If I place them together, it adds interest."

"Wow. That sounds great."

Olive brightened. "Thanks. And then, see these here?" She pointed to a miniature plant with chubby, rosette-style leaves.

"Yes?" Julia leaned closer and squinted to read the sign. "The one that says 'Sedum Golden Glow'?"

"Yes. That one. I'm thinking of getting a few of those guys and placing them on the dining table in these cool little glass-and-gold terrariums I found online. They have delicate little panes of glass set against metal frames that catch your eye, and they're fancy enough for Mom's taste. She's okay if I do rustic, but she always wants a touch of something expensive mixed in. The terrariums do the trick, I think."

"Sounds amazing." Julia was blown away. Here she'd assumed Olive wasn't too interested in pleasing her mother, but clearly the girl had taken Ginny's preferences into account and done her homework. Plus, as Julia could clearly see, it all excited Olive.

"Thanks!" Olive's rosy cheeks pushed back into a wide smile.

"You seem to know so much about all of this," Julia said, waving her arm. "Do you ever think about doing it for a job?"

Olive's face scrunched. "You mean work for a florist or something?"

"Sure. Why not? You obviously have an interest."

"I don't know. Yeah, maybe. I guess if the situation was right."

Julia studied her. "You know what someone told me once? That if you wake up and think about something more than anything else, then you're meant to do that thing." She wanted Olive to understand that having a passion for something was a rare and special gift. If horticulture or floral design was in the realm of Olive's interest, she should pursue it.

"Is that how you feel? About the news?"

Julia took a long pause. Ironically, she hadn't obsessed over the daily news alerts and updates from the office the way she had a week ago. *What does that mean?* she wondered. It had been years since she'd been able to freely set aside her work. Up until recently, she'd never wanted to.

"I suppose so. I mean, when I was your age, I couldn't think of anything else. I logged a lot of hours building my résumé and my career to get to where I am today. But—" She hesitated. Reflecting on her current predicament, with her career dangling in limbo, was difficult. Even at a distance. "My situation is a little different. I think I wanted it so badly, was so afraid of losing footing in my job, that I made a huge mistake. I lost sight of what was important. I hope no job ever makes you feel that way. It's no fun. Trust me."

Olive fingered the leaf of a nearby zebra-striped plant. She seemed to be working something out in her head.

"Gosh." Julia sighed. "I haven't said any of that out loud. To anyone."

Olive looked up. "How does it feel?"

"Strange." She'd carried such a sense of shame since arriving in Arizona. Sharing her problems with her family, or anyone, for that matter, wasn't easy. Look at how James had reacted when she'd tried to confide in him. From Julia's perspective, her fiancé hadn't wanted to accept her error. He hadn't wanted to accept her. Part of Julia worried that her sister might have a similar reaction. But Olive was different; she seemed to genuinely care.

"Maybe you just need a long break. Maybe that's what my mom needs too." Julia sensed a tone of sadness in her words.

"Is that what you think? That your mom has taken on too much?"

Olive shrugged. "I don't know. I mean, she did leave a lot of hectic, work-related stress back in New York. But she still has that perfectionist, workaholic vibe. Even way out here in the desert."

Julia nodded. She understood what Olive meant. Ginny did seem stressed. But she also wasn't convinced it was because she was still cooking for customers. She couldn't put her finger on it, but something told her there was more to her sister's tension. Plus, Olive's attitude toward her mother hadn't helped. Julia debated whether or not to say so.

"You know, your mom's path doesn't have to be yours. You can follow your own dreams."

"Ha! Really? Does she know that?" Her smile carried a touch of frost.

"I think so."

"That's nice, Aunt Julia." Something in her expression gave Julia the sense that a door had been opened but then shut. A curtain of heaviness had dropped. "Honestly, I feel like Mom's never going to let me go. Her business needs help. And no offense, but we all know you aren't going to stick around forever. Then what? It's back to me and Mom, locked in a battle."

Guilt swept over her. Here she'd thought staying on had been helping, but in Olive's view, Julia was only prolonging the inevitable. And she worried Olive was anticipating being abandoned by her aunt all over again.

A contemplative silence unfurled between them. Each studied the row of plants before them, lost in thought. After a while, Olive made a move.

"If you want to help me find some moss and small white rocks to use as filler, that would be great. I know they're around here somewhere. I just can't remember where I've seen them." She stood on her tiptoes and scanned the perimeter with wide eyes. "Ooh, I see some nice eucalyptus over there. I can pair it with a variety of succulents for a pretty table garland. I need to check that out next. Want to come?"

"Sure. You lead the way." Julia stepped back and gestured for Olive to pass. She was so glad she'd tagged along.

Observing her niece in this environment, practically her natural habitat given how Olive had come alive once they'd walked through the doors, made Julia realize two very important things. First, her niece really did have a passion. Julia wanted to encourage Olive to follow it wherever it might take her. Second, she believed there was still hope for her sister and her niece after all. Olive might not want to admit it, but her mother's opinion mattered. Somehow Julia needed to bring those two together and demonstrate how much they both cared.

Exiting the flower market, their cart full of purchases, Julia was surprised to find Shane Hemsley just outside the entrance.

"Shane!" she exclaimed, jostling an armload of wrapped eucalyptus. Olive nearly bumped into her back, caught off guard by the abrupt stop.

"Well, hey there, ladies," Shane said, smiling over a grouping of potted trees. "Busy morning of shopping, I see." He nodded toward their cart.

"Yes, some stuff for Ginny's restaurant. What about you?"

He jutted out a thumb. "Need to pick up some small trees for a new build. I don't normally deal with the landscaping, but today is the big reveal to out-of-town owners, and I thought it might be a nice touch."

"Oh, that sounds really thoughtful. I bet they'll be happy." Julia tried to imagine him at work, architecture plans in hand, overseeing the construction from the ground up, adding creative touches like small trees to complement the design. It warmed her to know he'd grown up into a successful, considerate man who appreciated the details.

Shane smiled again, dropping a hand into his pocket. Julia got the sense he'd be happy to chat longer, but she realized Olive was getting fidgety behind her. They needed to get back to the house and help Ginny prepare.

"Well, it's good to see you again. Maybe we'll run into each other more often." She didn't know why she said that. It wasn't as if they had mutual friends or anything. But still. Something inside her, much like a flicker of hope, ignited. She liked his easy manner and kind smile. It *would* be nice to see him again. She realized she hadn't made a new friend in quite some time—hell, she hadn't spent quality time with a non-work-related friend in longer than she could remember. Her life had been too consumed by getting ahead of the next lead, and even her outings with James somehow always revolved around showing face.

"Yeah, maybe we will. Good luck at your sister's, and enjoy your visit. See you around." He gave a little wave and ambled off toward a larger display of plants.

"Well, that was interesting," Olive muttered as they walked toward the car.

"Was it?" Julia feigned indifference. Her finger automatically went to touch her engagement ring, as if she had to remind herself that it was still there. She needed to hear James's voice. That was all.

"Uh-huh." Olive grinned and gave her a knowing glance. They loaded the trunk and headed back to the house. All the while, Julia replayed in her head the coincidence of running into Shane.

~

Dinner that evening was to be a cozy affair, with Ginny's reservation book indicating a small party of four. Compared to what they'd been used to, it should have been easy.

In the dining room, Julia busied herself by helping Olive separate stems and rearrange plants into artful centerpieces. It was fun, but she also felt distracted. Stepping away briefly, she phoned James. He didn't pick up. She'd have to try again later.

When she returned, Olive requested a second pair of cutters. Julia darted off and began rummaging through kitchen drawers, assuming that's where her sister might keep them. When she came upon a stack of mail with foreboding PAST DUE labels, she froze. Were these new? And if so, why had they been hidden in a drawer? Surely such things required immediate attention, whatever they were.

Glancing over her shoulder, she checked for her sister. Finding herself alone, Julia carefully plucked the top envelope between her fingers and peeked inside. To her surprise, it appeared to be a recent notice for an overdue mortgage payment. Her heart sank. Ginny's money problems went much deeper than not being able to pay Olive a regular salary. Her sister was behind on the house payments and who knew what else. And what's more, she was hiding this from everyone. It wasn't good.

"What are you doing?" Julia jumped as Ginny came up from behind, her tone barbed with accusation.

"Oh!" The envelope slipped from her grasp and back into the drawer. But before Julia could shut it, Ginny was upon her. "I just, I was looking for some gardening shears and stumbled across the mail."

"So you decided it was your business to go ahead and rifle through it?" Ginny glared at her and snatched the contents of the drawer, then thrust the envelopes behind her back.

Julia wavered. Ginny was clearly angry at her invasion of privacy. But she was also evidently in trouble. "Ginny," she said. "Why didn't you tell me it was this bad? Are you really not able to pay your mortgage?"

"God!" Ginny snapped. "It's none of your business. I let you into my home, after everything, and this is how you repay me? By snooping around in my personal life?" There was venom in her words. Like a great bubbling of red-hot anger now rising to the top, ready to explode with dangerous force if Julia wasn't careful.

"I, uh, wait, what do you mean, 'after everything'?'" She frowned. To what was Ginny referring, exactly? And how had this altercation taken such a sharp turn all of a sudden?

Ginny's eyes narrowed. "You know exactly what I'm talking about. Don't play naive, Julia. Why do you think I'm even here, struggling to run a business and make a living in the middle of the desert—the very place we left in order to find better opportunities? Do you think I just gladly gave up the big paycheck and my burgeoning career for the hell of it? To work my fingers to the bone, with no real resources, or staff, or following, for that matter, just because I wanted a change? You can be so clueless! Don't you realize I'm in this position because of you?"

What the hell was she talking about? How did they go from zero to fifty in only a matter of seconds? Julia stared, dumbfounded, at her roiling sister.

"Ginny," she started, "why are you blaming this on me? I didn't make you move back to Arizona."

Ginny sneered. "Didn't you?"

"No, I didn't." Julia felt herself bristling.

"So, when Mom and Dad died and left umpteen million loose ends to be handled—the house that took forever to repair and then sell, the debt, the funeral arrangements—you assumed that would all magically take care of itself? Clearly you did. Because when I asked you to come help me, you blew me off. Never mind that there wasn't an official funeral service to attend. You couldn't even be bothered to help sign the forms and send their ashes out to sea. You left me no choice. Someone had to come pick up the pieces, Julia. And when I did, my job didn't exactly wait around for me. I did the responsible thing while you ignored it all. You chose your career over your family. Well, I might have lost my reputation while scraping to get by, but at least I can say that I didn't do *that*."

What was happening? Julia smarted as if she'd been slapped hard in the face. This was absurd. She hadn't forced Ginny to do anything she didn't want to do. Plus, there was no way she could have left her journalism job at the time. She had commitments. Didn't her sister know this?

"I don't know what to say, Ginny. You sound like you already formed an opinion about all of this even before you asked for my side of things."

Ginny only huffed and folded her arms tight.

"I appreciate what you did for Mom and Dad. But you're laying it all on rather thick. I never asked you to take over. You just did. Like always. Because you're a control freak."

"Ha!" Ginny's rage was becoming manic. Julia shrank back, unsure of what might come next. "That's a joke. I only take over because you never do. *Ever!*"

"What's going on in here?" Olive appeared in the kitchen now, gardening gloves dangling at her sides. Both sisters looked from her to one another. Silence fell over the room.

"Nothing but the usual bullshit," Ginny hissed. "Never mind. I've got a party to feed and I don't have time for this." She stormed past them both and disappeared toward the back of the house.

Julia's shoulders fell as she leaned against the counter. "Your mom's just mad at me because of some stuff that happened after your grandparents died."

"Oh, that." Olive nodded as if she already knew. "Yeah, she could've used some help, that's for sure."

Julia slumped. Had it really been that bad? Had Ginny and Olive struggled while Julia went about her life in New York? Would things have been different if Julia had come earlier? Was she really as terrible as Ginny made her out to be? Suddenly, she wasn't feeling so great. Maybe she should go lie down.

"But you're here now." Olive interrupted her mounting downward spiral. "And that is a lot. You've stayed on to help with Mesquite, and my mom won't say it, but I will: it's been a big help. Really. Sometimes it's better late than never, right?"

Julia shook her head against the blood pumping in her ears. "I guess. I don't know, actually." She looked at her niece. "Olive, I'm sorry if it has been difficult. I'm sorry I wasn't a better aunt. I guess I didn't really know how stressful things were. Or if I did, I was in denial. Will you forgive me for not being around?"

Olive let the lids of her eyes fall before she met Julia's gaze. "I know you didn't do it on purpose, Aunt Julia. I'm okay with it. I understand. No one's perfect. But you might need to give my mom a second. She's said her piece, and now she likely needs to cool off."

"Okay, thanks. You're wise beyond your years, you know that?" Julia reached out and touched Olive's arm. She wanted to hug her but wasn't sure how it would be received. They were all feeling a bit raw.

"Thanks. I'm sure we'll talk more about it, but honestly, my mom is right. We have people coming tonight, and there's still stuff to be done. So I'm just going to get back to what I was doing. I'm sure Mom would appreciate it if you stayed and helped. I know her. Even if she's mad at you, she still needs you. Okay?"

"Okay." Julia offered a weak smile. She wasn't really sure, but she was going to stick around because Olive asked her to.

~

The dinner service was off all night. Because of the earlier blowup, the energy in the house had taken on a tense air. Nothing ran smoothly. The three women more or less ignored the elephant in the room and spent two hours catering to a cocky young guy and his even younger girlfriend, along with another couple they'd brought. It wasn't that the group of newcomers was high maintenance, per se. It just struck Julia as peculiar, the way the one guy kept asking pointed questions about the food, seemingly to impress his friends. He spoke with his mouth full and waved a fork in the air, trying to get Ginny's attention and strike up a conversation with her whenever she poked her head out to check on things. He said he'd heard of Ginny's preceding reputation. He wanted to know whether she missed her old chef's life back in New York and how she managed to keep such a clandestine spot in her desert home. Olive tried to run interference, to protect Ginny's cooking schedule and fragile nerves. Julia smiled politely and offered stilted information about the menu.

As the service rolled on, Olive mentioned that the guy kept ogling her and snapping a lot of close-up images of the food. The women had to remind him that while sharing photos was fine, Ginny preferred that guests not tag the location. They were met with indifference. No one seemed the least bit aware of who Julia was. While the women agreed that was for the best, it was strange that someone so curious would overlook the real subject of scandal right under his nose.

Ginny only shrugged and chalked the evening up to someone's overt interest in the industry. "Maybe the kid is an aspiring chef himself. Who knows? As long as I get paid and my guests go away happy, that's all I care about." Julia noticed the bitter coating to her words and pretended to ignore her own sense of unease.

When the night was finished, the three of them separated with awkward silence. Julia went to her room with a headache and a sense of gloom. What was she going to do when she woke up? Downing a glass of wine, she prayed for sleep to take over and for a dreamless night. She had no idea what the morning would bring.

CHAPTER TWENTY-THREE

JULIA

Julia had decided to stay on despite the lingering tension. She figured that, while she didn't like what Ginny had to say, especially the blame, it would be far worse if she left her sister and niece in the lurch. Again. There were overdue bills, and there wasn't enough manpower to run the business. It wasn't permanent, but something like loyalty kept Julia from leaving just yet.

It was now Saturday afternoon and the second weekend the three women had worked together to make Mesquite a success. They had fallen into a collective rhythm, tidying the house, preparing food, and entertaining a group of regular diners. Julia found herself getting lost in the business of it all. Perhaps it was convenient avoidance. She didn't allow herself to dwell too much. Otherwise, her thoughts would go dark.

Now, however, as she stood over the kitchen counter, absentmindedly snipping the delicate tail ends from a bowl of French green beans—or haricots verts, as Ginny called them—a faint sadness tugged at her.

"Hey," Ginny said, coming in from the other room. She met Julia with a look of trepidation. Her eyebrow arched. Julia pressed her lips together, worried she might say the wrong thing. Her heated anger had cooled off into the form of grief. Yet she wasn't sure how to get past it.

"Oh, hey." She did her best to act casual.

Ginny's gaze went from Julia's face and then down to the pile of untrimmed ends arranged on the counter.

"Watch your knife cuts!" she warned.

"Good grief." Julia let go of the razor-sharp paring knife, and it clattered onto the hard stone surface. It never failed. Every time she wielded any kind of a sharp edge, Ginny maddeningly appeared at her shoulder to scrutinize her work. She still couldn't quite mimic Ginny's hummingbird-like chopping methods. She feared getting nicked. "You can't scare me like that. I might chop my finger off if I'm not careful. Then what would you do?"

"I'd be down a helper, that's for sure." Ginny leaned in close. "Seriously, though. You're hacking up my side dish. You've got to pay better attention."

Julia took offense. In her opinion, she'd done a fine job. It was just a bunch of long skinny beans with the tops cut off. She inspected more carefully. It looked mostly right, so long as no one was holding a ruler to the beans.

"What's the problem?" she asked. Was it really just the vegetables, or was her sister still trying to punish her? "I'm trimming the ends just like you told me."

Ginny reached around with a huff. Julia noticed her sister had softened over the past week, but not enough to ease up on certain things, like the high standards of her kitchen. *Once a demanding chef, always a demanding chef,* she thought.

"This isn't good enough," Ginny responded. A single bean was raised, the rolled sleeve of her button-down shirt sliding into the crook of her elbow. Julia's eye caught the flash of pocked skin—a puckered cooking burn here, a deep knife scar there.

A clutch of tenderness gripped Julia's heart. She should have been more understanding; instead, she'd been defensive.

Her sister had gone through so much. Ginny's arms were a road map of years given over to difficult challenges and unforgiving cooking equipment. The work had consumed her whole life. The marks reminded Julia of how so many of Ginny's former kitchen staff had covered their own aggrieved bodies with sleeves of inky tattoos—some even of knives themselves—and only now did it all make sense. She supposed that many chefs chose to brand themselves because they literally wore their work on their arms.

Ginny's arms were proof that the scars didn't always fade away. She'd paid a price for her talent, and now these reminders would always be with her. And it had all been given up when she relocated to the desert.

"Sorry," Julia blurted out. Her sister had sacrificed pieces of herself. Perhaps Julia hadn't appreciated this about Ginny as much as she should have.

"It's okay, just start again."

"No, I mean I'm sorry about everything." Julia gulped back a welling of fresh emotion. She set down her knife and turned to face her sister. "I've thought a lot about what you said last night. About my not showing up after Mom's and Dad's deaths and about how you took on everything. I hope you know I never meant it to go that way. I didn't do what I did to hurt you. I just, I don't know, I was so invested in my career and assumed you'd be the same. When you weren't, I took it as an affront. Like you lost your drive and gave up, and it scared me. It made me realize that our hold on success—on life, even—is precarious and could end at any moment, so I suppose I threw myself into my work even more determinedly to fight against that. Does that make any sense? Anyway, I needed to tell you that I'm sorry. You've done a lot, and I appreciate it."

A crack in Ginny's tight expression emerged. Julia watched as she took a long inhale and rolled the apology around in her head. Julia hadn't known she was going to say those things in that way, but the delivery felt right. She wanted her sister to know that she regretted how she'd turned her back all those years ago. And that it hadn't been intentional. None of it.

"Thanks for that," Ginny murmured.

"Of course."

"I know you loved your job. I know how hard you worked to get where you are. I don't begrudge you that. I said some harsh things. I didn't mean all of it. You're here now. That's been helpful."

"I've tried."

"I know." Ginny eased over and rested against the edge of the counter. It was as if a wall was finally crumbling. Julia leaned back, too, allowing herself to be comforted by Ginny's familiar scent. Her clothes smelled of something sweet and tantalizing, like rich, caramelized onions. "Truce?"

"Truce."

A swollen bean was rolled between Ginny's fingers. "Now, about these beans. You can do better. Only the stems get cut. See here? And each of them needs to be uniform. Understand?"

Julia studied the green dart between Ginny's plump fingers. She didn't see what her sister saw: the imperfections. But then again, her sister had an eye for such things. That's what had aided in her success in the first place. That and hard, driving talent. But surely Mesquite's dinner guests wouldn't be so discerning. So far, they'd just seemed happy enough with how it all tasted. Julia, however, had been helping Ginny long enough to know she shouldn't second-guess. "I think so."

Appearing unsatisfied, Ginny met her eye. The deepening creases near her temples held worry. Something lurked just below the surface. Julia sensed it.

"Are we good?" Julia asked.

Ginny sighed. "Yes. I know you think stuff like this doesn't matter, but it's important to me. Even if it's on a subconscious level, diners register perfection. If you haven't noticed, it's kind of a big deal that I've conceded this much control already."

A chuckle escaped. It was true. Her sister had uncoiled ever so slightly in her new environment. "I'm surprised you let me do this much."

"Ha ha. Very funny." Ginny's tone was dry. "I was going to let you move on to dicing the shallots next. But after seeing this hack job, I don't think you're ready."

"Oh my god." Julia rolled her eyes playfully. "You really are impossible to please."

"Damn straight. How do you think I got that Michelin star?" Ginny winked. They were going to be okay.

"Yes, I know," Julia said. The Michelin rating had once been everything. It had taken Ginny decades to hone her skill and build upon her knowledge before reaching such an esteemed level. They both knew the recognition was what Ginny sought.

"So, let me see you do it the right way," Ginny instructed, interrupting Julia's contemplation. She inched nearer still. Julia could practically feel her expectant breath.

"I understand." Julia wondered if she might offer Ginny a loan. Their rift might have been fixed, but not the financial woes.

Julia clutched the knife and nodded. Solemnly, she began again, this time with much more care. She forced herself to concentrate on the task at hand and leave the worrying over her sister for later. Right now, Ginny was counting on her to finish.

Ginny wandered off, mumbling something about going into the garage to sift through a stash of extra pans.

In her absence, Julia sent up an acknowledgment of gratitude. This was progress. Now, how to make some progress between Ginny and her daughter? She reflected on yesterday morning with Olive. If only Ginny could have seen the way Olive lit up at the flower market and spoke of her uncertain future. Surely her sister would understand the need to let

Olive go and seek her own path. But Ginny's tunnel vision, as far as the tenuous supper club was concerned, was going to be difficult to break. Somehow Julia had to find a way to help Ginny see that getting closer to Olive actually meant cutting her loose. She just didn't know what would become of her sister if both she and Olive abandoned her at the same time. Was distance really the best medicine?

And then, as they usually did when she was left to the task of chopping in solitude, her thoughts went to James. He'd called once that morning but hadn't left a message. Julia wondered if it was because he missed her or if there was some new development regarding the Rossetti business.

Slipping her phone from her back pocket, she set aside her chopping and touched the screen. A list of news alerts cascaded downward. Scanning them, it wasn't until she read the last one that her eyes bulged.

Damn. Ginny's name appeared across her screen in a headline.

A few days earlier, just for fun really, she'd been discussing with Olive the idea of news alerts. The two women had punched in "Ginny Frank" as a lark. Julia thought she saw pride flash over Olive's face as the feed generated pages upon pages of headlines on her rock-star-chef mother's rise to stardom. Most of the articles had been dated before three years ago, after which there'd been a trickle of rumors about why she'd jumped ship and what had become of her. But now, as Julia frantically opened the article and skimmed the headline, she realized what she was seeing.

Her sister's secret supper club had just been discovered and reviewed online. And Ginny was not going to like it.

"Whatcha doing?" Olive came up from behind and peeked over Julia's shoulder. It caused her to jump a foot.

"You scared me!" she yelped. "Oh, Olive. I'm afraid something terrible has happened." The old, familiar flip-flopping of worry filled her.

Olive came around, her face scrunched with concern. "What's the matter? More bad press about you and the mayor?"

"No." Julia shook her head. She expanded the words on the screen and then shoved the phone under Olive's nose. "It seems bad press follows me everywhere I go these days. Remember that weird guy who was here last night asking all the questions? Turns out he's some big-time food blogger."

"What?"

"Yeah. He just published a write-up of Mesquite online! And"— Julia scrolled frantically with her finger—"it appears he has, like, *two hundred thousand* followers! These look like legit industry people too."

Olive went pale. "Oh my god! I thought there was something suspicious about that guy! Mom's gonna freak."

Julia nodded. "Yep. You should see this." They both bent over the phone. Quietly, they continued to read.

After a minute, Olive exhaled. "Did you read the part where he says Mom is a former Manhattan celebrity chef who now runs an illegal speakeasy for rich people, with her *disenchanted daughter* acting as sommelier and her *scandalous news-anchor sister* as food server? Oh no!"

"Yeah." Julia moaned. "I read it."

"Who does this guy think he is?"

Julia felt her knees buckling. Her career was already circling the drain, but she couldn't be responsible for taking Ginny down with her. Or Olive. This was awful. Had Julia being there put her sister's business in an even worse light? Clearly this guy had done his homework on the whole family. She moaned again. This was going to do some serious damage to all of them. But she didn't care about herself as much as she worried about Ginny. What would her sister's reaction be? What would happen to Mesquite? And what about Olive?

Something acidic rose in the back of her throat.

Olive studied the device. Her hair fell around her face, but Julia could feel the heat of Olive's anger rising. "And did you read this part, where he basically gives the street address of our house? I mean, people are going to find out. Mom could be fined or, worse, shut down!"

Julia realized they were both breathing heavily by now. Panic bloomed as she craned an ear and listened for Ginny. Where was her sister? They were going to have to tell her, weren't they?

As if on cue, Ginny came ambling around the corner. At the sight of their faces, she stopped short. A set of suspicious eyes darted from one woman to the other. "What are you two doing?"

Julia swallowed. "You'd better sit down and then we'll tell you."

Ginny shifted and obliged. Julia slid the phone gently onto her lap. "I just want to say I'm sorry ahead of time."

Ginny frowned. "You already said you were sorry." Julia could tell she was confused.

"I know, but this is about something different." How could this be happening now? Just when the two of them were back on even footing. She continued, "I know you don't need this right now, but there's something you need to see."

"Okay." There was concern in her voice. Ginny reached down with hesitancy. Both women looked on as Ginny read, wide-eyed and stricken, the color quickly draining from her face.

"Oh no!"

"I'm so sorry," Julia said for the umpteenth time, but it didn't feel like enough. Her hand went to rub her sister's tense shoulder. For the first time in her adult life, Julia understood what it meant—really meant—to be on the other side of the reporting fence. To be on the receiving end of a sharply pointed news angle. To be exposed. Without mercy. And it wasn't good. Julia was sickened for Ginny.

How the hell would she fix things for her sister and niece now that she was the source of their problems?

CHAPTER TWENTY-FOUR

GINNY

Despite Ginny's twist of raw nerves over the food blog, she knew the show must go on. There wasn't any other choice. Not really. Mesquite was expecting a group of diners very soon, and she wasn't going to let her emotions overtake her ability to work. It just wasn't her style.

A better part of her day had already been given over to analyzing the article, unpacking it piece by piece, and then poring over the long list of reader comments that followed. The blogger had written nice things about the food itself, but his focus seemed to be on the people in the room more than the ingredients on the menu. She couldn't decide whether the guy was trying to take her down in an act of arrogant defiance or pat himself on the back for stumbling across not only a clandestine outfit run by a former celebrity chef, but also a hideaway for her tarnished semicelebrity sister. He'd been after the salacious, and, according to the response from his audience, he'd found it.

So far, any attempt to reach the blabbing idiot had failed. Ginny and then Julia had written scathing messages demanding that he take down the post. They stressed the importance of the word *secret* in "secret supper club." They told him he should know better. Foodies were supposed to band together, not tear each other down. Ginny only hoped her guilt-inducing tactic would work. Otherwise, she'd be out of luck.

In all her years working in the industry, there'd been no shortage of crazy situations. Fights among sous chefs, heated exchanges with pushy restaurant owners, and the odd mean-spirited critic. But never before had she felt so exposed. So vulnerable. All it would take to end her business—and her only source of income—would be for the blog to be picked up by the local media or, worse, discovered by the health inspector. Mesquite was how Ginny paid her bills, supported Olive, and connected with the customers she so desperately needed. This wasn't just about bad press; it was so much more. Losing her business would mean losing everything she'd built up over the past three years. Having this taken away would be crushing.

Aside from her business, Ginny also worried about the impact this might have on Julia's position at GBN. True, she wasn't thrilled about her sister's presence adding fuel to the blogger's fire. Having Julia named in the piece, especially at this point in her sister's precarious career, would draw more unwanted attention. But Ginny realized just how negatively this could affect them both. No doubt the news network, and other press outlets, would soon learn about the write-up. She couldn't help noting the irony that the one time they were all finally in it together, they were in a big, boiling stew of disaster.

~

By the time the dinner guests arrived that evening, Ginny felt she at least had her kitchen under control. *Focus on what's in front of you,* she quietly told herself. Otherwise, she might go crazy with worry.

The service started out as usual. Six guests arrived together, mostly newcomers, except for Julia's high school classmate, Shane. He, curiously, had made the reservation himself. It appeared Shane had enjoyed his first meal so much that he wanted to come back with friends. Or was it something else?

Though she was preoccupied, Ginny wondered about him. He was nice-looking, with a laid-back, unguarded smile, and he had the naturally suntanned hue of someone who spent a lot of time outdoors. He was almost rugged in appearance. The group accompanying him was a small collection of friends, as she'd overheard them explaining to Olive. Men and women in their late thirties who'd entered with arms slung around one another. Their collective joviality gave Ginny a pang of longing.

The guests could be heard commenting on their adventure on the mysterious, darkened drive toward the foothills, into Ginny's remote neighborhood. They recalled how one of them had jimmied open a bottle of wine—sans opener—in the back of the chauffeured SUV and then splashed liberal amounts into everyone's cups. The women giggled while one of the younger men made playful jabs at their roadie bartender. It was the kind of lighthearted fun and friendship that Ginny had been lacking.

It had been a long while since she'd had the freedom—or rather, allowed herself the freedom—to go out for a night on the town with friends. Many of her customers returned with such regularity that Ginny now easily considered them friends. She supposed she had the best of both worlds in that regard. Mesquite had given her the chance to keep cooking and to be surrounded by likable people.

Except for one, that was. But she refused to think about the aggravating food writer for now.

Lingering in the doorway a minute longer, she listened as one woman declared that if it weren't for Shane, none of them would ever have known that any kind of underground dining like Mesquite existed.

"Shane here," the woman said, tapping him on the shoulder, "said this was the best food he's had in ages. And only he knew how to find it. So of course we all wanted to be let in on the secret!"

"It was the best," Shane gushed.

"To Shane!" Someone raised a red plastic Solo cup.

"To Shane! Cheers!" Four more cups were thrust into the air, along with a ripple of laughter.

Shane grinned as he ran a hand along his stubbled jaw and dipped his head bashfully. His friends paid no mind to his embarrassment and instead took generous sips of their drinks. They didn't see that Shane's focus was being drawn elsewhere.

Ginny hovered in the background and tracked his gaze. Ever so slowly, it drew along the table and over to where Julia was standing. Her sister, Ginny noticed, looked pretty that evening in a feminine, cream-colored blouse that dipped into a V along her collarbone. She wore simple black pants and ballet flats that perhaps belonged to Olive. Her hair was gathered loosely at the nape of her neck, showing off a pair of delicate gold earrings that sparkled as they caught the light. A hint of a smile curved upward on her glossed, pink lips.

The two appeared to lock eyes momentarily before Julia flushed and abruptly turned. With a hasty motion, she began pouring waters from a filled pitcher. Shane watched her for a second longer before moving on.

Oh boy, Ginny thought. Judging by that meaningful exchange, this guy had the potential to quickly make things complicated for her sister. She surveyed the room to check if anyone else might have noticed. Luckily for Julia, no one had.

The air encircling the group of friends continued to buzz with excitement. Olive stepped forward and raised a bottle of pinot noir. Everyone cheered and took their seats, letting the merriment spread.

Ginny uttered an abbreviated version of her usual welcome and then excused herself, returning to her stove. She was pleased for the new customers and grateful to Shane for bringing them. Yet she couldn't help but speculate about why this guy had returned to dinner so soon after his last visit.

Whether Julia would acknowledge his attention, she wasn't entirely sure. Ginny's probing would have to wait until dinner was over. At the moment, she had her hands busy plating the planned first course of locally grown butternut squash soup with farm-fresh goat cheese and miniature crostini. And just in case this crew required more than the usual amount of bread to sop up the alcohol, she grabbed a crusty baguette from a basket in the pantry.

~

Julia and Olive brought an extra energy of support that evening, which Ginny understood as reassurance. Each fell into her serving role. Olive produced several bottles of suggested wine pairings, explaining how each one would complement the various courses. Julia took her cue and announced that evening's menu. As usual, the crowd oohed and aahed at the descriptions and chattered excitedly as they waited to be served.

"Olive?" Ginny asked in an uncertain tone in between her prep tasks.

"Yeah?" Olive stood nearby, her hands pausing as she wrestled with a stubborn cork. A low frown hovered. Ginny caught how her daughter's blue eyes shifted ever so slightly, as if she was nervous about what she was about to say.

"I just . . . ," Ginny began. It was disturbing how foreign intimate moments with her daughter still felt. There was such an unease that had built up between them. They'd fought so much lately. It seemed most of their interactions came with a bitter edge. Ginny so wanted that to change. She wondered if Olive did too. "I just wanted to tell you I'm glad you're here. You know, aside from your support in the kitchen. I'm proud that people get to see that you're my daughter. I don't say it often, but—thank you."

Olive's mouth twitched before breaking into a restrained smile. "You're welcome."

Ginny swallowed back emotion and nodded. This was enough. At least for now.

Olive's attention returned to the wine bottle, and she moved from the room. Ginny watched her a beat longer, relieved to see that her daughter's shoulders had relaxed away from her ears, where they were usually glued in her presence.

Small strides, Ginny thought.

Things in the kitchen were, thankfully, going according to plan. Ginny's hands moved at a gratifying pace over the stove. She deftly controlled the four burners to simmer sauces with ease. A pair of solid wooden cutting boards were positioned at her elbow, piled with minced garlic, leafy herbs, and fresh root vegetables. A beautiful cut of Angus beef rested on the counter, coming to room temperature and marinating in rich juices. An elevated twist on a white chocolate cheesecake chilled on the packed refrigerator shelf. All in all, she had planned a fabulous meal.

This was how Ginny had always envisioned Mesquite running, smooth and well staffed, with happy guests at the table and herself at the helm. If she thought about it hard enough, which she rarely had time to do, Ginny would say this evening was damn near perfection.

Feeling sentimental, she allowed herself a pour from the bottle of chilled Oregon pinot noir in the refrigerator. She wiped her fingers clean with a nearby tea towel and watched as the golden evening light filtered through the windows, illuminating the translucent burgundy liquid in her glass.

This is how it should be, she thought to herself. Happy customers in the other room, her daughter and her sister all under one roof, and a warm place to call home. She'd be content if she knew it could last. But she wasn't naive enough to assume it would. Just look at what the previous few hours had been like. Nothing remained perfect forever.

Her thoughts were interrupted by a loud racket coming from the other room.

"Oh no!" Julia's voice cried out. There was a clamor of chairs scraping backward along the hard floors, followed by an escalation of voices. Case in point. Ginny set down her glass and braced herself.

Before she could move, Olive came flying into the kitchen, her eyes wide. An ashen pallor masked her daughter's worried expression. "Mom, you'd better come."

"What is it?" Ginny asked. Olive's urgent panic sent her heart leaping high into her throat.

"I—I don't know," Olive stammered. "One of the women just sort of lost her balance. Her glass cracked onto the table and then she slumped over in her chair."

"What? Is she drunk?" Ginny moved past Olive, whipping her towel away.

Olive shook her head. "They're all a bit tipsy, but she wasn't slurring or anything. It was like she fainted. Aunt Julia caught her before she went down."

"Shit. Turn off those burners, would you?" Ginny ordered over her shoulder as she raced into the dining room, leaving Olive with a face full of alarm. Both women knew they couldn't afford to have anything bad happen at the supper club. It would call unwanted attention, and they were already up to their elbows in that.

Ginny pushed the concern from her mind and burst into the other room. Her eyes cast about. The most important thing was everyone's safety.

The first thing she saw was a cluster of men and women up from their seats and hovering in a semicircle around a dazed-looking woman. Julia was there, pushing a glass of water forward and murmuring reassurances. Shane and a balding man were crouched on either side, examining the woman's glassy eyes. Red wine had been spilled, and a single appetizer plate was in pieces on the floor.

"Is she all right?" Ginny asked, approaching. Her skin prickled with the sensation of doom. A million frantic thoughts ran through her head.

Was the woman having an allergic reaction to the food? Had Ginny poisoned her somehow? Or was she having a stroke or heart attack?

Judging by the woman's features, which were slack, she was most certainly ill, but she wasn't old enough or out of shape in the way that Ginny might associate with cardiac arrest. There weren't any rashes or swollen patches on her porcelain skin. If anything, this attractive, well-dressed woman appeared drugged. "What happened?"

Julia's head popped up with an uncertain expression. The bald man was on his knees. He waved a hand in front of the woman's face and then snapped his fingers, trying to gauge her level of alertness.

"She's diabetic," Shane said. His voice was thick with fear. "She must have crashed and we didn't notice."

The other man, who wore a platinum ring on his left hand, rummaged through the woman's purse. "Sometimes her blood sugar goes off-balance," he said, almost apologetically. He had the calm authority of someone who'd experienced such a scare before. "We try to regulate it as best we can, but it still happens. It's been a while since I've seen her get woozy like this. I need to check her blood sugar. I'm pretty sure she needs a dose of fast-acting glucose."

"Oh gosh. Do we need to call an ambulance?" Ginny's heart rate ticked upward. She was suddenly conflicted. She wanted to get the woman the help she needed, but she didn't want to draw more negative attention to Mesquite. Summoning any kind of authority to the club would be a disaster in itself.

If an ambulance came, the police might accompany them and ask all sorts of questions. That was definitely not what Ginny wanted. She wasn't ready to explain that this woman was a paying guest in an illegitimate restaurant.

If that happened, she'd be hit with a crippling fine by the health department. Mesquite wasn't permitted, and what she was doing was considered illegal. If she was caught, the supper club would surely be shuttered. Her customers would lose trust and disappear; her only source of income would dry up. Ginny's entire dream could be yanked away from her in the span of one evening.

How was it that her business had now been threatened more than once in the span of a week? She had to wonder if Julia's sudden appearance had anything to do with it. While clearly she couldn't be held responsible for this episode, she did seem to usher bad luck through the door.

"I don't think we need to call anyone just yet," the man responded, breaking Ginny's panic-filled thoughts. "I've dealt with this lots of times; we just need to stabilize her."

A whoosh of relief filled Ginny's lungs. Olive appeared at her side, leaning against her arm. Ginny was grateful for the unspoken support.

The others remained quiet as they watched in hushed tones and the man retrieved what looked like a miniature doctor's kit from the woman's purse. With expert speed, he went to work.

"Angie? Are you with me?" he asked in a loud voice.

"Mm-hmm." The woman moaned and nodded lethargically. Her eyes were still open, but barely. Her slow, fluttering lids made Ginny well up with nervousness.

After what felt like an eternity, once Angie's husband had done some calculating of her blood sugar via an app on his phone, he administered a thick swab of gel onto her gums and rubbed. Within minutes, there was a noticeable improvement. Angie thankfully appeared out of the woods. Her eyes perked up, and she was able to speak in fluid sentences. Ginny nearly collapsed with relief at the sight.

She and Olive exchanged grateful glances.

"Wow, we're glad you're okay, Angie," Shane said, still kneeling down next to his friend. He offered a kind smile and thumped Angie's husband on the back. Both men passed a look of relief between them, and Angie colored.

"I'm sorry," Angie said, the life coming back to her. "I don't know what happened. I had extra wine, which was risky, I guess. And I didn't eat much today. The starter course didn't really fill me up."

"Don't be sorry," said a woman with a dark bob haircut. She leaned in and squeezed Angie's free hand.

"Yes, don't ever apologize for something like that, Angie. We're just glad you're okay."

"We love you, Ang!"

"Hear! Hear!" someone else bellowed, and they all—except Angie—cheered with exuberance and reached out to lift a glass.

Julia placed a tall glass of water in Angie's right hand, which she carefully sipped.

"Well," Ginny said, once the toast was made, "how about I get your main course going, along with some more bread? And then you can get some sustenance into you?" She looked at Angie hopefully. It was important to turn the evening around and make sure this woman left her house on a positive note, and with a full stomach.

"Sounds great."

Ginny turned back toward the kitchen with Julia and Olive right behind her. Suddenly, the doorbell rang. The three of them froze.

Oh god. No! Ginny's heart leaped back into her throat. Which one of them had gone ahead and dialed 911 anyway? The night was turning into a complete disaster.

"I'll get it," Julia said. Ginny nodded stiffly as she watched with terror. Her sister went cautiously for the door.

Wanting to head off whoever it was at the pass, Ginny tugged off her chef's coat before deciding to follow. She needed to make sure Julia could convince the emergency responders it was only a false alarm. There was no need for anyone to come inside. Rounding the corner, she arrived in the entryway just as the front door was jerked open.

Stopping, she blinked.

It was not the authorities after all. There weren't any men in EMT outfits or a vehicle parked out front with flashing red lights. No badges or buzzing two-way radios.

Instead, standing in the doorway was a smartly dressed man with a weary expression. He was at once a welcome sight and out of place.

"Who is it?" Ginny skittered forward, her brain ping-ponging between the crisis in the other room, the half-cooked ingredients in the kitchen, and the stranger at the door.

The strong pull of curiosity drew her closer. She couldn't quite make out his face, but the man seemed to know Julia by the way he stepped in, his hands instantly at her waist, and brushed his lips against her cheek. Ginny stopped and cocked her head.

Julia, one hand propping the door ajar, remained stiff. She murmured something that sounded like a question, but Ginny, a few feet away, couldn't quite decipher it.

"Julia?" Ginny frowned. "Who's this?"

At that instant, Shane also appeared in the foyer. A troubled look clouded his features. "Everything okay, ladies?" He came up between the women. "Julia? Need any help?"

Ginny caught Julia tense ever so slightly. Her glance darted to Shane. She felt sorry for him. She supposed he felt partially responsible for bringing a guest who'd created so much commotion. His tone was one of genuine concern, but Julia had become awkward in his presence.

"Julia?" Ginny asked.

"Yes, everything's fine." Julia's voice hitched, her back still to them. Hesitantly, she stepped aside to fully reveal the man in front of her. "Ginny, this is James. My fiancé."

All three of them stopped and stared.

CHAPTER TWENTY-FIVE
JULIA

The entryway filled with one giant, uncomfortable pause. Julia reassured everyone it wasn't emergency responders but her fiancé, who'd flown all the way from the East Coast to surprise her. She tried to present his sudden appearance as a grand romantic gesture, but she didn't think she was convincing.

"Hi there. James Townsend. A pleasure to meet you." James stepped over the threshold and jutted out his right hand. He fixed his gaze on Shane, who took his outstretched hand dumbly. James's voice was deep. "Sorry to barge in. I didn't realize Julia would have company."

"Oh, hi there. Nice to meet you too," Shane said, a crooked grin of uncertainty spread over his face.

James planted himself in her sister's doorway, still dressed in his work clothes, with a small overnight bag at his feet. Clearly, he didn't plan on staying long.

Julia swallowed back a new seed of dread.

"And you are . . . ?" James's brow arched, his response suspicious. He gave Shane a curious once-over.

Shane hesitated. He seemed to be putting the pieces together. A hand reached up as he nervously ran his fingers through his hair. "Oh,

right. Sorry. It's been a crazy night around here. I'm Shane. Just a guest."
His gaze flicked briefly to Julia. "But you didn't come to see me. I'll
leave you both to it. Good to meet you, man."

"Thanks."

Shane spun on his heel and strode back in the direction of the dining room. But not before Julia caught the confused look on his face.

"Crazy night?" James asked. "What, are you gals having some kind
of party or something?" The suspicious tone remained.

Ginny emitted a nervous laugh. It was clear she didn't know what
to make of James's arrival either. "Ha! Yeah, something like that."

"How did you find me here?" Julia cut Ginny off before she could
continue her sarcasm. Her fingers gripped the edge of the door for
stability. A swirl of shock and embarrassment threatened to tip her
off-balance if she were to let go. Her nerves were still frayed from the
upsetting episode with Angie. Now James had arrived, in *Arizona*. Two
jolts in one night. It was unbelievable. James had traveled halfway across
the country and was now standing there in Ginny's entryway. She didn't
know if she should be happy or utterly pissed off. "I didn't even know
you were coming."

"Well, it appears my surprise tactic worked," James said. He shifted
and returned her gaze with a tight smile. He was likely thinking of all
the missed calls she had yet to return. Julia needed a minute to recalibrate. How on earth had he found Ginny's place, anyway?

"I'm surprised, all right."

"I missed you. So here I am."

Ginny, clearly feeling like a third wheel, backed up. "Well, that
sounds nice. Why don't you come inside, James?"

Julia felt a firm hand on her elbow, leading her away. Ginny gra-
ciously gestured for James to follow. Though her thoughts were still
spinning, Julia felt a wave of gratitude toward her sister. Ginny was also
in disbelief and was likely overcome with stress over her guests and the

unattended dinner, but she'd put on a gracious-hostess hat for Julia's sake. She'd have to remember to thank her later.

But right now, Julia needed to understand what James was doing there in the first place.

"Thank you," James said, the muscles in his face relaxing. "You must be Julia's sister, Virginia."

Ginny plastered on a smile. "Everyone calls me Ginny. Nice to meet you. I've heard so much about you."

Thank god for Ginny, Julia thought. They both knew Julia hadn't mentioned James much at all. Instead, she'd brushed aside all inquiries into her love life. But Ginny didn't let on about any of that. Instead, she donned the old familiar role of covering for her younger sister. No questions asked. Julia's well of appreciation deepened.

"Sorry to show up unannounced like this, but I was worried."

"You don't have to apologize to me." Ginny shook her head. "Julia, why don't you take him somewhere quiet where you two can enjoy some privacy? I've got to get back to our guests." She sent a pointed look in Julia's direction, telling her it would be best to keep everyone separate for the time being.

"Sure, yeah. Let's do that. Ginny's busy cooking for some of her friends. She's probably got things burning on the stove by now." Julia placed a hand on James's back, hoping to steer him away from the growing din of voices in the other room. "You can put your bag in my room."

Ginny excused herself, and James politely thanked her. Julia led him down the hallway toward the bedrooms. More trepidation bubbled up with each step. Hopefully Olive—who had likely remained in the dining room to keep the dinner guests happy—could take over and help her mom get the remainder of the meal back on track. She'd have to, considering the late hour and James's overnight bag. They apparently had a lot to discuss.

"That's your sister?" James whispered, following close behind. "You two sure don't look alike."

Julia shot him a weary glance over her shoulder. It felt like a loaded question. James returned her gaze with a raised eyebrow, as if to say, *I'm only pointing out the obvious.*

"Yes." She wondered what exactly he'd meant by it. Was it the discrepancy in their ages? Something in his voice caused her to bristle. It was as if he was judging Ginny before he even got to know her.

Wordlessly, she continued down the hallway and ushered him into the den before shutting the door.

"You can set your bag down anywhere." She waved a hand, hoping he could look beyond the unmade bed and modest furnishings. "And then maybe you can tell me what you're doing here."

"Wow. It's nice to see you, too, honey." His mouth hung open as he paused, casting a curious gaze about the room. Julia watched him take in the southwestern decor, the traditional leather-and-twig chair, the brightly colored bedding, and the small window in the plastered wall that peeked out into the inky darkness of the desert night. It had become home to her over the past two weeks, providing a sanctuary where she could curl up and rest.

She wondered, however, whether James saw it that way. James liked things with straight edges and clean lines. His own taste in home furnishings was minimalistic, bordering on sparse. Ginny's home, on the other hand, was all rounded edges and a multitude of textures—exposed brick, natural-edged wood, and earthy clay. Every surface was adorned with Mexican art. It wasn't cluttered, per se. But seeing her surroundings through James's discerning eye, Julia had to admit that her sister's taste was the opposite of simple.

"So this is where you'd rather be than back home with me?"

"No. That's not fair." Julia shook her head and then dropped onto the daybed. The springs gave a little wheeze as she did so.

"No?" James raised a brow.

She gestured for James to take a seat in the only other chair in the room. "James, it isn't that I'm not glad to see you. I am. Truly. It's just that you showed up here like you were ready to storm the castle. I mean, why didn't you even call? Send a text? Anything."

He exhaled and tossed his bag to the side, creating a heavy thump on the rug. Julia noticed his jaw set as he opted to remain standing. "I *did* call. Several times. Do you not check your phone these days? I've been trying to reach you to no avail. I finally got fed up and hopped on a flight. A very full and expensive flight, I might add. This was no easy task, Julia. It's not like I could just grab an Uber to zip into the next town over. I came all the way out here, to Timbuktu, to find you. Doesn't that mean anything?"

Julia swallowed. He'd come here to make her feel guilty. He was doing a good job of it. Her eyes watered.

"Babe." His voice softened. "Talk to me."

"I'm really sorry. I've been busy helping Ginny. I guess I haven't checked my phone as often as I normally do."

The softness faded. "In other words, you haven't been too interested in communicating with me."

Julia met his eye. "That's not true." She suddenly felt exhausted.

"Isn't it?" His words were edged in fresh bitterness. "Or maybe other things besides your sister have been occupying your time. Maybe that Shane guy out there has something to do with it?"

Julia scoffed. "Oh, come on. Really? Just because another man is in my sister's house, you assume something? Do you really think so little of me? That's one of Ginny's friends. I only just met him." The lie rolled off her tongue in a quick, defensive reflex. One she believed, at least partially. Shane hadn't distracted her that much, had he?

"Whatever you say."

"James." Julia peered at him. "Why are you here?"

"To see you."

She stood up from the bed and came to face him. It dawned on her now just how long they'd been apart. Standing there, close like that, she could inhale the pleasing, familiar scent of his laundry detergent mixed with his woodsy aftershave. But she was able to see that his eyes were rimmed with a thinly veiled sadness.

Her actions had affected them both.

"I'm glad." A layer of frost thawed. She had missed him. It was just that she'd pushed him aside temporarily to make room in her heart for Ginny and Olive. In the process, she'd let the details of their lives gradually envelop hers. It had been a welcome break from her own tangled, self-induced worries, that was all. But it had hurt James in the process.

"I'm glad you wanted to see me. I really am. I just don't understand why the dramatic entrance, that's all." She reached for his arm and gently wrapped her fingers around him. His muscles relaxed. In this instant, Julia could sense herself being drawn back to him, back to the life they'd created.

James's expression mirrored her own. Tenderly, he wrapped his hands around her waist and drew her in so that their hip bones touched. The top of her forehead rested against his broad chin as she leaned in and exhaled. It had been a while since she'd been held like that. She felt a little weakening behind her knees as she closed her eyes.

"Julia." James's breath was soft in her hair. "I understand you had a rough go of it at work and you wanted to get away for a bit. I really do. But I need to know you're not going to run away whenever there's trouble. You just up and disappeared without even telling me. And then every time I tried to talk to you about it over the phone, it went badly." He held up a hand and placed it to his chest. "I'm not saying I didn't play a part in that. I'm just as guilty of being defensive, but it got to the point where I felt the only way we could talk was if I flew out here and knocked on your door. Well, your sister's door. I found her address online. It wasn't that difficult. So here I am, heart on my sleeve and everything."

Her face turned upward. A new welling of guilt rose up inside her. What had she been so upset about? Here was a man who loved her, had traveled a great distance just to tell her this, and was willing to work through whatever disagreements they'd had just to be with her. New warmth blossomed in her heart as she folded herself tighter into James's open arms. This was where she belonged. There shouldn't have been any doubt. Should there? Her career might be on shaky ground, but her relationship with James didn't have to be.

Pushing onto the tips of her toes, she angled her face and kissed him.

"There's one more thing," James said after kissing her back. A gleam played in his eyes.

"What's that?" she asked dreamily.

"You're going to want to sit down for this."

Her brows knit together. "Why is that?"

His hands slid to her elbows, as if bracing her for what he was about to say. "I think I've found a way for you to turn this Rossetti thing around. You may not be losing your job after all."

CHAPTER TWENTY-SIX
JULIA

Julia couldn't believe what she was hearing. She found herself waving James off. He had unspooled his story so quickly that her brain buzzed. It was clear he expected his buoyant energy to be contagious, lifting Julia up out of her stupor and giving her the final shove back to New York, where he thought she belonged.

"I think you're going to have to tell me again," she said. "And this time, go slower."

She found she had to sit up straighter in an effort just to take it all in. A slight jittery sensation ran down the length of her spine. The evening had been a series of unexpected jolts.

"You have a way out," he repeated. "There's legitimacy to this thing after all. And you could be the one to expose it."

She mulled the notion over in her head, saying nothing at first.

James took her hand and laced his fingers gently between hers.

Outside her door, the distant voices of Ginny's dinner guests rose to a final crescendo, Shane's among them. The sound of thank-yous and goodbyes being exchanged was followed by the click of the front door. The knot of anxious tension that resided in her lower back shifted and melted away. From the sound of it, everyone had left a happy customer.

James claimed he'd miraculously—and accidentally—found a way to prove she'd been right about illegal activity in Rossetti's office. Well, half-right. Julia was skeptical. The damage had already been done. She'd humiliated the mayor and been suspended from her duties at GBN. But the reporter in her hadn't been snuffed out altogether.

Information had come across James's desk recently that had piqued his interest.

"One of my buddies in the office came over to ask my advice on something, and long story short, we wound up talking about the details of his workload. He showed me a spreadsheet that had Rossetti's chief of staff listed as one of his clients. I recognized the name right away. I mean, how could I not after all that's happened, right?" He shifted eagerly and waited for a reaction.

"Go on."

"Well"—he hesitated—"this is all privileged information, and I could lose my job for telling you this, but maybe it will give you the lead you need. This guy, Evan Falsetto, Rossetti's right-hand guy, had my buddy make a million-dollar investment for him not too long ago. A million dollars! Do you know how much he makes working for Rossetti? I looked it up. Not enough to bankroll that kind of money. I did a little digging, and it seems he's got a side business—a consulting company—only my guess is he's been underreporting earnings and got into trouble. The timing is too coincidental. I think it's the mayor's chief of staff who's going to be indicted. I say it looks highly suspicious. Don't you agree?"

"Unbelievable."

"Anyway, this is the proof you need!" he said. "All you have to do is follow up, make some inquiries, let Peter know there really was a grain of truth to your story after all. Surely, with this kind of scoop, you'll get your job back. Goodbye suspension, hello promotion! Then we can get back to normal." His eyes lit up as he looked at her expectantly.

"Hmm." Julia rolled the idea around in her head. She envisioned what it would be like to march into Peter's office with fresh confidence and reclaim what was rightfully hers. To eject that Hannah O'Brian girl from her seat at the desk and stun a smug-faced Miller, putting him in his place once and for all. If what James was telling her was true, and if she could get her hands on concrete proof, then GBN would have to put her back on the air and agree to let her break the story. Wouldn't they?

Getting her job back and getting back into Peter's good graces was what she'd wanted. But still . . . A nagging dread lingered at the back of her mind. Something within her that, over the course of the past couple of weeks, had altered. Julia wasn't about to share this feeling with James just yet. She needed time to think.

"It's tempting, I'll give you that," she mused. Her brain started to turn over the list of possibilities. She ran over the various angles she could take, the headlines that might be born from breaking a story of this magnitude. She considered the gratification that would come along with it—a kind of satisfying redemption that comes with uprooting the truth after everyone thought it wouldn't be possible.

She could do it. *Maybe.* If the stars were aligned just so. She'd need corroborating evidence, a solid source, someone credible who would go on record and admit to all of this. Who was going to do that? James's coworker? Someone in the AG's office? Not likely. Julia understood that would be the most difficult hurdle to cross, finding someone to come forward.

As eager as James was for his fiancée to redeem herself, Julia knew this kind of story would prove tricky no matter the conditions. Politicians didn't like to show their cards. Ever. And neither did their chiefs of staff.

Julia tapped her upper lip with her index finger, mentally sorting through the narrative. This was big, but getting it packaged up and airtight enough to go on the air wouldn't be easy. At the moment, she had little street cred left. If any.

James scoffed. "Tempting? How about a sure thing? An ace in the hole? This is what you've wanted, right? To redeem yourself with the network and prove you didn't make up a false accusation? To shed your image of 'fake news' and reaffirm your reputation?"

Julia sighed. She could tell he was becoming incredulous. "Yes." She nodded. "Of course."

"Then why are you even debating this?" he asked. "If I were you, I'd be shoving my clothes into a bag as we speak and then catching the next flight out of here. Pronto." His breath came out in short bursts, a kind of frenetic energy radiating off his now-taut frame.

Julia could tell he'd wanted nothing more than for her to leap to her feet, throw her arms around his neck in gratitude, and begin packing up her suitcase so they could both flee back to the city. James didn't like how she'd derailed both of their lives with her reckless actions. That kind of behavior wasn't what he expected from her. It was time they got back to the business of being a couple.

Back to normal, as he'd so succinctly put it.

But Julia didn't budge. She had the distinct feeling she was being pressed into a corner. Only she wasn't sure how to wriggle out.

"Julia?" he asked. "Why aren't you saying anything?"

"James." She inhaled, drawing courage into her lungs. If she were to utter anything other than full agreement with his plan, it would once again create a fissure between them. Yet something stronger, almost visceral, began to churn inside her gut. She knew she wouldn't be able to explain it, not yet anyway, but something kept her rooted to the ground.

She wasn't ready to make her next step.

"You are amazing," she began. "I can't thank you enough for bringing this information all the way here, and for trying to save my career. It's overwhelmingly generous."

"I'm glad." His breathing slowed and he narrowed his eyes, as if he was trying to make a careful calculation. She'd seen this look on him many times before. As when gauging an unpredictable stock or tricky investment, James was trying to predict the outcome. "So? Why aren't you as enthused as I am right now? I thought you'd be leaping out of your skin when I told you."

She shifted. "And I would be."

"But what?"

She hesitated. If she told him the truth, about all the things she was questioning in her mind, it would surely be the start of yet another fight.

"I'm just tired, is all. It's been a long day—for both of us, I'm sure—and I think I just need a decent night's rest. Can we go to bed and talk about it more in the morning?" Her voice caught as she inwardly prayed for him to agree. It was true, she was maxed out. At this point, her vision was beginning to blur with fatigue.

He nodded in slow agreement. "Sure. I guess you're right. Maybe it's best to tackle this thing when we're fresh. But . . ." He paused, his eyes grazing over the compact daybed. "Where am I supposed to sleep? That tiny bed of yours can't possibly hold both of us. Should we go to a hotel?"

Julia smiled in spite of herself. "I guess it is a little cramped in here for two people. How about I make up a spot on the couch in the living room? Ginny won't mind. It's not perfect, but it's a better option than you driving around in the dark, searching blindly for a hotel. This isn't the city; things aren't as easy to find out there in the desert night."

"You're telling me. It's kind of desolate out here." He shuddered. "Once I turned the rental car away from the airport, I wasn't sure where I was headed. How does she stand being so removed from it all? I mean, it's nothing like Manhattan, that's for sure."

Julia smiled. "Yes." She was about to say that's what was so nice about the place, but she decided against it. James wouldn't understand and had zero interest in sticking around long enough to try to.

Together they gathered up extra bedding from a linen closet and made a temporary bed for James. Julia said good night and flicked off the last remaining lamp. Tiptoeing back to her own room, she prayed for clarity to come in the morning. Because at that moment, she didn't know what she wanted.

And that was what frightened her the most.

CHAPTER TWENTY-SEVEN

GINNY

Last night's surprise arrival of Julia's expensively dressed Wall Street fiancé had set the whole household off-kilter.

Not that it hadn't been headed in that direction anyway.

After tending to Shane's ill friend, executing the remainder of her dinner menu—thankfully rescuing the mushroom puree from the oven in time to liquefy it with a dash of milk—she and Olive managed to get everyone fed and out the door in one piece. The entire episode, paired with her looming angst over the food blogger, had left Ginny frazzled and worn out. She could only imagine how Julia felt.

By Julia's stunned look, she hadn't exactly been thrilled to see their new houseguest. *And,* Ginny thought, *neither had Shane.* The poor guy had slunk back into the dining room after meeting James and then proceeded to sulk in his chair like a forlorn adolescent all through dinner. Even Olive had noticed his change in demeanor, asking gently if he was worried over his sick friend. Shane had smiled pitifully and said everything was "just fine, thank you."

And this morning in the living room, sitting on a half-made sofa, was James. The mysterious boyfriend. Ginny found herself wondering what to say.

She was still groggy-eyed and doped up on the half of a sleeping pill she'd allowed herself the night before. It wasn't a habit she practiced often, but when the pressures got to be too much for her exhausted brain, Ginny succumbed. If she didn't, she would spend the whole night tossing with worry.

The prior evening had been a near miss with the Angie disaster. What if the authorities really had come? There wasn't enough money in Ginny's bank account to pay her most recent food bill, let alone whatever penalty would've resulted if the cops had been called. Once again, she'd overextended herself. It wasn't as if she set about to do it, but she held herself to such a high standard and wasn't willing to sacrifice the quality of the food she served. It was a mistake she had to stop making. She knew this.

Throw yet another prying stranger into the mix, and recent events had felt downright out of control. She'd needed a solid night's sleep to forget it all until the morning.

"Good morning," James said now, rising to greet her as she entered the room. Ginny closed the gap between them with palpable unease. She hastily smoothed her wild hair. Being half-drugged might not make the best impression. She supposed she should have at least brushed her teeth.

"Good morning."

"I hope you don't mind that we made up your sofa at the last minute. Julia thought it was better than me looking for a hotel at all hours of the night." James's hand went to the back of his neck and rubbed. Ginny noticed his button-down shirt was rumpled and a thatch of his thick brown hair stood on end at the crown. The whites of his eyes were vaguely bloodshot. She studied him, standing there, shifting on socked feet. He was certainly handsome, but in a way that was overly manicured, like a forty-year-old Ken doll with dark hair and a suit. She supposed this was Julia's usual type. The professional kind with a strong jaw and piercing gaze.

Ginny shook her head. "No problem. Hope it was comfortable."

"Oh yeah, just fine. Thanks." He offered a crooked smile, revealing a noticeable dent in the confident armor he'd worn last night.

"Julia still sleeping?"

"Yeah, I guess so. I've just been out here answering emails on my phone. I didn't want to wake her just yet."

Ginny nodded. Feeling slightly uncomfortable with this stranger, her fingers tugged at her pullover sweatshirt. She'd at least had the foresight to get dressed before emerging from her room. Something had told her she wouldn't be alone. She caught his eyes moving in the direction of the kitchen.

"Coffee?" She tipped her head.

"That'd be great," he said, with a lopsided smile of relief.

Well, at least they could relate over the importance of a strong cup of coffee to start the morning; the rest of his lifestyle, she'd had to leave behind long ago.

~

A half hour later, after Ginny and James had indulged in several refills of dark French roast and a crumb-filled plate of day-old scones, Julia emerged. At the sight of her, Ginny and James brightened in unison.

"Hi, you two." Julia padded in with bare feet. A long cashmere sweater was draped loosely over a wispy nightgown. She blinked repeatedly against the glowing morning light. As she drew nearer, Ginny noticed circles of red rimming her sister's eyes. She wondered if Julia had been crying. It was difficult to tell, considering her perky smile. Either her sister was truly happy to see them, or she was good at faking it.

Ginny's gut told her it was the latter. She was a trained TV personality, after all; that smile could be tacked on with the snap of a finger.

"Hi, babe." James jumped up, his voice a touch too eager. With quick strides, he was at her side and gave her a peck on the cheek. Julia returned the gesture robotically and then went for the coffee maker. There was something in the way James moved, almost fidgety, that Ginny took as anxious anticipation. She assumed he couldn't wait to get out of there, away from obsolescence and back to the familiar city. She wondered if Julia wanted the same thing.

"Have you both been getting to know one another better?" Julia asked, choosing to lean on the counter and cross her ankles rather than hover over their table.

"Oh yeah." James pumped his head, the tuft of hair still standing up. "Your sister was nice enough to make me breakfast."

"Oh no. That's not a real breakfast; I'm sorry to say I wasn't exactly on my game this morning. It was a long night. Just had some leftovers from the bakery."

"Oh, I love anything from the bakery. I'd have their pastries every day if I could," Julia mused.

"Ha! I pretty much do. And now look at me!" Ginny snorted and patted her belly.

James suddenly appeared squirmy. "Well, whatever it was, I appreciated it."

"Anytime." Ginny sensed he didn't entirely mean it. The two of them had endured the forced exchange of superficial small talk until Julia arrived. She and James had swapped reports of the weather— Arizona's and New York's—and brief updates on life in Manhattan. Ginny had smirked inwardly. She might as well have switched on the television. James didn't seem to be interested in any kind of in-depth conversation.

Perhaps he wasn't sure where the sisters stood in their relationship, and he wanted to protect Julia. Or, Ginny feared, maybe there just wasn't much substance to the guy. If that was the case, she hoped her sister would see him for who he was and move on. She couldn't imagine being married to someone who was all business and no heart.

But then again, she'd fallen for Will all those years ago. And he was all heart and no business. Look where that got her. Ginny pushed the thought aside. What did she know, anyway? She hadn't dated anyone in years. She was no expert on relationships; that was for sure. All she knew was that she wanted her sister to be happy. That was all that mattered. That and Olive's happiness. They both deserved that much.

"So," Julia broke in, "I think I'll take James outside onto the back patio so he can see the view. C'mon, James. We can take our coffees out there and talk some more."

"Great."

Ginny took this as her cue to give them some privacy. She imagined James was there to take Julia back home. She wondered if her sister would leave sooner than she'd planned. She had to admit, she'd be crushed if Julia did. They'd just begun to get into their sibling rhythm again. Ginny had enjoyed having her sister around. And she knew Olive did as well. Her daughter's volatile attitude had completely turned around over the past several days. It was almost as if Julia's presence had shed a whole new light on Olive. Ginny had to admit, it had done the same for her.

Now James was there to bring all of this to a close, and she felt the curtain dropping.

"Sure. Of course. You both go out and enjoy the morning. Take a load off. You've earned it, Julia. I'll see you in a little while." Ginny collected the short stack of dirty dishes and deposited them into the sink. Backing out of the room, she gestured for James and Julia to go on.

Just before she turned to leave, she glanced at her sister. There was conflict in Julia's face; she could tell. It would be up to her whether she stayed or went. Ginny supposed Julia would have had to make that choice eventually anyway.

Making her way down the hall, she stopped at Olive's room. She pressed a palm silently against the door. If she listened hard enough, she thought she could hear the rustling of her daughter's downy covers as she turned over in bed. It was coming up on nine in the morning, far too early for Olive to emerge from the fog. Her daughter was nothing if not consistent with her need to sleep late after a night of work.

But unlike on so many other mornings, Ginny was comforted that just on the other side, her daughter remained in her somnolent cocoon. Having Olive under her roof felt nice. It wouldn't last forever; Ginny knew this. Her daughter was a grown woman now, most likely with plans and dreams of her own. It was only a matter of time before Ginny would have to let her go. She couldn't hold on to Olive forever, expecting her to serve the guests of Mesquite and help grow a business that wasn't her own, especially not for paltry wages. It wasn't fair. Olive had been trying to tell her this for years, only Ginny hadn't listened. She saw that now.

Maybe it had taken the presence of her little sister to help Ginny recognize this about Olive. They each had to find their way, wherever that might lead.

Moving beyond the door, Ginny trod unhurriedly to her own room. Things were beginning to shift; she could feel it. And she needed to be prepared. In response, a plan was beginning to form.

CHAPTER TWENTY-EIGHT

JULIA

"I don't think I'm going home just yet," Julia blurted out. She fiddled with the frayed edge of a patio cushion while James lowered himself into a teak chair and gaped.

The heat of the day was just beginning to descend, the sun's glowing rays casting a peach-colored hue on the earth below. James tilted forward and squinted against the increasing brightness. Julia could tell he was having a difficult time processing.

Her metropolitan fiancé seemed so out of place here, surrounded by the natural landscape of scrubs and cacti, with his dark wool slacks, deeply creased designer shirt, and polished shoes. None of it fit with the relaxed setting of the desert. And, she woefully realized, James's all-business attitude didn't quite fit with her current frame of mind either.

For all intents and purposes, Julia had shed her city skin to adapt to her new environment. Or maybe it was just coming home, like putting on a well-worn sweater that was moth eaten and stretched but still the coziest choice of all. She'd found that doing so had brought on a welcome kind of ease, one that allowed her to settle into herself more deeply.

And she wasn't prepared to give that up.

"What do you mean?" Dismay dropped down over James's unshaven face. This was going to be a lot harder than Julia had thought.

"I don't mean to just spring it on you," she said. "But I'm not ready."

Fumbling with her ring, she felt a pang of something between guilt and regret. They'd been through so much together. Even so, there was resolution in her decision. She hadn't been sure when she'd gone to bed the night before. But now she knew. James's arrival had confirmed what she'd suspected for some time but had been too afraid to admit. They both wanted different things.

"Oh."

I've disappointed him, Julia thought. And it occurred to her then, as she searched his face, that she was tired of being a disappointment. She was tired of the weight it carried. Of course James hadn't ever meant for his expectations of her, *of them,* to be more than she could handle. Julia knew this. But somehow they were. And they both deserved to be with people who accepted them for who they were, *where* they were, at the present moment. Instead of constantly wishing for more.

Somehow she needed him to see this. She also needed to accept responsibility.

"I know it's been terribly unfair to keep you in the dark. I ran away without warning. It wasn't right. I'm sorry. You deserve better."

He shifted. "Yeah, it hasn't been easy."

"I needed time. I didn't realize how much I needed it until I went away. You know," she stalled, her voice cracking, "things—our lives in particular—have been pretty crazy lately. And then that disaster with work happened, and it all became too much."

His frown deepened. "So you're saying things with me became too much? I was part of the problem?"

"No." She shook her head. "Not at all. You're not the thing I was running away from. I was escaping my own mess. But in the process of untangling it all, of getting quiet and figuring out what I really wanted, I discovered that my outlook has changed. *I've* changed. I no longer want the same things for my career, for my environment even, that I once did. And I know it's hard to hear. But part of my realization is that you and I are not in the same place we once were either. If we're honest with ourselves, I think we want different things."

He swallowed, his eyes drifting downward. She watched as he grew quiet. Only his mouth twitched as he considered her words.

"That doesn't mean I don't love you." She swiped at the silent flow of fresh tears, noticing James's eyes grow misty as he listened. "And it doesn't mean I don't love all the time we've spent together. You and I shared something special. It's just that . . . it's just I don't think what we shared can evolve in the direction I'm going. I believe it's best if we both go after what we're passionate about, not just what we're comfortable with. In all honesty, I think it would be better for both of us if we moved on. I'm so sorry." A lump settled high in her throat. As necessary as it was to admit the truth out loud, doing so felt like experiencing a death of sorts.

James's shoulders rose and fell. His expression was full of sorrow. "I've been thinking too," he said. "While I still had hope for us, I guess some of what you're saying is true. We do seem to want different things. I mean, seeing you out here, at your sister's place, feels like visiting a stranger. It's surreal. Here's my fiancée, but suddenly she's someone I no longer recognize. I'm not saying this in a bad way. Quite frankly, you seem more peaceful, more comfortable in your skin out here. And I hate to admit you found a way to be so content in my absence. I'm not going to lie. It hurts."

Julia nodded. "I'm sorry."

"I know it sounds self-centered," James continued. "But that's how I feel. It just sucks to discover you that way without me. And I certainly don't embrace this environment the way you seem to have done. It all feels so foreign. The opposite of exciting, if you know what I mean."

"I know," she said.

James chuckled softly. "It's beautiful and all, don't get me wrong. But it's so damned quiet. So remote. I couldn't live like this."

"I know you couldn't." For the first time, she grinned. She knew exactly what James meant. He was far more comfortable in the center of the action. He was the kind of person who thrived on other people's— lots of other people's—energy. He liked the hustle and bustle. He sought it out wherever they went. She didn't fault him for that. It was just in his makeup.

"And I don't want you to be anywhere you're not happy," she said. "That's where we differ because I discovered that I like being back here. My sister and niece are a big factor. I feel at home again after all this time away. It didn't come at once. But I found a comfort here. I found I'm okay with the quiet. Perhaps I was running from being alone for so many years. I never allowed myself to even try. But once I did, I enjoyed it. Does that make any sense?" She so badly wanted him to understand. To be okay with her decision. Somehow, if he was, she might not feel so guilty for being the first to let go.

"It does," he replied. "It hurts like hell, but I understand. I really do."

As difficult as it was for James to accept defeat, Julia believed he knew that what she was doing was the right thing. They didn't belong together. Not anymore.

"Before I came to Ginny's, I was losing sight of who I am. I wasn't eating, I wasn't sleeping, and I certainly wasn't enjoying any kind of meaningful personal time. We never even got around to planning our wedding. That should have been a signal to us, shouldn't it? I mean, think about the last time we did something together that didn't involve our jobs or networking. That didn't involve dinner with clients or posing for photographers on the social circuit."

"We spent every night and morning together."

She shook her head. "Not really. Our morning rituals consist of you grabbing a bagel and me liquefying spinach in my juicer. And then we get dressed for work and we're off to the races. Just because we bump around in the same kitchen doesn't mean we're spending time together. There isn't any quality conversation spent over a shared meal. Honestly, James. You can't tell me I'm wrong."

"You're right. I guess we just let the busyness of our lives take over. Like you said, maybe we lost sight of each other. Or what we really want." James gazed out into the distance. Their lives had taken unpredictable turns. It was time for reflection, on both their parts.

"James?" She leaned in. Small spiderwebs of lines deepened at the corners of his eyes. She realized the trip had left him weary, and now he'd be going away empty-handed. A ripple of regret shot through her. She'd somehow managed to derail both their lives. "I'm so sorry. I know this wasn't what you envisioned when you boarded the airplane yesterday. I really do appreciate your bringing news all this way. Truly. I'll do something with it. I just need to make sure I'm ready before I do."

He offered a sad smile. "I get it."

"I'm grateful you do."

He held her gaze for a moment longer. "You know I can't stay. I have to go back. There's too much going on at the office. And we both know I don't really belong here anyway." He inched forward and placed his hands on his knees, as if to stand. They weren't going to sit there and dwell. It would be much harder that way.

"Thank you for everything." She slipped off her ring and placed it in his palm. Before letting go, she gave his hand a squeeze.

He stood, his mouth turned down. With a slow nod, he pocketed the ring. Perhaps he knew words were no longer needed.

After he gathered his things, they walked down the driveway together and said their goodbyes. Julia hugged him a final time and then watched him drive away. Running the fabric of her sleeve under her damp nose, she told herself to be strong.

She was going to have to navigate the choppy waters alone. But while she was losing James as a tether, she was at least comforted to know that she had Ginny and Olive to keep her company. Reconnecting with her family had given her more than she'd ever expected. It had given her a new kind of courage: the courage to stand alone.

CHAPTER TWENTY-NINE
JULIA

She'd chosen to stay, which was either selfish or self-preserving. Julia really had no clue. It was too late to second-guess her decision now. For better or for worse, she was going to take a new path.

Turning on her heel, she shook off the unsteady feeling and wandered back into Ginny's. The front door closed with a satisfying click, and she leaned up against it, feeling the weight of her decision sink down into her bones.

Now what? she wondered.

As if on cue, Olive emerged, peeking around the corner with her usual topknot of messy honey-colored hair. She blinked twice and glimpsed around. Not seeing anyone else, she shot Julia a hesitant smile.

"Hey, Aunt Julia."

"Hey, yourself."

Olive ambled out into the foyer, a pair of black yoga leggings and a faded tank top hugging her beautifully tanned body. "I wondered where you went off to. I was worried for a minute there that you'd jumped in your boyfriend's car and driven away without saying goodbye."

Julia smiled. She could've sworn she felt her heart beat in double time. Seconds before, she'd come back through the front door with a rumbling of doubt. But hearing the sincerity in her niece's voice, all the worry now fell away. This was why she'd chosen to stay. For family. It was because of this lovely girl standing in front of her. Olive, she believed, needed her. And so did Ginny.

And, Julia realized, she needed them too.

~

Later that evening, as a patchwork of rosy pinks blended together in a dusky sky, the three women sat on the patio and clinked glasses. They had the night off from work and had rewarded themselves with an impromptu happy hour in the backyard.

Ginny had inquired earlier about James, pressing her hand on Julia's with a concerned look. She'd asked about the details of the broken engagement and whether Julia was going to be okay.

Julia batted a tear away and shrugged.

"I don't know, to be honest," she said. "I guess only time will tell."

Ginny had nodded in return and suggested a drink.

At Julia's prompting, they'd agreed to forget their recent troubles in the interest of taking a much-deserved break. To live in the moment, despite any silent fears of tomorrow.

A pleased-looking Olive, dressed in her favorite boho-style denim overalls and tank top, had gleefully presented the women with a tray loaded with freshly made drinks. In addition, Ginny had brought out an artful arrangement of goat cheese, fig jam, and thinly sliced prosciutto, accompanied by delicate wine grapes and rice crackers.

Julia cut into the cheese with the flat edge of her cracker, feeling momentarily guilty that she hadn't brought anything to the table other than her appetite. Ginny seemed to read her thoughts and gestured for her to help herself.

"This might be your dinner tonight," she said with a grin. She leaned forward and pushed the cheese board a little closer. The sleeves of her linen button-down gathered in folds around the muscles of her forearms. Julia watched Ginny pluck a handful of juicy grapes from the bunch and then pop one into her mouth. Her teeth bit down. "The kitchen is officially closed."

"Fine by me."

"Yeah, me too. Just keep the drinks coming."

Icy tumblers filled with fresh-squeezed juice, vodka, and citrus wedges glistened in the changing light. Julia grasped hers and rubbed away a layer of frost with her thumb. She lifted the rim to her thirsty lips and then took a long, luxurious sip. Her eyes closed. It tasted like heaven.

Crunching on a mouthful of ice, she smiled. "Mmm, that's really good. I love this cocktail, Olive."

"Why, thank you." Olive dipped her head in a mini bow. "I'm pretty proud of it myself. Do you taste the basil? I muddled a little from Mom's garden. It complements the lemon well, don't you think?"

"Yes, honey. Good job." Ginny had already gulped down one-third of hers. Clearly she'd needed to unwind after a crazy couple of nights.

Beyond her, along the edge of the patio, a rainbow of color danced in the evening breeze. Olive's backyard efforts had gone well beyond the leafy herb garden. Arranged in sweet clusters, with a backdrop of desert sage and tall grasses, sat well-tended terracotta pots brimming with yellow snapdragons, deep-violet lobelia, and powder-blue pansies. Even in the dimming evening light, Julia noticed a couple of butterflies flitting near the bright arrangement of petals. It was such a charming sight, and her niece had been responsible for the entire thing. There was no doubt this girl had a serious green thumb.

"I love the hint of basil, Olive." Julia smiled over her glass. The ice bobbed to the top of her drink. This cocktail-hour distraction was just what she'd needed. "Nice touch. I'm impressed! What other hidden talents do you have?"

Her niece beamed, sitting cross-legged in a chair to her right, her eyes bright and her toes wriggling like a blissful child's.

"She is talented," Ginny added. Julia could tell by the way Olive's eyes widened slightly that she wasn't used to hearing this from her mother. Ginny wasn't normally one for compliments, especially directed toward her own kid. Perhaps Ginny was now trying to change all that.

"Thanks, guys."

Julia tipped back in her chair, her head resting against the smooth wooden slats. The vodka was beginning to take effect. Everything around her seemed to adopt a tranquil, velvety softness. Even the air was soothing, encircling the three of them in a calm of earthy sage.

She glanced upward, grateful for the view.

"I have to say, I've missed these kinds of sunsets," Julia mused. Bright pinks had morphed into intense shades of lavender, fading into the night sky.

"It's the best," Ginny chimed in, raising her glass. "And I agree with your aunt. This is one of your better cocktails, Olive."

"To the best!" Olive said, and they clinked glasses once more.

Julia relaxed, sensing a colorful ripple of happiness thread its way among the group. Glancing to either side, she looked from one face to the next and told herself to hold on to the feeling.

It was the most uncertain and yet the most content she'd been for a long while. Would it continue?

"You're looking awfully pensive." Ginny cocked her head with a raised brow. "Are you having second thoughts about not leaving to go back with James?"

Julia hugged her knees to her chest and considered the question. Was she sad? Did she regret putting James back into his rental car and sending him off to the airport alone? In doing so, she'd ended a chance at love and also left the opportunity wide open for another reporter to snatch up a news story in her absence. Possibly. Her career, or what was left of it, might very well be negatively impacted by her lack of action.

But these were all risks Julia was willing to take. She'd gone into work once before with guns blazing, and look at how horribly that had turned out. This time she was going to be smart. If that meant taking her time, then so be it. The world was going to have to wait.

She shook her head. "No. I think I did the right thing. I'm not going to lie; it was heartbreaking to watch James go without me. That's the person I promised the rest of my life to. And now that's over. But that doesn't mean my life is over, and truthfully, I don't regret my decision to stay longer. I didn't realize how much I needed this break until after I got here. I've got some more thinking to do, and I'd rather do it here."

Ginny studied her, appearing to absorb the explanation. With a faint tip of her head, Julia saw that her sister understood. And she even possibly agreed.

"Well, we're glad you stayed, Aunt Julia," Olive said, kicking her long legs over the arm of her chair. Her bare feet swung back and forth, the muscles of her calves stretching. "And for the record, Mom's a lot nicer when you're around."

"Oh my god." Ginny's eyes rolled toward the sky and back. She scoffed, but Julia knew she secretly didn't mind. Olive's playful comment meant they were getting along. And that was a big step from where they'd been a couple of weeks ago.

Julia laughed. She suspected Olive was right. Ginny's demeanor had lightened up considerably since she'd first arrived. But that also had to do with Olive returning home and altering her adolescent hostility. "Glad to help."

Julia took another sip and gazed out into the distance. The truth was, Ginny and Olive were the ones who'd helped her. It took jumping into someone else's life to let her step back and look at her own. So much more needed to be sorted out, including her job and her future. But for the first time in a long while, Julia had the sense of having both feet firmly planted on the ground. She felt her roots reestablishing themselves, spreading back to the earth and back toward her family. There wasn't any price tag that could be put on such a gift.

"I'm just thankful to be here," she admitted. "Even with all the baggage I brought through your door—literally and figuratively—you let me stay anyway. I want you to know I'm grateful. To both of you."

Ginny pressed her lips together, pausing before she took another sip. Olive watched them carefully, perhaps wondering what secrets her mother and her aunt had carried from their past. After a minute, Ginny spoke.

"You know," she began, "I think you came here for a reason."

"Uh, yeah. It's called running away from my problems."

"Okay," Ginny continued. "Like I said, I think you came here for a reason. Yes, you needed a break from your work fiasco and possibly a place to hide. And you needed to sort through things with James. But you could have gone anywhere: Bora Bora, the coast of France, Antarctica, anywhere!"

"Those all sound like good options."

"But you didn't take any of them. You wound up on my doorstep, to be with Olive and me. You came back home."

"Yes, I did. And so far I haven't regretted it, so don't make me start now," she jested in an attempt to lighten the mood.

At least one of her decisions had been right. Time would only tell about the rest.

CHAPTER THIRTY
GINNY

By midweek, Ginny had been stewing on a plan. She wasn't sure how it was going to work out, but she felt compelled to move forward regardless. Too many troubling events had happened lately. If Julia's visit had reminded her of anything, it was that nothing was guaranteed and life was about taking chances. Ginny had taken a chance when she'd opened a supper club. That had been fulfilling to a degree. But money was tight, and it had taken a toll on her relationship with Olive. Not to mention her nerves.

In addition to this, not once but twice, her business and its secrecy had been threatened as of late.

Ginny recognized it was time to take another kind of chance. It would still involve food, of course. Her heart would always remain in the kitchen, but perhaps this next time around she'd do things a bit differently. Ever since that night when James had shown up, offering to whisk Julia away, back to the city to resuscitate her old life and her career, Ginny had been simmering on an idea.

Picking up her phone, she dialed a number she'd come to know well. As it rang, she clicked her bedroom door shut and went to sit on the end of her bed. After several seconds, the other line picked up.

"Hello? Roger?" she asked. Knowing what she was about to propose sent an uptick to her already-thumping heart rate. "It's Ginny Frank."

Roger immediately gushed on the other end. "Oh, Ginny, my girl! How are you? I've had the nicest visit to a local sheep farmer who had the best cheeses. You've got to get out to this place. I'll send you the address. This kid would be a great vendor for your restaurant." Ginny could hear the wide smile in his voice.

She imagined him sitting outside somewhere, wearing his signature khaki pants and collared shirt, probably looking out over his well-tended vegetable garden or collection of beehives. While she'd never been to Roger's home, she imagined he was the type to grow multiple varieties of his own heirloom vegetables or raise bees for batches of his own honey. Fully retired and in his seventies, Roger now had the freedom to dedicate his time to his passions. He was just that type of man—a foodie right to the core.

"That sounds great, Roger. I'd love to have the farmer's information. Sheep's milk is very on trend as of late, especially when so many people are moving away from traditional dairy. But I'm calling because I have something else I want to run by you."

"I'm all ears."

Ginny shook her head, even though she knew he couldn't see her through the phone. If she did this, she wanted to do it right. "Oh no, I mean I want to meet in person. Maybe we could get together for coffee this week? In town? It would be my treat."

Roger chuckled. "Well, this does sound mysterious. I'd be happy to meet you, my dear. You name the place and time and I'll be there."

"Great. Thanks."

"Anything for my favorite chef!" This exclamation was exactly the incentive Ginny needed to move forward. She was convinced Roger was the best person for what she had in mind.

After giving Roger the details of their coffee date, Ginny hung up and did a tiny fist pump in the air. They'd arranged to meet in two days.

She could barely contain her excitement. While all the details had yet to be sorted out, she had a pretty good sense of what her proposal would include. And Roger's willingness to meet was a good sign. Letting her gaze drift out the open window, she told herself that if it was meant to be, it would be.

In the past few days, she'd been hunting around online, doing research. She'd googled everything from writing a business plan to crowdfunding options, and even poked around at local real estate. If she was going to make a move, she needed to be educated. After that, it was up to the universe whether or not she'd succeed.

What Ginny did know for sure, however, was that her next move wouldn't involve Olive. Sure, her daughter would always have a place to stay. The extra bedroom would be open to Olive whenever she wanted it. But Ginny knew it was time both she and her girl learned to stand on their own two feet. As individuals.

Olive would no longer be required to work at Mesquite. Which meant she'd be free to pursue her own passions without the burden of her mother's expectations. It wasn't fair for Ginny to lean so hard on her daughter for support. She knew this now. The best way to keep her from relying too much on Olive would be for Olive to get a job of her own. Life had to move on. Both Ginny and Olive needed to evolve.

If they remained stagnant, they ran the risk of living unfulfilled lives, and Ginny certainly didn't want that for her daughter. Or for herself, for that matter.

The next part of her plan involved looking at the week ahead for Mesquite. Three dinner services had been booked for the upcoming weekend. The same went for the week after that. Ginny wondered if she could count on both Julia and Olive to stick around to help. The reservation calendar took them into mid-February, and the promise of a full dining room table meant the chance to pay off her credit card debt. The high tourist season would be in full swing all the way through spring break, when the temperatures climbed back up and locals began cranking their air conditioning.

If she could just limp along until April, then maybe she could close Mesquite and concentrate on her next move.

CHAPTER THIRTY-ONE

JULIA

Julia was seated at the dining room table when Ginny found her. She'd arranged a messy but workable makeshift office there earlier that morning. Her laptop lay open, its screen brightly displaying open news sites and a bullet-point-formatted document of notes. Within her reach was a steaming mug of coffee that held her second refill of the morning. Remnants of a blueberry muffin and a chewed melon rind occupied the plate adjacent. Ever since arriving, Julia had found her appetite reawakened, and the yearning for breakfast was a daily sensation that she happily indulged. There wasn't any need to starve herself for the cameras anymore. Not really.

And while this detail meant she wasn't working, this was just fine with her.

Despite the muted sunlight streaming through the far window, a low fire glowed in the room's kiva fireplace. Julia liked how the crackling hunks of burning wood kept the chill off during the early-morning hours. Plus, the smell was heavenly. It was a mix of charcoal and cedar that reminded her of childhood campfires and cups of marshmallowed hot chocolate.

With James's newfound information still buzzing in her brain, she couldn't help but rise early and do some exploring online. If what he'd said was true, that the mayor's chief of staff was being investigated for tax evasion, then Julia suddenly had the potential to serve up a significant story to her boss.

A bigger question loomed. Did she want to be the one to do it? Did she really want the attention thrust back onto her? After everything that had happened?

Of course, the opportunist in her wanted to break the story in the worst way. It would be an act of redemption, an opportunity to shed her unwanted image as a hack reporter.

Yet ever since the botched Rossetti interview, certain aspects of the job had soured for Julia. A considerable amount of loyalty had been lost, on both sides of the deal. Gone was the driving need to please Peter in an effort to hurtle her way to the top of the GBN pecking order. Gone was the idea that the network would put its powers behind her blossoming career.

Was this really the place Julia wanted to be? Was this the brand—as the executives so succinctly put it—that she wanted to represent? For the first time in years, Julia wasn't so sure.

But throwing away a juicy lead went against her very nature. Thus, she'd thrown herself back into work that morning, taking notes and writing down questions regarding Rossetti's staff and the inner workings of his downtown office. And about the consultancy that James had mentioned. There were still too many holes in the story that required filling. Julia had to be prepared either way. The only difficulty was what she'd do with her findings once they were gathered.

"Someone looks hard at work." Ginny came in behind her, dressed for the day with a collection of reusable shopping bags hanging off her right arm. "Whatcha doin'?"

Julia rotated in her seat. She felt caught in the act somehow, even though she wasn't doing anything wrong. Still, a guilty grin played at the corners of her mouth. "Oh, I just thought I'd catch up on a few things. James had a lead on a story I was working on, and I thought I might look into it myself."

Ginny's brow arched. "I thought you were still on leave for another couple of weeks."

"Yeah. I am. Technically. But I want to be prepared for when that changes." She paused, chewing on her lower lip. "Strike that. *If* that changes, I guess I should say."

Ginny deposited her bags onto the table and pulled out a chair. A look of concern crossed her face. "Are you thinking you might not have a job when this period is over? Has your boss said anything more?"

Julia shook her head and slumped in her seat. It was true; she really had no idea whether she'd have a position to go back to at the network. The last exchange she'd had with Peter hadn't been encouraging. In fact, it had been downright depressing. Peter had stopped short of "You leave me no choice." And Julia still hadn't figured out exactly what that meant. Rather than press him for clarification, she'd gotten off the phone as quickly as possible before he decided to fire her right then and there. Ever since then, a constant dread had accompanied her wherever she went. Ginny might not want to board her any longer. And then what?

But admitting this out loud felt like too much of a risk.

"No. Peter hasn't communicated with me beyond the instructions to sign documents and make sure I keep my distance from GBN." Julia shrugged. "He hasn't said I'm not welcome back either. So, who knows? But then again, some much younger woman has been whisked in to cohost in my absence. *Daybreak* has continued on as if nothing happened. It's unnerving, if I'm totally honest."

Ginny cocked her head. "But you're out here working anyway?"

"Yeah, I guess I am." Julia offered an unsure smile and then made small circular motions at her temples. Just thinking about work made her head hurt. "It's all I know how to do. If I learn of a good story, I can't help myself. It's part of my DNA at this point. But I'm not sure what to do with it all. I'm pretty disillusioned at the moment, if that makes any sense."

Ginny studied her. Her arms lay folded across her chest, and her lips were fixed into a tight purse. Julia knew how her sister felt about such things—the dangers of selling out to an establishment just to get along. Without a shadow of a doubt, Ginny didn't approve. "It makes a lot of sense," her sister finally said. "You've been through a lot. You made a mistake, but you've also been turned out without the chance to defend yourself. You're conflicted. I get it."

"Yeah, that about sums it up."

Ginny loosened her arms and cast Julia a reassuring glance. "Take it from me, sometimes it's healthy to step back and reflect. I think that's what you've been doing out here, thousands of miles away from home. Whether you intended it or not, you came to Arizona to get some perspective. I'm confident you'll figure it out."

"Ginny?" Julia felt the salt rising at the back of her throat. She swallowed.

"Yes?"

"Thanks for understanding. I mean it. You have no idea."

Ginny reached out and patted Julia on the back of her hand. "Trust me, I have some idea. You're going to be fine. I just know it. I want you to know it too."

A thought occurred to Julia. "What about you?"

"What about me?"

"Well, obviously something else has been worrying you. Besides the ebb and flow of mother-daughter tension with Olive. You're clearly stressed over money."

It was a risk, and maybe Ginny would once again say it wasn't any of Julia's business.

"You're not wrong." Ginny's face turned sad. "Money has been more than tight. I can't deny it. Lord knows I've tried, though."

229

This time it was Julia who reached forward with a hand. She hated to see her sister this way. Now she was glad she'd pushed. Ginny was perhaps in real trouble. "How long has this been going on?"

Ginny groaned. "For a while. And I'm embarrassed to say it's only getting worse. Mesquite has been amazing and I love doing the supper club, but if I'm completely honest, it's sucking my bank account dry. Food is expensive. Booking the supper club dinners for only two or three nights a week hasn't exactly been bringing in as much cash as I'd hoped. It's no secret I haven't been able to pay Olive what she deserves. But up until now, I've kept to myself how dire my finances really are. Olive doesn't know. Not fully. I didn't want to place that burden on her. Our relationship has been fragile enough without the added stress. You're the first person I've told."

A thickness filled the space between them.

Julia watched her sister's face fall in shame. While this was news to her, she couldn't really say she was surprised. Ginny's dinners of artisan ingredients and high-end fare had to have taken a toll on her bank account. But Julia had just assumed the supper club's customers covered the price tag. Her heart broke for Ginny.

"Oh, Ginny. I'm so sorry."

"Thanks." Ginny swallowed, her throat bobbing. Julia watched as she blinked back dampness from her eyes. Her sister had been holding so much worry inside. It must have been difficult without any support system to lean on. A pebble of guilt settled in her gut. At least Julia had had James to listen to her worries and hold her hand. Who did Ginny have if she'd kept it all from Olive?

Julia should have been around. She suddenly realized she would've liked to have been there for her sister. Instead she'd foolishly let so much time go by.

Ginny continued. "I've been working out a plan to turn things around. I'm still a long way off from making it work, but the good news is there's hope. And please . . ." She paused. A look of consternation masked her features. "I don't want this to affect your choice to stay or leave. Truly. Don't set your life aside just to hang around here and help me out of a mess I created. That's not why I told you. I'm telling you the truth because you asked. Your help with the supper club has been amazing. But honestly, you don't owe me anything, in spite of how I may have made you feel guilty before. I was carrying around years' worth of hurt, and probably resentment, that I needed to get off my chest. But I'm ready to get rid of it."

"Well, you're not getting rid of *me* quite yet. I'm planning on sticking around a bit longer. And I intend to help out while I do." Julia smiled. She snapped her laptop closed and gathered her loose papers into a pile.

"Thanks," Ginny murmured.

Julia fixed her with a searching stare. "You're not alone, you know, Ginny. I'm here. So, what do you say we go into the kitchen and you tell me what I can do to help prepare for your next round of guests?"

Ginny returned the smile, and together they went into the other room to plan.

CHAPTER THIRTY-TWO

JULIA

Thursday brought an onslaught of surprising phone calls. Julia had been taking a dustrag to Ginny's living room when the phone in her back pocket buzzed. Ever since James accused her of being a poor communicator, she'd kept the device on her at all times. She couldn't run this risk with work. With the exception of showering and sleeping, Julia had gone back to her regular practice of scanning her screen for messages. The updates she'd turned off, in an act of self-preservation. The notifications of people trying to reach her, however, she monitored.

She was surprised to see that the number illuminating her screen belonged to Catrine from work. Brightening, Julia picked up after one ring.

"Cat," she said. "Hi!"

"Hey yourself, stranger." A gravelly female voice greeted her on the other end. Julia smiled and imagined her makeup artist friend hunched over in a knee-length puffy coat and stylish boots, planted on a bench in the smoker's area behind the studio. It was a nice little hideaway, actually. Except for the cloud of cigarette smoke emitted by stressed-out staff.

A muffled breeze sounded through the line. Julia thought of her friend, braced against the chilling temperatures on the streets of New York. It might even be snowing there. Glancing down at the drawstring linen shorts and stretchy cotton V-neck she'd borrowed from Olive, she understood just how vastly different her surroundings were from Catrine's. Julia had traded overcoats and wool mittens for bare feet and sun hats. Suddenly, the idea of returning to winter conditions on the East Coast was terribly unappealing.

Finding a spot on the sofa, she ditched her dustrag and flopped down. "Ha! I know. I've kind of been MIA. Sorry I didn't call. I hope you can forgive me."

"Jeez, girl. I'm just glad to know you're alive and well. Where the hell did you run off to, anyway?"

Julia rolled her eyes. She wasn't surprised that she was a watercooler topic throughout the building. Part of her didn't care, and the other part wondered what else had been said in her absence. "I was suspended over the Rossetti interview. Peter and the big bosses are upset with me, so I guess you could say I'm taking the time away to find myself. As corny as that sounds. I just needed to put some space between myself and the city. Does that make sense?"

"Yup, I get it." There was the sucking sound of Catrine's long inhale, followed by a forceful exhale. Julia sensed tension in her friend's voice. "I'd leave for a while if I could too. This place is getting more insane by the day. Did you hear that Miller asked for a promotion after you left? There's chatter that he marched upstairs and asked to take over hosting *Daybreak* on his own. Then they sent in that Hannah chick and he went nuts. The whole team has been overcome by his bad energy. It's not been good."

"Wow." Julia had no idea. She knew Miller thought highly of himself. And she knew he believed that he'd rise up in the ranks faster than she would. He'd practically announced this outright on more than one occasion over the past year. But to assume he could just have the whole show to himself was pretty ballsy. Even for Miller. "I didn't know. I gather he's been giving my replacement a hard time?"

Catrine let out a low, wicked snicker. "Oh my god. You don't even know the half of it. The poor girl's hands shake under the desk for most of her tapings. The production assistant says Miller refuses to speak to her when they're off the air. He's made the whole environment downright hostile. If this keeps up, I doubt she'll last. She's okay, bright and bubbly, if you like that kind of thing. But she's not you."

Julia's heart expanded. "Oh, Cat. You're the best. I'm sure that's not true, but I love you for saying it anyway."

"I miss having you sit in my chair and be the one normal person in this damn place. Now I'm stuck gluing false eyelashes on Hannah while she sips her coffee out of a baby straw all morning. Oh yeah, and she does voice exercises in the makeup room. Loud, annoying ones that make her sound like a gerbil that's sucked all the air out of a helium balloon. I'm inches away from stabbing her with a lip pencil."

"That sounds pretty awful." Hearing that she'd been missed and that the environment had changed gave Julia the tiniest slice of gratification. While she didn't want her friend to have to endure the toxic actions of her coworkers, Julia was glad that she hadn't been forgotten. Otherwise, she would have felt as if her time at GBN hadn't been about anything.

According to her friend, it had.

"When are you coming back?"

Julia bit her lower lip. That was the million-dollar question. In keeping with the parameters of her suspension, not for a couple more weeks. What she did after that, however, remained a mystery. "I don't know, to be honest. I suppose I'll need to meet with Peter and see what the network has in mind. I've been keeping my distance on purpose. Just to clear my head."

"Yeah, I hear you. I wish I could join you, wherever you are."

"Arizona. At my sister's place."

Catrine snorted. "That's nice, you're probably somewhere warm while I'm out here freezing my ass off."

"Sorry about that."

"Yeah, no worries, girl. I just called to say hey and tell you I miss seeing you around. Keep me posted when you get back, okay? We can catch up."

Julia nodded into the phone. "You bet. Thanks for checking on me. You're the best."

They hung up and Julia remained on the sofa, going over the details of their call. So Miller had been shot down, and now he was taking it out on Julia's replacement. That sounded about right. As much as Julia detested Hannah on paper, in reality, she felt sorry for the girl. Broadcast news was a cutthroat business. Show any sign of weakness and you didn't stand a chance. She wondered how it would all turn out. For everyone.

She'd stood to gather up her dustrag when her phone buzzed a second time. Thinking it must be Catrine again, so soon after hanging up, she picked up quickly. "Hi."

There was a beat of silence followed by an unsure voice. "Um, hi yourself."

Julia frowned and pulled the phone back to study the caller ID. It just read unknown number. "Sorry, who's this?"

"Julia? It's Shane. Your friend from the crazy dinner party?"

She laughed. "Oh, hi, Shane. How are you? Are you calling for my sister?" Although, now that she'd said it, that really didn't make sense either. Why would Shane have Julia's number but not Ginny's?

Another drawn-out silence ensued. Maybe he was regretting making the call. "Oh, no," Shane finally said. "I was actually calling for you. Ginny gave me your cell. I hope that's okay. Really"—he was rushing now—"I just felt like I needed to apologize for the other night. That was a total disaster, with my friend getting sick, then me barging in on you and your boyfriend. Fiancé, rather. I just hope I didn't cause any trouble. I guess I just wanted to say that to you."

Julia found herself dropping back onto the couch. Well, this was surprising. Shane had been worried enough to seek her out and apologize. "That's so considerate of you. But there's nothing to be sorry about. You didn't do anything wrong. Neither did your friend. I hope she's okay. No more health scares after dinner was over?"

"Angie's fine. Thanks. Despite what happened, my friends all raved about your sister's cooking. And how nice you and Olive treated them, considering everything that went on. I just wanted you to know. You were a great help. So calm amid the chaos. I guess that's what makes you a good reporter. You can perform under pressure."

"Don't I wish." She grinned into the phone. It was nice talking to him like this. As if they'd been friends all along. There was an effortless, easy warmth to it that Julia liked. "But you're sweet to say so."

"Seriously, you impressed me."

"Thanks." Her gaze drifted out the front window. A pair of lovebirds flapped around on the ground near the front walkway, their velvety gray feathers like smooth overcoats as they moved in unison across the gravel path. Julia relaxed into a dreamy state, taking in the warm sound of Shane's voice as he spoke.

"So, are you staying in town for much longer? I gathered from Ginny that you didn't go back with, um, James." From the strained way he posed the question, Julia got the sense he felt awkward asking. Perhaps he felt it wasn't any of his business. Or maybe he wanted it to be his business but was embarrassed to be so bold. Either way, Julia was intrigued.

"You're right. I didn't. James and I . . . we broke things off, actually." It felt strange to say it. Almost like a betrayal. But this was her new normal. Julia and James were truly no longer a couple.

"Oh gosh. I'm sorry to hear that. Are you okay?"

A warmth bloomed in her chest. She could tell Shane was sincere with his concern. It was nice to talk to a friend. "Yes, thanks. We had a long talk and realized things just weren't working. It was difficult, but I think it's for the best. We just want different things."

"Well, good for you for knowing what you want. Best to get out before it's too late, I suppose. I'm sure it wasn't easy, though."

"No, you're right. I have time off from work at least, so it's helping to spend it with my sister and my niece. The sunshine doesn't hurt either. That's definitely a plus."

"Yeah, this is a nice time of year. It's nothing like the intense heat of the summer, which comes a bit later. You know that from growing up here. You chose a good time to come."

"And you guys have the best skies for stargazing too. We can't see all of that in the city. Too many lights."

"Well, maybe sometime . . ." His voice became unsteady and dropped off. Julia very much wanted to know what he was trying to say.

"Sometime what?"

There was rustling on the other end. Shane seemed to be choosing his words. That, or he was distracted. "Oh, nothing. I forgot what I was going to say. Anyway, I should let you get back to it. Maybe I'll get to see you around before you go."

Julia deflated some. "Sure. Thanks for the call. It was nice to hear from you."

"You too," he said. "Bye."

And then he was gone. Julia stared off into the distance and tried to imagine the words Shane had stopped himself from saying. And she wondered if she'd ever find out.

CHAPTER THIRTY-THREE

GINNY

Ginny pressed the gas pedal as she sped into town, her knuckles blotched with white against the hot steering wheel. She checked the time once more on the car's dashboard. Eight forty a.m. Good, she wasn't late. But she wanted to arrive well before Roger in order to secure a corner table and collect her thoughts. It was important to be buttoned up. She might be meeting with a friend, but today was about business. Ginny needed to treat this meeting seriously.

They'd agreed to meet at nine o'clock at the local bakery. For the past couple of days Ginny had been cautiously optimistic. Now, however, as she raced down the road with the foothills fading in her rearview mirror, she found herself twisting into a bundle of nerves.

It had been a long while since she'd put herself out there.

Earlier that morning she'd showered and dressed, then made rushed excuses to Olive and Julia that she had an appointment in town. Olive, who'd barely peeled herself from her bed, didn't bat an eye. Her sleepy daughter was too preoccupied with getting the coffee maker to start. Julia, on the other hand, cast her a sidelong glance.

"Okay, but don't we have stuff to do for tonight's double booking?" Her sister stood in the dining room, folding table linens. It was Friday night and Mesquite had reservations for two separate seatings, which meant double the food and double the work for all three women. It was risky for Ginny to be flitting around town on such a busy day for the supper club.

"Oh yeah. I know. It's going to get hectic later. But this was on the books and I don't think I can cancel. I shouldn't be gone more than an hour or two. I'll be back soon. I promise. Thanks for setting the table," Ginny called as she gathered up her tote bag containing her laptop and printed notes, then headed out the front door.

Now, as she eased into a parking spot in the bakery's back lot, Ginny glimpsed at her reflection in the visor mirror. She wasn't normally one to wear makeup, but today she'd applied a conservative amount of black mascara and powdered bronzer that she'd located in Olive's bathroom drawer. With a quick swipe of her organic lip balm, Ginny straightened her shoulders and exited the car.

You can do this, she told herself. *Just do it like you practiced, and remember, Roger is your friend.*

Her mind quickly went over a checklist of papers and computer documents in her bag. Her plan was to impress Roger with a brief PowerPoint presentation, followed by some real estate photos and anecdotal scenarios that would paint a broad-stroke image for him. Her hope was that she'd walk away from the meeting having piqued his interest, at a minimum. Anything more would be a victory.

The sugary aroma of freshly baked pastries welcomed her into the boutique eatery like a warm hug. The tinkle of an overhead bell announced her arrival as she slipped through the doors and made her way across the black-and-white checked floor. After waiting in a short line, she paid for an Americano, heavy on the cream, and a healthy-size savory breakfast muffin loaded with sausage, spinach, and cheddar cheese. It was an indulgence, but a protein-filled snack sounded like a good idea. She needed to be sharp for this meeting. Afterward, she settled down at a two-top table near the front. Sliding into her chair, she glanced around. Not too full and fairly quiet—perfect. Now all she had to do was wait.

For Ginny, waiting was always the hardest part.

Her head popped up at the bell. Roger emerged, striding through the entrance wearing a neatly pressed plaid shirt coupled with khaki slacks, Italian leather loafers, and a metallic Rolex that glinted in the light. Ginny knew enough to recognize expensive clothing when she saw it, even though Roger's uncomplicated, casual appearance was anything but flashy. He had money but didn't show it off. That's what she admired about her friend.

In addition to this, despite his age, which was somewhere in the seventies, Roger was certainly an active guy. With his cinnamon-hued suntan and muscled forearms, which he'd once told her was from hours spent on the tennis court, he looked like he could quite possibly outrun Ginny in a race—though that wasn't saying much considering she didn't really work out, ever. She also liked that Roger was one of those retirees who kept himself so entrenched in the passions he loved. So far, she knew him to spend his free time on a mixture of travel, country club sports, and gourmet food. It was the latter interest that Ginny wanted to capitalize on.

She only hoped Roger would feel the same.

Spotting her, he held up a hand and waved enthusiastically in Ginny's direction. He crossed the room. "Hello."

"Hi, Roger." A faint ripple of grief suddenly went through her. Roger was around the same age Ginny's father would have been if he were still alive. She wondered if these kinds of coffee dates were something she and her father would have enjoyed together. They'd been close, but the geographical distance had split them further apart than she'd liked. And then, before Ginny knew it, her parents had been killed. Ever since then, Ginny had chosen to tuck the sadness away in the background.

Seeing Roger now gave her a kind of nostalgic feeling of what it used to be like to have parents.

"What fun to see you out and about, away from the confines of your natural habitat," Roger announced.

Ginny shook off the sadness and chuckled. "You make me sound like an animal near extinction. I do leave the house every now and then, you know. But yes, I'm not often out of my chef's coat, away from the kitchen." She glanced down at her tunic shirt and white pants with a brief air of self-consciousness. She wasn't about to admit that before she left the house, she'd had the fleeting thought to wear her chef's coat in order to make her presentation seem more professional. But at the last minute she'd decided against it. It was better to appear more casual and not give any indication that Roger might be her only hope for a successful future.

"Indeed," he said, skimming the bakery with a playful grin. "Although we are still in a restaurant, so I guess I didn't get you too far out of your zone."

"Ha! That's the truth. I'd have breakfast here every day if I could. One skill I lack is baking. I admire all those fancy cakes in the display case. A dessert chef I am not."

"But you do everything else so well."

"Thanks, Roger. Can I buy you a coffee? A muffin perhaps?"

"Sure, I'll have what you're having. Looks perfect."

After they were both settled again with their matching orders, Ginny cracked her knuckles under the table and decided to dive right in. She wanted to keep Roger's attention while she had it. Who knew how long he had to meet with her. For all she knew, he had a tennis match or some other appointment to keep.

"So, Roger," she began, clearing her throat. "I've actually asked you here today to present a proposal of sorts. To cut to the chase, the short of it is that I think I'm going to shutter the supper club."

"Oh?" He frowned. "But why? It's such a wonderful experience you provide in that cozy adobe home of yours. And I've seen firsthand that you've curated a nice little customer base of regulars. Don't you enjoy it anymore?" She could tell by Roger's concerned expression that he didn't approve.

She shook her head. "It's not that I don't enjoy cooking for intimate groups, because I really do. In some ways it's been the best of both worlds for me. I get to experiment and try new menus without the worry of a large staff and oppressive overhead to contend with. I've kept it fairly simple with Mesquite. The fact that what I do resonates with people has been a dream come true."

Roger's face remained scrunched into a question. "So?"

"So, the downside to that scenario is that pop-up restaurants and underground supper clubs don't usually make a profit. And"—she hesitated—"if I'm totally frank, I've kind of dug myself into a financial hole."

"You're in debt?"

Ginny nodded, swallowing back an upwelling of shame. "I'm not able to pay myself or Olive. I just make enough to stay afloat. But that's not really working anymore."

"I see." Roger squinted, the rim of the coffee cup hovering in front of his lips. He took his time with his drink, sipping it in a preoccupied manner, as if he was contemplating something. His gaze moved to the middle distance, his brow furrowed. After a minute, he looked at her. "So what do you need in order to keep going?"

A burst of hope bubbled up. This was the reaction she'd hoped for.

Ginny shifted in her chair. Now was the right moment to open her computer and dazzle him with her presentation. She reached down to retrieve her things from her bag. As she did so, she reminded herself to keep calm. To speak with confidence, in the hopes of impressing her friend.

"Well," she said, bringing the device to life on the table between them, "I've asked you here because I've been working on a business plan. I think, with the right backing, I'd like to open a boutique restaurant no bigger than the one we're in right now." Her right hand waved in a swooping motion around the cozy bakery.

Roger's gaze followed her hand. The beginnings of a smile emerged as he perked up. "You want to open up a dinner spot? To the public?"

"I do. And I believe there's room in the local market for me. I've looked around. No one else is offering what I can do. I have some ideas on how to make it happen. It may be presumptuous, but I thought that of all the people I know, you'd be the most likely to be interested. Or, at the very least, perhaps give me some feedback. You are my favorite foodie, after all. If you'll allow me, I'd like to share my ideas." She bit down on her lower lip and waited.

"Because you think I might be the right 'backer,' as you say?"

"Yes, I do." Her lips practically tingled as she'd said it. All Roger had to do was listen. But Ginny couldn't help but feel excited. She'd taken the first step. Saying it out loud had made her wish suddenly seem real.

Ginny had announced she wanted to get back into the restaurant game. And this time, it would be on her own terms. All that stood in her way was the money.

~

An hour and a half later, after they'd drained several cups of coffee and outlasted most of the bakery's morning clientele, Ginny and Roger ended their meeting with a handshake. They left together, breaking off into separate directions toward their cars. Ginny's feet felt as if they weren't even touching the ground as she floated through the parking lot and into the driver's seat. Her meeting with Roger couldn't have gone any better.

He was going to sleep on some ideas about how he could possibly support her new restaurant. While he hadn't committed to anything yet, Ginny had hope.

She couldn't wait to get home and tell her family the good news. A new chapter was about to begin, possibly for all of them.

CHAPTER THIRTY-FOUR

JULIA

It was Friday evening, and Ginny's place was hopping. Boisterous voices mixed with raucous laughter filled the rooms, bouncing off the walls and encircling everyone in a cloud of merriment. Julia wound her way through the guests, busying herself with topping off cocktail glasses. Olive had created a signature cocktail she'd named Mesquite, after the supper club. Olive was also tending to empty drinks and offering small dishes of an artfully plated amuse-bouche before the dinner service began. Men and women mingled, gathering in chatty clusters by the fireplace, on the living room sofa, and out on the back patio as they waited for Ginny to announce dinner.

She'd arrived home in a flurry earlier that day, beaming with happiness, claiming she had some fun news to share.

While she was away, however, the well-used dishwasher had practically exploded and sent copious amounts of dirty water flooding onto the previously cleaned kitchen floor. The disaster had thrown the women into a slight panic. A hose must have become disconnected, because it took Julia and Olive the better part of the morning to sop up the mess. They'd elected to call a plumber out to the house the following day for fear of putting them all further behind schedule. Repairs would have to be made.

It would be a full night of service at Mesquite. There wasn't time for any sort of crisis.

Ginny's news was temporarily put on hold as the three women scampered around, trying to make up for lost time before the first group of guests arrived. So much still needed to be done: prepping the food, setting up the bar, and deciding on the various wine pairings. It wasn't like Ginny to leave so many critical elements of her menu to the last minute. But by the way her sister cheerily went about cooking that afternoon, Julia had assumed there must be a good reason.

Julia herself was presently caught between a confusing mixture of happiness and trepidation. On the one hand, it was evenings like the one Mesquite was having—the cozy rooms of the adobe house full of joyful people, her sister and her niece contentedly working close by, and the desert night air trailing in from the outside with an intoxicating mix of sweet sage and rich earth—that made Julia feel alive.

Somewhere along the line, desert life had regrown on Julia. And more than that, it made her happy. She'd come to peace with the things she'd run from as a young adult—when she'd hoped life in a big city would somehow legitimize her dreams and her career—and now could appreciate the beauty of this place from a more grounded perspective.

Yet still looming was her unfinished business with work and her future. Her old life. Never in a million years would she have guessed that those two subjects would ever be pushed into the background. For so long, they'd been the only things she poured her energy into. Gratefully.

But everything had shifted. And now Julia feared what had once meant so much to her had altered. She felt like the mysterious cactus flowers she'd seen that suddenly opened up in the desert night, blossoming into something more than their previously closed-off shape had allowed.

She felt herself transforming into something new under her circumstances. And the realization was both heartbreaking and invigorating at the same time.

"Thinking about one of your many suitors?" Olive sidled up beside her and took the empty pitcher from her hands.

Julia turned, flushed. "Oh my gosh. You don't give up, do you?"

Her niece pivoted, her long ponytail whipping as she went. "Just wondering, that's all. I'm going to open the wine, but maybe you can tell me what had you looking so dreamy when I get back." She winked and trotted away, appearing pleased with herself.

Julia scanned the room. All the guests still seemed happy. Excusing herself, she hustled into the kitchen. "How much longer?" she asked Ginny, who was sliding a baking sheet of glistening caramelized figs from the oven.

"Five or six minutes, tops. Then you can seat everyone. Are they all okay out there?"

"Yes, totally fine." Which they were, but Julia couldn't help but wonder if this late seating would run into the second shift of diners, expected later that evening. Being late wasn't ever an option. She knew Ginny well enough to hold her tongue. She didn't want to sink her sister's buoyant mood with excessive worries.

"Okay, great. I'll get this banged out in no time. We'll be okay." Ginny jutted her chin in the direction of the baking sheet, indicating the first course was nearly ready. A sugary aroma trailed through the air. She seemed to have everything under control.

"And maybe in between courses you can tell me where you were today?" Julia broached. The question had been burning a hole in her ever since Ginny had arrived home practically bursting with delight, but she'd remained tight lipped.

"Yeah, Mom. Why all the mystery?" Olive asked, snatching up the basket of warm bread to deliver to the table.

Ginny ignored them. She began plating dishes of buffalo mozzarella with glazed figs and fresh mint. Julia looked on as each plate
was drizzled artfully with olive oil and sprinkled with crunchy salt
and black pepper just before Ginny nodded that they were ready to
go out.

"Quick, get them all into their seats!"

"We're on it!"

Julia and Olive hustled out and gathered the group with a brief
announcement that dinner was served. It was a choreography they had
perfected over the past weeks. And as she and Olive stepped aside to
make room for the guests, Julia realized she was going to miss having this experience with her niece. She'd enjoyed living and working
together in such close proximity. It had brought on a new kind of
intimacy that she had come to cherish.

And then it dawned on her. Julia didn't want to pack up and return
to New York. She didn't want to risk missing out on this feeling. This
was where she most wanted to be. With family.

It was as if she'd been washed over with a wave of sudden clarity.
Gone was her desperate desire to make it at GBN, gone was her desire
to commit every waking hour toward gaining recognition and respect
from a corporate culture that had showed little loyalty in return, gone
was the yearning to be in the epicenter of busy city life. And perhaps
most surprisingly of all, gone was any lingering worry she'd made the
wrong decision about James.

This was a big one.

What mattered to Julia was love and family and peace of mind.
If she had stayed with James, Julia feared she'd have lost herself and
become a version of what he wanted his partner to be, and that wasn't
her true identity. Not any longer. A tiny voice inside her head told her
she might be more clearly seen for who she really was by someone like
Shane. As strange as it was to admit, Julia just got that sense.

This thought gave her hope. An optimistic enough feeling to stick around and find out. Not because of a man, but simply because of a feeling.

It was good to tap into her authentic self, finally. And she wasn't about to let that sensation slip away.

Olive peered inquisitively at her and then went to retrieve the waiting plates. She tugged on Julia's sleeve as she passed by. "Okay, let's get the first course out fast." And then she paused. "Everything okay? You seem lost in thought tonight."

Julia blinked, suddenly aware she'd been daydreaming for the second time. "Oh yeah. Perfect. I'm ready."

"What's the deal with you and Mom?" Olive pressed, leading Julia away. "You both have a similar far-off look on your faces. Is there some kind of big news or something I don't know about?"

She really was an intuitive girl.

Julia entered the kitchen and glanced from her sister to her niece. "Yeah, I think there is, actually."

~

Four hours and many dirty dishes later, the three women sprawled out wearily on the living room furniture. Their shoes had been kicked off, and each cradled a stemless glass containing a hearty pour of red wine. Shirts had been untucked and ponytails loosened. Low music trailed throughout the house, the volume turned up a notch now that the guests were all gone. A dull crackle remained in the fireplace, the remnants of a wood-burning fire that had been fed all night. Julia scanned the scattering of empty cocktail glasses that littered the surface of the large coffee table.

They were all too tired to clean a single thing more.

Julia, Ginny, and Olive sank farther into the cushions and reflected on another busy but successful night of work.

"Sorry, but that scallop dish I made tonight was the bomb, if I do say so myself," Ginny mused, looking over her glass.

They giggled.

Julia, feeling the lure of sleep calling, gazed back at her with her eyes at half-mast. "Mm-hmm. It was. I tasted it. So buttery it was ridiculous. Well done, sister."

"I filled up on a lot of mozzarella and bread. That cheese was so good, Mom. You should order it from that place all the time."

Ginny nodded.

"So," Julia began, "are you going to share whatever you've been waiting to tell us?"

Ginny took an idle sip of her wine. Both feet kicked up as she readjusted herself on the deep sofa. "I have some news. It's a little premature, but I'm going to tell you both anyway. Hopefully I'm not jinxing myself by doing so."

"Well, now you have to tell us."

"I met with Roger Mendelsohn today."

Olive frowned. "Roger from the supper club?"

Ginny nodded her head. "Yep. That's the one. Anyway, he's kind of been my biggest fan since I opened Mesquite. We've become friendly. He has a great palate, so I trust his taste. Anyway, he also has money, which is why I met with him." She paused and glanced around the room.

"Okay . . ." Julia wasn't sure where this was going. Was her sister going to start dating a man who was old enough to be their father? Was she that desperate for money?

"Well, you both know that the supper club has had its challenging moments. It's no secret I'm not pulling in a ton of revenue. And while it's been fun, it's also been rather risky. That thing with the diabetic woman the other night really scared me. The evening could have taken a much more drastic turn for the worse. Think about what would have happened if the authorities had actually been called to the house. It would have been a disaster."

"I know." Julia shuddered at the memory.

"And then there's the matter of that stupid food blogger who won't even respond to my emails. I'm still so ticked off about that. And"— Ginny sighed—"I didn't tell you guys this, but another reporter has left two messages asking for a quote. It seems she's found the blog. She wants to write about Mesquite."

They all took a collective inhale, reflecting.

"I've ignored her for now. And I still plan to pursue this guy in hopes he'll take down the write-up. Anyway, to make a very long story short, I'm being proactive. I approached Roger and asked him to be my primary investor in a new space. Believe it or not, I want to open a boutique dinner spot. Roger has tentatively agreed to help me." A whoosh of breath followed Ginny's speech; clearly, she'd been holding in a big secret. She searched their faces with expectant eyes.

Julia sat up. "Wow! Are you serious? That's amazing, Ginny. Really. I had no idea this was something you were thinking of doing."

"Yeah, Mom. Jeez. You never really mentioned this before. Not since New York."

Ginny shook her head. "I left the city to take care of family business, but I have always missed the collaboration and energy of a working restaurant. And this time I'll be in charge. This will be my restaurant, with no one looking over my shoulder. Roger will be like a silent partner. I'll have minimal staff, high-quality food, and a small enough space so that there won't be a giant overhead. I really think it could work. I've slowly made a name for myself around here and collected a bunch of loyal customers. Hopefully they'll follow me to my next spot. And I won't have to be in hiding anymore."

Both women were quiet, soaking in Ginny's announcement. This was big. It would change the dynamic of so many things.

"That sounds cool, Mom . . ." Olive trailed off, as if she might be concerned about something else.

Ginny must have understood because she quickly answered her daughter. "And Olive, this also means a new chapter for you. I don't want you working for me anymore. I want you to find your own way. I won't push you, but if you want to go to school for landscape design or floral arrangement or something else, I would gladly help you figure out how to fund that. You deserve to follow whatever interests you."

Without hesitating, Julia jumped in. "I second that!" She turned to face Olive. "Olive, honey, I would love to help finance your going back to school if that's what you want. You're so talented. It would be great to see you chase your passion."

Olive gaped. For a moment she said nothing. "Wow. That's amazing. Thank you."

Julia noticed something like a light turning back on in her niece's eyes.

Ginny and Julia smiled back at her in unison. They'd both seen Olive's potential and wanted to see it fulfilled, but only if it would make Olive happy.

Julia believed it would.

Ginny turned to Julia then. "It's all going to move pretty fast in the next few months. Thank you, Julia, for sticking around and helping me during your visit. Olive and I both appreciate everything you've done. Promise you'll come back and visit again? It would be fun to have you see the new business when it's ready."

Julia looked back at her sister. A warmth filled her heart. "I won't need to do that."

Ginny's face fell. "Oh, I just thought that—"

Julia cut her off. "What I mean is that I won't need to visit because I've actually decided I'm not going back."

"You're not?"

"No. I'd like to stay. In Arizona. I'm quitting my job, and I've already ended things with James. My old life doesn't fit me the way it used to. I can't explain it. It just doesn't. Things have changed. I've changed."

"Wow, so what does that mean?"

Julia took a big breath. "If it's okay with both of you, I'd like to find an apartment in town and move closer. That is, if you'll have me. I didn't realize how much I missed having family around until I came here. I didn't realize how much of myself I'd lost over the past few years. I want to change all of that. I believe by staying I can do that. And I have some ideas about a slight shift in direction with my work. It's nothing concrete yet, but I'm mulling over some plans. What do you think?"

Before she could wait for an answer, Olive leaped up and crossed the room. She flung her arms around Julia's neck. "Oh, Aunt Julia! You're staying! You're staying!"

Tears pooled in her eyes. She'd hoped for a positive reaction, but she hadn't expected such a big one from her niece. Craning her neck, she peered over Olive's tight embrace at Ginny. Julia worried her sister might not feel the same because she'd yet to say anything.

From where Julia sat, however, she noticed that Ginny also had moisture in her eyes. Her sister appeared to be just as choked up.

"This is turning out to be a day of new beginnings." Ginny beamed.

"I agree!" Olive darted off in search of more wine, and the three women toasted to a new chapter. Julia's heart had never been so full.

CHAPTER THIRTY-FIVE

JULIA

Breaking the news to GBN wasn't difficult. Before flying home to pack up her things, she'd emailed the office that she'd be stopping by. Although Peter appeared slightly stunned at her resignation—most people did not willingly walk away from an opportunity as prestigious as GBN—he claimed he understood. Julia explained she'd had a change of heart and planned to relocate. Her boss nodded, was cordial and kind, and wished Julia the best.

"Thanks for the opportunity, Peter."

"Absolutely. I'm only sorry things are ending the way they are. You have great potential, Julia. You've learned a valuable lesson with the Rossetti incident. I'm sure you'll go on to do good things."

Julia smiled and accepted his well-wishes. It meant a great deal to part with GBN on decent terms. Thankfully there hadn't been any legal mess to clean up. Peter promised a letter of recommendation, but she knew that her boss was secretly relieved he wouldn't have to go through the ugly business of firing her. After all that had happened, her chances of staying, let alone rising, at GBN were rather slim, and they both knew it.

She hugged Catrine goodbye and promised to keep in touch. She'd miss their talks. "If you ever need a vacation with lots of sunshine, you know where to find me. I'd love to see you," Julia offered.

"Thanks." Catrine hugged her back. "I just may take you up on that. It sounds fantastic."

"I mean it. You've been a good friend. Call me if you need to vent. I'm just a phone call away."

"Deal." Catrine smiled wide as Julia turned to go.

Before leaving the office, she had one more thing to take care of. She made her way to the busy newsroom floor, glanced around, then dropped a folded note on Hannah's desk. Julia didn't personally know her replacement, and she wasn't sure if the girl was capable of keeping up with Miller, but she decided Hannah should have a fair shot anyway.

In the note were the few details Julia had gleaned in her research about the scandal in Mayor Rossetti's office. It included specifics on Rossetti's chief of staff, the consultancy, and a brief timeline of events. Whether anything would become of her notes was up to Hannah. Julia found herself hoping the newcomer would have the courage to break the story herself, putting Miller in his place and bringing in a victory for GBN. Maybe even clearing Julia's name in a roundabout way.

It was nice to think of the underdog winning for a change.

It was even nicer to know she might have a small hand in that happening.

Julia was finished with big network life. In the end, it wasn't for her. She'd already put out some feelers in Arizona. A couple of meetings had been placed on the calendar. The idea of having a more low-profile job with a smaller news outlet appealed to her now. Time would tell if she'd get the chance. Then again, if she could have a second chance to begin with Ginny and Olive, she had to hope there'd be room for a second chance for her career, and maybe even love too.

CHAPTER THIRTY-SIX
JULIA

Five weeks later

Julia shifted in the passenger seat of Olive's Jeep and turned a key over in her hand. Its jagged angles poked into the skin of her moist palm. A fizzing of nervous excitement moved steadily through her. Today was moving day. And there was no turning back.

"Thanks again for driving me," she said to Olive.

"Of course. I'm excited to be one of the first people to see your place. I can stick around and help when the movers come as well. It could be fun!"

"That's okay." Julia smiled. "You'd better scoot. I know your mom wanted you to stop by the restaurant with an estimate for the flowers. You can't be late for your new gig!"

Olive laughed. "No, I guess not. Even if it's just Mom."

Olive had taken everyone's advice and enrolled in a local floral school. Her first class had begun a week earlier. There was a larger, more prestigious floral school—where all the heavy hitters in the floral industry trained—located in New York that Olive had her eye on. But for now, she wanted to remain in Arizona. Julia assumed that, like her,

Olive was taking advantage of the repaired relationship she finally had with Ginny and felt strongly enough that it was worth pursuing.

Ginny, clearly thrilled that Olive had chosen to stay, offered her daughter a monthly retainer to keep the new restaurant in fresh arrangements and to tend to the outside planters in the summer months. The landlord of the little brick building that housed the restaurant and small offices also offered to pay Olive. He'd asked her to revive a string of planter boxes out front and maintain them regularly.

It was a nice starter salary. Julia knew both mother and daughter were pleased with the arrangement. Soon, Olive hoped to have saved enough to get her own apartment.

"Well, here we are!" Olive rounded the corner of a downtown street known for its great shopping and dining. A brand-new, modern condominium project, complete with a state-of-the-art workout facility, pool, and smart systems, had just been completed the season before. Julia, not yet ready to abandon the trappings of city life altogether, had chosen to purchase one of the contemporary residences that featured impeccable finishes, culinary-inspired appliances, beautiful wood floors, and private patios that offered up to seven hundred square feet of outdoor living space.

Letting go of her portion of the pricey lease in Manhattan had allowed her to make the offer in Arizona's reasonable market. She was also able to sell some of her furniture, including a small but significant piece of art that James had once gifted her. Though she'd given back the ring, he'd insisted she keep the art. Thus, she was able to deposit a tiny cushion into her bank account, along with some savings, which would come in handy while she figured things out.

The new condo was within walking distance of Whole Foods, a slew of trendy retail shops, a scenic bike path, and popular restaurants, including Ginny's newest endeavor. This fact alone had been the biggest draw for Julia. She could walk down a handful of blocks to visit her sister anytime she wanted. Just like in the old days.

"I can't wait for you to see my patio," she told Olive. "I bet you'll have some great ideas for a low-maintenance garden. It's got a spectacular view of the mountains too. I plan to spend lots of time out there."

"Let's go!" Olive hopped out eagerly.

Julia slid from the passenger side and shut the door. As she glanced up, the gleaming new building seemed to smile down at her. Julia shaded her eyes and took it all in. The sun refracted in a high window and winked down onto the street below.

This is my new home, she thought to herself. She gripped the key harder, filled with a surge of gratitude. Somehow, Julia knew this move had been the right decision. Despite what she'd had to let go of to get here, she was glad.

～

Later that evening, Julia sat at a long community-style table in Ginny's yet-to-open restaurant. Her cheeks pushed back into a wide smile. All around her were the people who would become her new friends and family. Her new tribe.

To her right was Olive, looking very grown-up in a long dress with her glossy hair in a high twist. A young man, whom Julia had just met, sat close by Olive's side. He was apparently one of Ginny's vendors and had a tight friendship with Olive. This was the "friend" Olive had stayed with whenever she'd fought with her mother.

The pair looked cute together, whether her niece would admit they were a couple or not, and Julia found herself glad for them. There was nothing like young love.

To her left was Shane, who'd come alone. Sweet, genuine Shane, who'd arrived with a bouquet of flowers for Ginny and a bottle of prosecco for Julia as a housewarming gift.

"To your new home." He smiled, handing over the bottle. Julia's heart did a little flip at seeing that the delicate silver bow had been tied with a note that read "Love, Shane."

"Thanks for this," she responded. "But you'll come over and have a glass on my new deck, won't you? The place isn't furnished except for the bed and some kitchen stools. But as soon as I acquire a patio set, you'll be my first guest!"

He gazed at her for a long second, their eyes locking. "I would be honored." Julia's heart did another flip as she settled into her dining chair.

At the last minute, she'd rung Shane up and invited him to her sister's menu-tasting party. She'd explained that the guests who attended were encouraged to vote on the best dishes as part of Ginny's research. The restaurant wouldn't officially be open to the public for another month, due to a list of unfinished build-outs in the back of the kitchen. Her sister, however, was moving ahead anyway. No surprise there.

Now, skimming the long table, where a flicker of soft candlelight and enough cutlery to satisfy an army shone, Julia couldn't help but feel a burst of pride for her sister.

Ginny was actually doing it.

Roger was there, with his kind-faced wife and one of their curious neighbors. Julia gestured across the table in greeting. Seated next to them were Beverly and Phil, who'd turned out to be Shane's aunt and uncle, and also a smattering of Ginny's other regular diners from Mesquite. It was an eclectic mix of young and old, creative and conservative. But altogether happy.

A young woman also sat near the end of the table, appearing to take in the merriment. Julia didn't recognize her but deduced she must be the reporter from the newspaper who'd been reaching out to Ginny. Inviting the reporter was genius, really. While Ginny hadn't been able to convince the food blogger to delete his article, she had managed to get the local news in her corner. Ginny had shared earlier that she'd promised the reporter an exclusive interview if she'd come to the new restaurant and try the food. Julia already knew her sister would be able to put a positive spin on the story. It was a clever idea, and she wished she'd thought of it herself.

Miraculously, there hadn't been much more buzz around the blog. Larger stories were taking over the airwaves that week. As a result, the blog had been buried beneath the noise from other, more attention-grabbing headlines. Julia had yet to see any further mention of her in the New York papers, aside from the quickly fading Rossetti episode. The industry, and its audience, were fickle like that. One scandal would eventually be traded for the next. That's just the way it worked.

Julia thanked her lucky stars for that.

Everyone was there to support Ginny's beautiful new business, Bistro G.

"Welcome, everyone!" Ginny emerged, dressed in her chef's coat. She came around the back counter, which was still covered with a sheet of loose plywood, electrical cords hanging at all angles. The place still required plenty of work, but Ginny was able to cook with working appliances despite that.

"Hello!" the group chimed back.

"I'm so glad you could all come tonight. I can't tell you how excited I am for this! I've been cooking for days, so you better have brought your appetites!"

"Hooray!" someone called.

Ginny tossed back her head and laughed. Julia noticed that the lines of worry around her now-glinting eyes had faded. That the tight expression from before was now gone. Her sister was basking in her dream, and they were all there to witness it.

"But first," Ginny continued, "please join me in raising a glass. Bistro G could not have been possible without the help of some very important people. First, my business partner, Roger. I am forever grateful to you for believing in my vision, and I couldn't have picked a friend with a better foodie palate!"

Roger beamed as his wife leaned over and pecked his cheek. "Hear, hear!"

"And," Ginny went on, her glass still lifted high in the air, "to my beautiful and talented daughter, Olive. I couldn't have done this without her help and support. I'm so happy you're here, honey. I love you!"

"Thanks, Mom." Olive's smile took up her whole face. Julia reached over and squeezed her arm lovingly.

"And finally"—Ginny stepped closer to the table, her eyes finding Julia's—"to my sister, Julia. Welcome back to your home in the desert. May you find love and light and everything you've ever wanted. Your being here means more than you'll ever know. I love you."

"Cheers!"

"Bravo!"

"To Bistro G!"

The crowd clinked their glasses together in a burst of joviality. As friends and family sipped their champagne, Julia took in all the faces. This was a night she never wanted to forget. It was the start of a whole new life.

And she couldn't wait to see what would come next.

ACKNOWLEDGMENTS

This book stems from my love of sister stories. A big hug goes to my two sisters, Aimee and Heather, for all the laughter, listening, and general good support they've given.

Thank you to my unfaltering literary agent, Abby Saul. You answer every call, email, and writerly plead for reassurance. I'm so grateful you're in my corner. To the team at Lake Union Publishing, especially Danielle Marshall and Alicia Clancy, thanks for seeing the vision and guiding me along the way. Gabriella Dumpit, thanks for your marketing know-how and day of fun in Seattle! Working with Sarah Murphy during the editing stage was a dream. Thank you for "sniffing out" what I was trying to say and making the book that much better.

To Gretchen Schaffer, my dear friend. You've offered a keen eye for everything from sample chapters to cover concepts, and I adore you for it. Thanks goes to Sandi Kahn Shelton for being an early reader. To my Hive of Bees: You gals are forever the best. Thank you for the years of support. A shout-out also goes to the Ladies of the Lake. I'm not sure another group of like-minded authors exists where so much is shared, championed, and promoted all under one imprint. I feel lucky to be a part of this network. Thanks to the booksellers who've featured my books in such lovely ways (Roundabout Books and Powell's, to name a few!).

Last, but never least, is my family. Greg, Natalie, Lauren, and Ben, I love you. Thanks for sitting in the front row. It means the world.

ABOUT THE AUTHOR

Photo © 2017 Benjamin Edwards

Nicole Meier is the author of *The Girl Made of Clay* and *The House of Bradbury*. She is a native Southern Californian who pulled up roots and moved to the Pacific Northwest, where she lives with her husband, three children, and one very nosy Aussiedoodle. Visit her at www.nicolemeierauthor.com.

herself for not stopping her when she'd had the chance the other night. But how could she have known?

"She's fine," Ginny said. "I have been texting her. Olive likes to keep me hanging by only responding with one-word texts. But she confirmed she's still mad at me and she confirmed she's safe."

"Huh." Julia didn't know what to make of it. Ginny seemed somewhat resigned to the fact that her daughter liked to keep things vague. A part of her understood that this might be a young person's desire to strike out on her own. To push against the confines of a small town and yearn for something bigger. It was what Julia had done when she'd first left Arizona, after all. Perhaps her niece was feeling the same way. "So, if you don't mind me asking, why not hire someone else to take her place? I mean, you must be pretty desperate if you had me fill in. We all know I'm more than rusty when it comes to service."

"Ha! You've got that right. But yeah, you could say I'm desperate."

"So?"

"So, I can't afford to hire new help. I'm strapped as it is." The arms were back across her chest. The invisible wall was up.

Julia frowned. This wasn't necessarily the answer she'd expected. Surely life out here in the desert had only a fraction of the high cost of living in New York. Didn't it? And Ginny had established a business. If you could call it that.

"Can't you use whatever it is you pay Olive for a new person?"

"No." It came out in almost a whisper.

"No?"

"I don't exactly pay Olive in a consistent manner," Ginny said, her gaze drifting to the ground. Julia detected the shame in her sister's response. "I don't have the money for that. Not now, anyway. Olive gets free room and board in exchange. And some cash on the side. That's pretty good for a twenty-one-year-old. She gets to eat and sleep here for free."

Julia laughed out loud. She couldn't help herself. Her sister could be pragmatic to a fault. "Well, that explains a lot! Oh my god, Ginny. No wonder she's pissed. Come on, let's go inside and make some coffee and you can tell me when your next group of diners is expected. Because I now have a million more questions."

"Okay." Ginny dropped her arms in concession. Julia sensed a crack in the wall her sister had built. Perhaps there was hope for the weekend after all. The future was a whole different matter.

CHAPTER FOURTEEN
JULIA

Julia pressed the phone to her ear and paced the tiny guest room. After talking things over with Ginny, she'd realized she was overdue for a phone call with James. No doubt he'd be worried about her well-being, and she wanted to assure him she was fine. Only, at the moment, she wasn't able to get a word in edgewise. Her fiancé was too busy listing all the reasons why she should jump on the next plane home and begin the arduous task of repairing her damaged career.

"But the network specifically asked me—ordered me, actually—to steer clear. They don't want me coming in to work just yet." Her voice sounded whiny and she hated herself for it. James was making her feel incompetent.

"But I just told you a retraction was read during Friday night's evening news. Actually, they're calling it a correction, and it's been blasted all over GBN's social media accounts all weekend. Haven't you seen any of this? They're making it sound like it was a statement from you and hinted that a formal apology to Rossetti might be coming next. What's more, Rossetti is on Twitter calling for your immediate firing. Doesn't that bother you? Don't you want to speak up for yourself? You could lose your job." He was incredulous, his speech climbing toward a frenzied pitch.

Julia blew air through her nose. She knew James meant well; he only wanted her to keep a firm hold on her career. He also liked things to have forward momentum, steps to be continually taken toward goals. It was bad enough he couldn't get Julia to commit to a wedding date. The state of limbo this caused drove him crazy, but she'd had her job to consider. Up until now, she hadn't been willing to take time off. Now that she'd been forced to take a leave, though, James wasn't happy about it.

His urgent reasoning, in the form of fearmongering, certainly wasn't helping. If anything, it was making her more sickened than she already was.

Running back to New York to get beaten down again in the form of public humiliation was the least appealing option. Yet she was conflicted.

"I obviously can't control what the network does, or doesn't do, in my absence. They're a big company and I'm a tiny cog in the wheel. Peter has made it pretty clear I made a costly mistake, and they want me to stay away until it's sorted out."

"But did you make a mistake? Are you sure there isn't any validity to the Rossetti story?"

"I don't know."

"And why did you have to go all the way to Arizona to visit a sister whom you literally never talk about? I don't understand. I'm the one who actually cares, and you ran away from me."

Julia sank down on the edge of the daybed, folding over to cradle her achy head in her hands. Poor James. He had a point. She hadn't mentioned her sister much over the past year. James knew the basics about her parents' deaths and the famous older sister who'd abruptly crumbled under her grief and given up her culinary career for a quieter life. And he knew that there'd been some kind of blowup between the